GUARDIAN'S HEART

Fire and Snow
Book One

KHLOE WREN

Books by Khloe Wren

Fire and Snow:
Guardian's Heart
Noble Guardian (Release: 5 Feb '16)
Guardian's Shadow (due out Mar '16)
Fierce Guardian (due out Apr '16)

Dragon Warriors:
Enchanting Eilagh
Binding Becky
Claiming Carina
Seducing Skye
Believing Binda

Single Titles:
Fireworks
Jaguar Secrets
Tigers Are Forever
Bad Alpha Anthology
Scarred Perfection (Release: 4 Feb '16)

ISBN: 978-0-9945190-3-0

Cover Credits:
Photographer: Eric Battershell
Model: Michael Gleason
Digital Artist: Jay Aheer of Simply Defined Art

Editing Credits:
Content Editor: Rahab Mugwanja
Line Editor: Ami Deason

Acknowledgements

First and most importantly, a massive thank you to my infinitely patient husband; without your support none of this would be possible. To my girls, thank you for sharing Mummy with the world inside her head. To my parents, your continual unconditional love and support means the world to me.

My sincere thanks to everyone who has had a hand in helping me create this story. Since first writing it three years ago, so many people have helped me refine it to what it is now. There are too many to name but you all know who you are.

An extra special shout out to my editing team who really had their work cut out for them with this project. I think every hurdle that could have arisen, did but we conquered them all and got it done in the end!

Finally to you, the reader. Without you, books go nowhere. So thank you for purchasing my book and I sincerely hope you enjoy the Fire and Snow world.
xo
Khloe Wren

Biography

Khloe Wren grew up in the Adelaide Hills before her parents moved the family to country South Australia when she was a teen. It was there that Khloe followed her father's footsteps and joined the volunteer firefighting service at 18. A few years later, Khloe moved to Melbourne which unfortunately meant she had to give up firefighting but she's always missed it. After a few years living in the big city, she missed the fresh air and space of country living so returned to rural South Australia. Khloe currently lives in the Murraylands with her incredibly patient husband, two strong willed young daughters, an energetic dog and two curious cats.

Khloe has always loved big cats, especially Snow Leopards. So it seemed only natural that when she began writing her first novel after having major surgery that left her on bedrest for six months, that she chose these beautiful creatures as her first shifters.

Glossary

Alpha (of a Leap): The leader of the Leap.

Continental Leap: The Leap chosen to represent their continent at the Council of Alphas. Each of the seven continents has a Continental Leap.

Council of Alphas: The Alpha of each Continental Leap form the Council of Alphas. It is their job to oversee all aspects of shifter life.

Dream Bonding: After the female turns twenty-one, shifter pairs can pull each other into a dream. Useful for when mates are apart from each other.

Chaton: French for kitten.

Comet Shifters: Those shifters newly created from Halley's Comet's passing of Earth.

Firie/Firies/Firie's: Nickname for a firefighter

Halley's Comet: When the shifters were first created. Halley's Comet passed as the magic was welded. Now, every seventy-five years when the comet passes over Earth, a new pair of shifters is conceived on each continent.

Jaws of Life: Apparatus Firefighters use to cut open crashed vehicles in order to save the occupants

Leap: Leap is the name given to a group of Snow Leopards.

Lost Ones: Shifters who are not part of a Leap and often don't know of their heritage. Lost Ones are often alone and scared of what they are, not understanding there are others like them.

Maman: French for Mum/Mom

Marking, The: After mating, the couple mark each other with permanent scratch marks to show their claim on the other. The mark looks like four wide scratch marks that reveal Snow Leopard spots beneath.

Mating: The process a couple goes through to bind themselves together for life. Mating forms an unbreakable bond.

Ma chère: French endearment, my dear.

Mon amour: French endearment, my love.

Petit fille: French for little girl/daughter

Search, The: On of the Council of Alphas' main purposes is to go looking for Lost Ones and Comet Shifters.

Shifter Magic: Because shifters were created with magic, they hold a low level of magic which they can weld on occasion.

Tibetan Monks: Tibetan Monks are the ones who originally cast the magic to bind a man and a Snow Leopard together.

Trigger: Trigger Corporation is the enemy to the shifters.

Ute: Similar to an American Pickup Truck

Dedication

To You.

May you find the one who will guard your heart, the one who will always be there shining bright, helping you through all your darkest days.

Prologue

Rosebery, Tasmania, Australia
November 2007

Conner let loose a low whistle as Dominic walked into the station house kitchen.

"Damn, you look like shit, Dom, why don't you go crash out back for a bit? I'll come get you if we get called out."

"Thanks, little brother, so feeling the love right now."

Dominic said in a voice heavy with sarcasm as he strode over to the coffee machine. Conner leaned back on his seat, taking a sip from his own caffeine fix. He furrowed his brow as he took in the sight of his older brother. Dominic wasn't standing tall and proud like he did ordinarily, instead, he appeared to be inches shorter than his actual six foot six height with the way his shoulders were slumped and his head hung down. His short black hair, normally clean and neat, looked greasy like it was at least a few days overdue for a wash and his face had, Conner guessed, at least a couple of days' worth of beard growth roughening it.

Conner and his only brother had always been extremely close. They could read each other's moods and body language so well that often it appeared to others that they could communicate telepathically. A very handy skill set when they were out fighting fires. It also meant it hadn't slipped his notice that over the last few days Dominic had been getting worse, looking more wrecked each day. He was worried about his big bro, both on a personal level and a professional one. With summer and the bushfire season just around the corner, none of them could afford to be off their game. Conner placed his can of Coke on the table as Dominic sat across from him and took a long drag of his coffee with his eyes closed.

"I'm serious, Dom, something's up. Has been for a couple days. You gonna spill? Or do I have to sic Dad onto you?"

"Yeah right, like to see you try pulling that one off."

Dominic chucked as he'd spoken but it wasn't long before his brother's features grew serious—finally, they were making some progress.

"They're just dreams, Conner. I'm fine."

Conner wasn't fooled by his brother shrugging his shoulder or by his casual tone.

"Bullshit you're fine. What dreams?"

"My mate turned twenty-one about six weeks ago."

Bloody hell! Conner held Dominic's stare as shock pinged around his skull.

"You're dreaming of your mate already? You only turned twenty-one eight months ago. But hang on, why has it got you so stressed out? I thought once you started dreaming of your mate, life is all sunshine and lollipops or some shit? Did you meet her and stuff it up or something?"

Lifting his can to take a drink, Conner recalled an earlier conversation with their father. One about the shifter's version of the birds and the bees. Their father had explained to them how when a male shifter's mate turns twenty-one, he would start seeing her face in their dreams. As time goes by the nightly visions reveal what she looks like from head to toe and, if after a decade or so the male still hadn't found her, he would begin to see places, people and things that she holds dear. Basically, the dreams provided a male with all the information he needed to go searching for his mate, the longer he took to find her, the more facts he received to assist him. Although, generally speaking, fate put mates in each other's path long before a male needed to go actively searching for her.

"Six weeks ago when they began, it was beyond amazing. After the first dream I felt so alive and had a buzz in my system, you know how it feels after you go for a good solid run? Like that, but twenty-four/seven. And at night, every night, she's all I see. She's so damn beautiful..."

By the glazed look in Dominic's eyes, Conner guessed he'd lost him to memories of his dreams, which wasn't going to help him work out what was wrong. It was time to pull Dominic back to reality. Conner cleared his throat and hoped his voice would stay steady.

"Yeah, yeah, don't need my nose rubbed in it. So what changed?"

"I'm not sure, it's like—damn it—I think she's in trouble or in pain, but I don't know how to find her. I've never seen her outside my dreams and it's still too early for me to see anything other than her. I just don't know where to start or what to do." Dominic scrubbed his hands over his face on a sigh.

Conner's gut churned as he fought the jealousy rising within him. He didn't want to feel like this. He knew he had most likely years until he would dream of his mate, it made sense that his elder brother would find his mate first, but his emotions weren't listening to logic.

"Have you spoken to Dad about it? I'm pretty sure he'd have some advice for you. He did tell us to let him know when we started dreaming of our mate."

"Nah, I haven't. He has his hands full at the moment, you know that. With fire season around the corner, he's flat out getting everything ready, and then there's The Search; I mean, hell, they've only found three pairs globally. That means there are still four pairs out there, including one in Australia. They all would have got the shock of their lives on their fifteenth birthdays in 2001 when they suddenly shifted to snow leopards at nightfall don't you think? It's important that we find them before they lose their minds. Six years not knowing what is going on is a long time. That's more important than my mate issues."

Conner rolled his eyes, he couldn't help it. Dominic was being a coward, looking for excuses so he didn't have to admit weakness to their father.

"Bullshit, bro—you're scared, that's all. You know as well as I do that Dad is *never* too busy for family. Hell, he's never too busy to help anyone who needs it, and he manages to multitask just fine. He'll be pissed if you don't go to him for help when he finds out you needed it."

Shaking his head in resignation, Conner got up and using every ounce of his supernatural strength, he hauled his brother's butt out of his chair. Dominic might be older, but Conner had more muscle. Before Dominic could come to his senses and stop him, he had him half way out the door. Pulling his arm free, Dominic growled at him.

"What the hell, Conner?"

"You need to go ask Dad for advice, and I want to hear what he has to say, so I'm coming along."

With a sigh, Dominic allowed Conner to usher him down the hall and into their father's office. He hated when his brother saw through his defense mechanisms and made him deal with things when he just wanted to hide. Hiding was good. Safe. He knew he should have told his dad when the dreams first started. It was, after all, what his father had asked them to do and Dominic had been meaning to tell him. It's just that other things kept happening and he hadn't got around to it yet.

His dad looked up from his desk, cocking an eyebrow when he saw them enter. Dominic was sure the sight of his nineteen-year-old, six foot two son, trying to muscle his twenty-one year old, six foot six son through the door would keep his dad chuckling for some time. Despite the fact Dominic wasn't in the mood for humor, he could see how others would think the image they made looked funny as hell. He would if he were watching it.

"What can I help you boys with?" he asked in a voice laced with more than a touch of humor.

Before Dominic could speak, Conner spoke up.

"Dom has something he needs to discuss with you."

The smirk dropped off Conner's face when their father turned his full attention to him.

"So you're here because…?" their father queried with a raised eyebrow.

"I, ah, I'd really like to hear your answer, Dad."

Conner almost sounded sheepish. It was so unlike his normally confident brother that Dominic found himself biting back a chuckle. He understood where his brother was coming from; he'd want to know too if he were in Conner's position.

"Alrighty then, you've got my curiosity spiked. What's up, Dominic?"

Dominic shut the door then dragged himself over to sit in the couch near his dad's desk. Conner dropped down next to him.

"Well, I've started dreaming of my mate…" Dominic

proceeded to tell his dad about his dreams and how they'd recently changed.

"Hmm, that explains it. Your mother and I had been wondering about what's been eating at you lately." He paused to scrub his hand over his face. "I haven't been as diligent in making either of you aware of our ways, have I? For that I am sorry."

He got up from his desk and came around to sit in the chair next to the couch.

"So, you boys are curious about mating and all it entails? Hmm, where to start...do you boys remember what I told you about the dreams starting when your mate turns twenty-one, and that you'll see more as time goes on?"

Dominic gave a quick nod as Conner sat forward and rested his elbows on his knees. Thanks to that little snippet of information, every night after he'd turned twenty-one, he'd gone to sleep with his stomach in knots of anticipation until he'd finally dreamed of her sweet face.

"Okay, I guess we'll start there then. As Dominic has found out, you are linked with your mate on an emotional level. Her pain will become yours. Now, I'm not talking about her stubbing her toe or crying over spilled milk, but when she truly suffers, like the loss of someone close, a major car crash that leaves her severely injured, that kind of thing, you'll know about it."

Angry heat rolled through Dominic. So, he had no

way of finding his mate but would know when she was hurting...that was plain cruel.

"But, Dad, what good does it do me to be able to feel her pain but be unable to do a damn thing about it?" Dominic could hear the frustration in his own voice and wasn't surprised when his father glared at him.

"Don't get yourself so worked up, Dominic. There is a way that you can possibly help her. It's called Dream Bonding. You can use your shifter magic to appear in her dreams, or pull her into yours, but you must be careful; it is just as easy to do or say the wrong thing in a dream as it is in real life. Leave a bad impression in her dreams, she'll shy away from you outside of them."

Right. Visit dream. Stay quiet. Got it, he could *so* do that. A kernel of hope lit up inside his heart as he leaned forward in his seat.

"How exactly does it work?"

His mind stilled and the churning in his stomach settled. He instinctively knew if he could just see her and touch her, offer her some comfort—even if it was just in a dream—it would ease both of them.

"As you're drifting off to sleep you need to focus on her, forming a connection with her subconscious. When she's asleep, you'll find it's easy to link together. Once linked, you can either push yourself into her dream or pull her into yours. But, be aware that she will think it is just like any other dream, that it is hers alone and formed from her imagination."

Taking a deep breath, Dominic ran the process

through in his mind. It sounded easy enough. He hoped like hell it worked. Frowning, he wondered what he'd do if it didn't. The fact his mate was hurting and he wasn't with her to fix it, ate at him. His dad cleared his throat, grabbing his attention. There was more? He'd thought his dad was done.

"While we're discussing mating, I may as well educate you on other areas. Like the Marking."

With that one word, his father had Dominic's full attention. He had seen his dad's mark before but his parents had never explained how it got there, and he was definitely curious.

"Now, obviously it has something to do with sex. I'm going to skip over the 'birds and bees' part of things because I'm pretty sure you boys know all you need to know about what goes where and what can happen as a result. So, when you are inside your mate, and you both climax at the same time, your right hand will partially shift. Only your right hand.

"Your claws will sprout from your fingertips. Once your claws are fully extended, you need to scratch your mate. Now, don't worry about hurting her, it uses shifter magic so you are not cutting into her. You can leave your mark anywhere on her body but traditionally speaking, mating happens with the male taking his mate from behind and leaving his mark here." He paused to place his palm inside his right hipbone. "Once you scratch her, you need to place your palm over your mark until the magic cools. For a minute or so, you'll feel the heat radiating from the mark. Your magic will then flow through to your mate. It doesn't matter if she's wholly human or one of us, she will still sprout claws on her right hand. Like you, it will only happen to her right hand.

"At that point, you need to leave her body so you can turn her to face you. Placing her hand over your heart, she will curl her fingers into your skin, dragging down to leave her mark. Just as you did with her, she'll put her palm over the mark until it is cool. Once both mates are marked, the mating is complete and is forever binding. The two souls will irrevocably be joined."

Dominic jerked in his seat when the loud shrill of the emergency phone filled the room and ended the conversation. Without missing a beat at all, Dominic followed Conner out the door; he was rather grateful for the break. He needed time to process what they'd discussed and to try his hand at Dream Bonding.

Sunshine, Victoria, Australia
Cancer.
The Big C.
Adele allowed the words to echo around her mind as she struggled to breathe through her grief. The disease was so far advanced there was no hope of finding a suitable treatment. Guilt had her stomach roiling and bile rising up her throat. Had she been so preoccupied with study she hadn't noticed how sick her mother had become? She'd noticed her mother looking tired lately,

but when she asked her about it, her mother told her how working two jobs was tiring and she just needed some more sleep. It was nothing for Adele to worry about. According to her mother, Adele had enough to worry about with her University exams. Had her mother known? Had she hidden it from her? Her only daughter?

Now, Adele was the one who was bone-tired. Her stiff and aching muscles reminded her she'd been sitting by her mother's bed for the past four days. She was praying and waiting for her mother to wake up or give her some kind of sign that she was still with her.

She hated the way the nurses and doctors looked at her with big sad eyes. Adele wasn't ready to accept her new reality. It was too much for her to bear on her own. At least her mother wasn't in any pain. The doctor had assured Adele of it and it had eased the vice on her heart a fraction. She'd seen the staff making sure her mother had enough morphine in her system to ease her pain. During her Nursing Degree, she'd learned about Palliative Care and she'd thought it seemed like such a nice and easy concept. Now, those two words tore her heart and soul to shreds quicker than she'd ever thought possible.

With silent tears tracking down her face and falling on the crisp white hospital sheet, she said a quiet plea, using her mother's native French in an attempt to rouse her.

"S'il te plaît, réveille-toi maman, ne me quitte pas sans dire au revoir."

Please wake up, Mama...don't leave me without saying goodbye.

Weariness tugged at her mind until she gave in and laid her head down next to her mother's hand, which she held in her own. Tears stained her cheeks until her exhaustion pulled her into sleep.

Adele woke to the sounds of the bush. Birds called and wind rustled leaves. Opening her eyes, she found herself surrounded by some of the tallest, straightest gum trees she'd ever seen. She was lying on her back on soft native grass in a small clearing and directly above her was a gorgeous cloudless blue sky. Tension eased out of her body as she allowed herself to relax; this place was beautiful and so peaceful. The sun felt so warm on her face and bare arms. She closed her eyes to enjoy the warmth as she took a deep breath of clean country air. With each exhale, she calmed more while all the real world stresses began to fall away. She had no idea how her mind had managed to create this place, one she had never seen before, but she was grateful for it.

She flicked her eyes wide open as she sensed someone watching her. She held her breath as she slowly sat up, turning her head to each side to look around the clearing and over the lake in front of her.

Her movements froze when she heard a noise that sounded distinctly like purring. Very loud, very close purring. She swung her head toward the sound and came face to face with a cat. No, not a cat, or at least not a house cat. This was a wild animal and he was huge and extremely beautiful. His large head was level with hers as he sat watching her with an intense stare. His fur looked so soft. His chest was pure white while the rest of his coat was tinged with brown and had black-grey spots.

Adele's gaze got caught in his once more. Ice blue orbs glowing with intelligence, protection, and compassion. A wave of calm flowed through her as she sat mesmerized, which was plain crazy. After all, she was sitting in front of a snow leopard, for crying out loud! Even for her imagination, this was astounding.

She wondered if she should be afraid, run as fast and as far away as she could, but this was only a dream, so it was safe. That, and for some strange reason she felt compelled to remain close to this beautiful animal.

Purring, the leopard slowly stood and padded over to her. Her heart racing in anticipation, she remained frozen to the spot as she waited to see what he was going to do next. He nuzzled his head up her leg as he lay down by her side. He pushed his back into her as he continued to nuzzle against her thigh.

It felt so good and within moments her heart rate settled back to normal and the tension flowed from her muscles once again. Speechless, she gazed down his long body, and he was definitely a boy leopard. She reached out and rubbed his fluffy ear and stroked his soft cheek, pushing back his thick white whiskers. His purring got louder and he closed his eyes as he nuzzled against her palm.

Totally surreal.

She couldn't put her finger on how she knew, but she was certain he was her guardian. There was definitely a connection between her and the animal, like her soul recognized him. It was a bizarre feeling knowing this snow leopard was somehow hers.

Her chaton, *her kitten.*

After stroking and petting him for several minutes, she was so relaxed that her mind began to wonder. Reality crept in on her thoughts and she couldn't help the sob that escaped her throat. Her mother, her whole world, was dying. She let go of the leopard, brought her knees up, and buried her face in her hands. And let out gut-wrenching sobs that shook her whole being.

The sudden coolness against her leg let her know the leopard had moved away from her. She guessed he didn't appreciate a crying woman. She didn't care. She needed to let out all the pain that was tearing her apart inside and eating her alive.

While lost in her pain and tears she gasped when warmth surrounded her. He hadn't left her at all. He'd just moved so he could curl himself around her so she was cradled between his front and back legs. Butterflies took flight in her tummy as she realized the leopard was trying to cuddle her. Hiccupping as her sobs receded, she raised her head out of her hands and wiped her eyes with her fingers. A nudge at her arm followed by a whimper had her looking into his face through her watery gaze. Her throat tightened at the concern and kindness that shone from his ice-blue irises. Was he for real? This didn't feel like a normal dream. Could the animal understand her, could he actually care for her?

"Are you really here? Just for me, my chaton*?" she whispered.*

He responded by nuzzling her shoulder and giving her neck a little lick that tickled. A snort broke free from her unbidden and had the animal purring.

"You like me giggling, do you?"

A small smile tugged at her lips when he nuzzled his head under her arm, until he was resting on her lap.

"You're just a little pushy, my chaton*," she said, lowering her legs to make room for him. She stroked the silky soft fur on the top of his head, between his ears.*

She could really use a hug. She moved herself down so she could lie with her head on his shoulder. He moved with her so she lay on her side against his hind leg with her head positioned just behind his shoulder. She stroked the thick fur down his front leg and paw, tracing his spots then the pads of his foot.

She watched as her tears landed on his soft fur. Words tumbled from her lips before she realized it.

"She's dying. My precious mother is leaving me," she whispered.

"She's all I have. I'm going to be so alone once she's gone."

As she poured her heart out, her chaton *gently nuzzled her cheek and shoulder. Eventually her tears ran out and with the sun warming her from above, and her* chaton *warming her from below, exhaustion made her heavy eyelids close. With his purring filling her mind, she felt safe and protected. Maybe she wasn't totally alone in the world after all.*

Dominic watched Conner hoe into his breakfast of bacon and eggs as he came into the kitchen. Their mother put a plate identical to his brother's down on the table for him as she gave him a quick kiss on the cheek.

"You're looking better this morning, my darling son, did your father's advice help?"

Dominic chuckled softly as he noticed Conner had stopped with his fork halfway to his mouth. He watched Dominic with avid interest. Obviously, he was desperate to know if the Dream Bonding their father had told them about had worked. No doubt he was trying to soak in all the information he could, hopeful that he would soon dream of his own mate. At nineteen, Conner still had at least a couple of years to go. Male shifters were always older than their mates.

"Breakfast smells great, thanks, Mum." He gave his mum a kiss on the cheek before he sat down. "Yeah, Dad's advice was definitely helpful. I managed to get the Dream Bonding to work last night. Took me a bit to get it started but, damn, was it well worth the effort," he answered with a broad grin.

This morning he'd woken feeling lighter and more relaxed than he had been in weeks. A little shiver ran up his spine as he recalled how good it had felt to have her hands in his fur. The knowledge that she wasn't in any imminent danger was a huge relief, although he hated that she was emotionally hurting.

"I'm glad to hear it, Dominic. Next time you won't wait so long before going to your father for help, will you?" She didn't wait for him to answer before she continued, "I've got to get moving, so I'll leave you boys to it. Shopping doesn't do itself and with the way you boys and your father eat, you have no idea how much I wish it did. I'll catch you both later."

She gave both her sons a kiss on the top of their heads.

"Now don't you boys forget to put your dishes in the dishwasher before you leave."

"Shall do, Mum."

Dominic smirked when he and Conner spoke at the same time. Then silence filled the room and as Dominic continued to eat, he barely held back from laughing. Clearly, Conner wanted to ask him about what happened but was trying to act cool. He knew his little brother wouldn't be able to resist for long.

Sure enough, after a few minutes Conner cracked and started the anticipated questioning.

"So, what happened, Dom? Is she all right? Do you know where to find her now?"

Dominic remained silent for a minute while he finished off his mouthful, enjoying the show of his brother squirming in anticipation. But he could only torture his little brother for so long. Besides, he really wanted to share what he had learned with his brother, who was also his best friend.

"I was right, Conner. My sweet mate is hurting something fierce. She told me her mother was dying and that it's always been just the two of them. She's feeling like she's going to be alone when her mother dies."

Conner frowned at him.

"She told you all that? In one dream—to a man she's never seen before? Dream Bonding's that strong, huh?"

Dominic barked out a laugh. "Hell no, even in dreams women don't tell strange men anything. I did try to join her dream as a man while she was dreaming of a public place, but she just moved past me, refusing to even look at me even when I called out. It was obvious she has little interest in men in general. I'm thinking maybe she's been hurt by a man at some point; her dad maybe? If it's just her and her mum, her dad's obviously not in the picture." He didn't want to even contemplate it being an ex-boyfriend. "So anyway, when that didn't work I tried pulling her into my dream. That worked perfectly. I took her to the little field up near the lake and met her in my leopard form."

"Oh man, you trying to make the woman run?" Conner's voice was laced with humor as he slapped his thighs.

"It wasn't like I had much choice, Conner. It's either man or leopard, and she didn't want the man. But she didn't run. After a little bit she cuddled up to me, spilled her story, had a good cry, then closed her eyes and relaxed with her head over my heart and her hand buried in my fur. Man, was I one happy cat. I got to see all of her, from head to toe and, Conner, she looks just like an angel. She had her dark wavy hair spread across my fur, and her ivory skin looked so soft. Even with her warm chocolate-colored eyes closed, I could still feel their warmth." Dominic's eyes glazed over as he sighed.

"Don't know that I ever want to be mated if I have to look like you do right now, bro. You look like a bloody lovesick kitten."

Conner rolled his eyes with a dramatic shudder Dominic knew he was putting on. Dominic's lips quirked into a lopsided grin as he remembered his mate's nickname for him.

"You know, that's what she called me. Her *chaton*. I looked it up this morning. It's French for kitten."

That had Conner instantly roaring with laughter, and Dominic couldn't help but join his brother. He just hoped like hell that he didn't have to wait too long before he would meet his mate in real life.

Chapter One

The gravel crunched under the soles of Adele's shoes as she walked through the cemetery. She slowed down as she approached the row where her mother's grave lay. She rubbed her fist over her aching heart; she still struggled to accept her mother was really gone. Her vision blurred with tears as she left the path to walk over the grass toward her mother. Frustrated, she swiped at the tears with her free hand. Surely after four years she shouldn't continue to fall apart at the mere thought of her mother?

Adele didn't bother looking where she was going. She'd been to her mother's grave so many times she was quite sure she could now find it while blindfolded in the dark. Her stomach twisted in knots of grief, she reached her mother's grave. Doing her best to push aside her roiling emotions, she set about cleaning the tombstone off and neatening it up. Then she carefully placed her six deep purple roses, her mother's favorite, in the special vase built into the top.

Once that was taken care of, she crumpled to her

knees on the grass and let the tight hold on her emotions go. As her tears began to flow, she buried her face in her hands. Four years later, the wound to her heart and soul still felt so fresh, like it had remained open and continued to bleed.

"Ma chère maman, tu me manques beaucoup."
My precious mother, I miss you so much.

As she'd always done, she spoke to her mother in French, taking comfort in using her mother's native language.

After several minutes, she managed to rein in her emotions. She pulled out a tissue, dried her eyes, blew her nose, and took a few deep breaths. She had things to tell her mother but she couldn't afford to sit here all day in the sun, she had studying to do. Opening her eyes, she looked up at the tombstone, reading the words she had so carefully chosen four years ago:

'In Ever Loving Memory Of
Fleur Petit
26-5-1972 - 20-11-2007
Loving Mother of Adele
As a mother you cared for me,
the Lord will now care for you.'

In a quiet whisper, Adele told her mother everything that had happened since she visited a fortnight ago.

"I'm nearly finished, *Maman*. My last exam is on Thursday, then I'm all done with Uni. You'd be so proud. I got my honors completed too. Your *petit fille* will soon be a qualified nurse and paramedic. If only I could find a job." She sighed. "I think I'm going to have to leave Sunshine."

The thought of leaving left her heart aching, but staying here surrounded by memories and reminders of her mother wouldn't be any easier. It had been unbearable at times over the last four years. Now, with University nearly over, she could feel the beginnings of depression claw at her. She needed to get away, get a fresh start or she would remain stuck in her mother's shadow, forever grieving and never moving on with her own life.

"I've found a few openings coming up in Tasmania. I've applied in Devonport, Strahan, Rosebery, and Hobart. I'm sure I'll be able to land one of them. I think I'll like Tasmania. It doesn't get as hot in the summer, for one thing. You know how well me and summer heat get along. Most of the jobs aren't going to start until the new year so I've got time to finish up Uni before moving over. I figure, new year, new start—what better time to go."

Tears pricked her eyes again when she realized she wouldn't be able to come for her fortnightly visits with her *Maman* anymore. But maybe that was part of the problem; she needed some distance to allow her heart to heal.

"I'm going to miss being able to visit you. I thought maybe if I take a photo, I can still sit and talk with you. I spoke with Chrissy and she's going to come visit on your birthday each year and tidy up for us."

Brushing away tears, Adele glanced down at her watch and gasped at how much time had passed. Time always seemed to fly when she was with her mother.

"Okay, *Maman*, I've got to get moving. I need to study for my exams. I don't think I'll be able to visit as usual, but I promise I'll come and see you again before I leave."

Adele stood and with a wince, stretched out her muscles that were cramping from sitting down for so long. With a lump in her throat, she laid a soft kiss to the top of the tombstone before heading back toward her car.

As Adele reached for her car door a tingle of awareness run up her spine. With a frown, she turned back toward the cemetery and froze as she tried to wrap her mind around what she saw. Was that a leopard under the tree near her mother's grave? She rubbed her eyes, before she looked again. Nothing out of the ordinary was there. She shook her head and climbed into her car. She was getting way too caught up in her dreams if she was imagining leopards in real life.

Cradle Mountains National Park, Tasmania, Australia

Dominic's muscles relaxed as he took a deep breath of cool fresh mountain air. He didn't get to do this nearly as often as he would like to. In his teenage years, after he first shifted at fifteen, he would go for runs through the mountains regularly, but as he'd gotten older adult responsibilities had filled his time.

Nothing felt better than having the wind over his face as he ran through the scrub. Or the way water splashed up on his paws and stomach cooling him off as he loped through the creeks. He arrived at the top of a high cliff and a shiver ran down his spine as he took in the natural beauty of the Cradle Mountains. Awareness seeped into him a moment before he heard a quiet growl to his right. He grunted but stayed still when Conner head-butted his shoulder.

What's up, Dominic? I can feel your anguish.

Some days Dominic could do without the connections shifters had when in leopard form. Since members of the same Leap could project their thoughts to each other, they could also get a sense of each other's emotions. Today of all days, he didn't want everyone knowing how he was feeling.

My mate was really hurting yesterday. It was the fourth anniversary of her mother's death. Just like Dad told us, I felt her pain like it's my own. I just wish she'd come to me or given me some hint to where she is so I could go get her. It's driving me insane being able to feel her pain but not being able to do anything to comfort her.

Wow. It's been four years already? Surely you'll meet her soon, bro. How long until you go search for her?

Soon, I can't wait much longer. After the fire season is finished I'll head over to the mainland and start searching. He didn't want to leave Rosebery, this was his home and where his Leap was. It was tearing up his insides not being able to hold his mate. *Come on, let's go for another run before it gets late and we have to head home.*

Conner nipped the back of Dominic's hind leg before leaping off through the bush. With a playful growl, Dominic took off after his brother— Conner was so going to pay for that cheap shot.

Dominic let Conner lead the way for a few minutes before he sped up and leapt onto his back, grabbing his neck with his teeth, gently of course; he would never intentionally hurt his brother, and rolled to the ground with him. Dominic loved mucking around with his brother. They both gave in to their inner kittens and rolled around play fighting, growling, and purring. It was a good ten minutes before Dominic decided to end things and pinned Conner down.

C'mon, Conner, sun's setting. We better get moving. Thanks for the game, bro.

After lightly tapping his head against his brother's, Dominic leapt to the side, releasing Conner before they leisurely prowled back to the carpark. As they got near, they stopped to listen for any humans close by. Dominic couldn't sense anyone close but it always paid to play it safe. They shifted back to human form before emerging from the trees. Better if they got busted as naked humans than as snow leopards if there was anybody around.

Dominic led Conner through the tree line and was

relieved to discover they were indeed alone. A shiver ran through him as the wind whipped around him.

"Damn, it's cold with no fur," Dominic complained.

"Tell me about it."

Dressing quickly, he wasted no time jumping into his car so he could crank on the heat before he drove his brother home. Dominic felt a hell of a lot better after their day out and a quick glance at Conner confirmed that he too was looking more relaxed and at ease than he had looked before they went out.

Cole Jones was hot and frustrated. Neither of those things helped his mood, in fact, they sent it straight down the drain. Just like every other damn day down at the Strahan Docks, he'd loaded and unloaded containers all day. What made today particularly crappy was that summer had kicked in early, throwing a stinking hot day at him in November. Out on the docks under the sun, it felt like the inside of an oven and that always put everyone on edge. Which meant, not only was he in a hellish mood, but so was everyone else, and he didn't have the patience for any of it.

Maybe he should have finished school, gotten himself a fancy desk job in a climate controlled office. Damn, what he wouldn't give for an air conditioner right about now. His belly tightened as his mind wondered to other things.

Finding a way to cool down wasn't the only thing that would improve his terrible day. He cracked his knuckles. A good solid workout followed up with a hard fuck would definitely improve his mood. Thoughts of how he'd spend his evening kept his mind happily occupied for the rest of the day. He didn't bother saying goodbye to anyone, that would take time and he just wanted to get home. Jumping in his ute, he wasted no time in cranking over the engine and roaring out of the carpark. His blood buzzed with anticipation of what he would do when he arrived home.

When he turned into his driveway, his left hand started to tremble. He took a deep breath and tamped down his excitement. He wanted his fun to last tonight, so he needed to settle down before he got started.

After parking his ute in the garage and making sure it was locked up, he walked up the path and pushed through the front door. His house wasn't huge. The main living area was open plan, with the kitchen at one end and lounge at the other. Three bedrooms and a bathroom came off the main room, and of course, the downstairs basement that had a small hallway and two rooms. The open plan suited his needs perfectly. It meant that by collaring the slave and chaining her on a fifty-foot chain she could do all he needed her to, but couldn't get out the front door and escape.

As he entered, he saw the brat silently slide into her room. Good. He didn't want to deal with her tonight. He wanted the slave. He rolled his shoulder anticipating his workout, hearing her screams. He continued his way through the house until he found what he was looking for. She was in the kitchen, trembling by the oven. He stalked over to her until he stood over her much smaller body, relishing her fear soaked wide eyed expression she looked up at him with. She was right to fear him in this moment. He was in one hell of a ferocious mood tonight. He cracked his knuckles, loving how she shuddered in response.

"I - I - I've made dinner for you, just like you wanted," she stammered.

Perfect. He grinned as a thrill ran through him. She was trying to placate him into not taking her downstairs; after all these years she really should know better. His moods were only placated by working her body over and fucking her.

"Turn everything off. You've got somewhere else to be."

Even he could hear excitement in his voice. Which made sense. He couldn't wait to get her downstairs. Arms crossed over his chest, he watched her hands tremble as she struggled to turn off the oven before taking the pot over to the sink. As soon as her hands left the metal, he pounced on her. Wrapping his fingers in her soft hair, he used it to drag her to the door that led to his basement wonderland. He only paused long enough to unlock the chain from her collar and carefully hang it on the hook by the door. His OCD could be such a bitch but he knew if he left it in a mess, he wouldn't be able to fully focus on what he was about to do. With each step he took down, his blood burned hotter as he thought over exactly what he was going to do.

Detective Alex Ross stared down at the reports he'd spread out over his desk. His heart clenched. So many lives cut short. Each of the eight profiles had a confirmed identity so they had photos of how each woman had looked alive. Grainy driver's license photos and blurry year book snaps glared up at him, as if the victims knew their killer hadn't been brought to justice yet. Then there were the police photos. The ones of beaten and battered bodies dragged from the river or ocean.

The first time he'd read these damned reports he'd thrown up. Each time he had to work on them bile rose up his throat. Alex was raised to respect all life, but in particular to protect women and children. He entered the police force so he could uphold those beliefs and every time he had to deal with domestic violence or a particularly horrific murder, his soul screamed at the injustice. Especially when they couldn't catch the damn perpetrator and the bastard kept doing it.

This particular bastard had to live around Strahan somewhere. He'd been raping and killing women for ten years, at least. Alex had always believed these cases were linked, and so did most of the cops who'd had anything to do with any of these murders, but they had no proof. Each of the bodies had been found in either the river or the ocean near Strahan so any evidence was compromised with water damage. Unfortunately for the perpetrator, technology was getting better at pulling DNA from the smallest of samples. A thrill ran through him as he looked over the newest report. The DNA profile of the killer. They nearly had him. All they needed to do now was find the match. Naturally, it wasn't in the system. Alex rolled his eyes, even though he was alone. That would make things way too simple.

But they did have a profile on him. One that stated the man most likely worked near the water. That he was middle-aged and would have control issues. Alex had already compiled the list of businesses that were on or near the coast or river. The biggest was the Strahan Docks, which thankfully ran random drug tests on their employees. Alex was hopeful he could get a judge to agree to give him an order for the Docks to hand over their next round of tests for DNA analysis. Hopefully he'd find a match and put this killer behind bars where he belonged.

As he moved to his computer to fill out the relevant paperwork, the photo on his desk caught his attention. He'd taken it on their last family holiday, his wife and two beautiful teenage daughters were smiling at him, looking happy and carefree. Something these eight women would never be again. His resolve to find this bastard before he could strike again strengthened. He had to catch him before he took any more lives.

Blood and pain always makes sex better. Hell, they made life better, Cole mused to himself. He unhooked the slave's cuffs and watched with satisfaction as she slumped down on the floor. Damn, he felt good. So much better than earlier.

He pulled his pants back on as the slave attempted to stand. His lip curled into a sneer; she was so weak and unworthy of a master like him. He needed a stronger slave, one that could handle the workouts and rough fucking. Although, this one had lasted longer than most. She was still lacking in so many ways. Growling, he grabbed her arm in a tight grip and roughly hauled her back up the stairs. She tripped twice but he refused to slow or allow her any time to get her feet back under her. He simply kept a tight grip on her and dragged her up. Once out, he closed the door and carefully reattached the chain to her collar before shoving her aside.

"You've got fifteen minutes to get cleaned up and serve me dinner, or back down you go."

He needed a drink, but couldn't stand the thought of the slave getting blood all over the bottle. The only mess he allowed was downstairs. Keeping that room bloodstained helped him torture his slaves so much better. Everywhere else was a different story. He required his home to be meticulously clean and he certainly wouldn't stand for drinking from a dirty bottle.

He tore open the fridge and snatched a cold bottle of beer before he headed to the lounge for some chill out time in front of the TV. A haze of red clouded his vision for a moment when he noticed the TV was already on—

bloody cartoons, damn little brat. He wondered where she was, before shaking his head. Who the fuck cared. He did appreciate that the brat knew to hide, knew to stay silent. He'd always hated kids, detested having to put up with their noise and mess. But this one's sad, lonely, desperate mother, who had no family or friends had been too easy to entrap to resist. No one had noticed her not hanging around town anymore. No one had filed a missing person's report on either of them. He took a long swallow of beer, letting the cool liquid calm him further. He supposed the slave's little brat wasn't too bad. She was certainly pretty, with her black curls and big round grey eyes. Such a pity she was too young for his tastes. He was sure she'd make a better slave than her useless mother. Those big grey eyes wide in pain would be a thing to see. That got his mind ticking over, maybe when the brat was older and her mother had passed being useful, he could get rid of her and train the brat to be his slave, properly. His very own virginal slave...he chuckled, yeah that sounded fucking ace.

Kelly silently closed her door as she heard his evil chuckle, the one that always made the hairs on her neck stand up and her body shudder. She'd heard his heavy footsteps on the stairs as he'd dragged her mother back up minutes ago. As always, she'd been listening for it and silently fled to her bedroom away from the lounge where she had the TV on trying to drown out the sounds of her mother screaming. A violent shudder ran through her body. She heard those screams in her nightmares each night.

Once safely in her room, panic had her sweating. She'd forgotten to turn the TV off. Her heart had just about beat out of her chest as she'd waited on his reaction. Thankfully, she'd been lucky this time. All he'd done was curse before changing the channel.

A ragged sigh escaped her lips. He hadn't come looking for her like she feared he would one of these days. He'd never touched her. He rarely even spoke to her. But she could see the violence in his eyes. Saw the condition her mother was constantly in from his *attention*.

Kelly slid down the wall, sitting with her knees up and her head back against the plaster. Instinctively trying to make herself smaller. The shirt she wore pulled tight against her throat and she tugged at it. She'd outgrown her stolen clothing again. She needed to sneak out and get herself something bigger. No doubt, her mother would need new clothing after tonight too.

A couple of years ago, after going out while he was at work, she'd discovered a clothing bin a few streets away. Since then, she would sneak out every six months or so and get herself bigger clothes. She also brought some back for her mother each time. He was always ripping her mother's clothes, wrecking them. He didn't allow them to leave the house, didn't provide anything more than food. Fortunately, he didn't pay any attention to what they did or didn't wear either, so he didn't notice when she'd been out to get more.

She closed her eyes and floated back in time. Five years ago, she and her mother were on the run from her father when they'd met Him. Her mother, tired of running, of being alone, was desperate. When he offered them the use of his 'unused small house on the outskirts of town' her mother told her this was a sign that all their problems were over. Yeah, right. Problems over. She grunted. The house was meant to be empty, just the two of them living there, starting afresh. When they arrived to move in he'd been there waiting for them. Had a collar and chain on her mother in a flash and since then they had both been enslaved. Kelly could leave, she wasn't physically chained, but she could never abandon her mother. Her mother would always need Kelly to help her. Just like after her father had finished with her, Kelly would clean up her mother when He was done. Help her recover and heal up. She needed to go to the bathroom to see how she could help.

She had learned how to move without a sound soon after she learned to walk and the skill continued to serve her well. She silently made her way to the bathroom. She didn't want him to notice her. She was getting older now, starting to develop lady parts. If she wasn't careful, he would notice and then she would end up being dragged down those horrid stairs to where very bad things happened. And she was quite certain she wanted to avoid that outcome at all costs.

Chapter Two

Adele finished packing up the few remaining possessions left of her mother's life, and her own. She was determined to snap out of her downward spiral. If she didn't soon, she feared she never would. Tomorrow she was packing up her little Toyota Corolla and driving off to find her fresh start. She didn't have much of a plan. All she had organized were four job interviews at various hospitals in Tasmania. She closed her eyes and hoped like hell she would manage to land one of the jobs. She didn't have a lot saved up so being able to find work quickly was her top priority. She'd figured New Year's Eve was as good a day as any to start a new life so she'd bought herself a ferry pass and by tomorrow night she would be in Tasmania. Glancing at her watch, she saw it was getting late so she headed off to bed. She would need a good night's sleep before starting her adventure in the morning.

The moment her head hit the pillow her eyelids slid shut and she drifted off to sleep with a smile tugging at her lips. Knowledge she was going into the magic world that had kept her sane over the last four years filled her with bliss.

She opened her eyes and grinned at the sight of their field. Tonight she really needed to see her chaton, *needed him to reassure her that she was doing the right thing by leaving. It was strange but it felt right to share her secrets with him and seek his approval of her plans. Maybe because he was an animal and couldn't talk, or reject her, that made her feel safe to tell him everything. Although, she hadn't told him anything about these plans yet. She'd been saving the surprise until now.*

Unable to stand still for all her nervous energy, she paced around the field looking for him. She froze when she found him and put her hand over her mouth to muffle the giggle she couldn't hold in. Apparently, he was feeling playful today. He was on his back with his paws in the air, squirming back and forth. Rubbing his back on the grass and sunning his tummy like a dog would. He stopped squirming, tilted his head back so he could watch her upside-down with his ice-blue eyes. She jogged over to him laughing out in pure joy.

"You want a tummy rub, my chaton?*" she said as she kneeled beside him and ran her hand over his tummy and up his chest. He rewarded her with a loud purr.*

"Like that, huh?"

She allowed herself to get lost in the sensation of his fur on her skin for a few moments before she dropped her bombshell.

"I'm leaving tomorrow."

The purring stopped suddenly as he quickly rolled over and sat up in front of her, head cocked to the side.

A grin tugged at her lips at his actions.

"You really can understand what I'm saying, can't you?"

His reply was an adorable little growl sound.

"Don't fret, I'm not trying to change the subject on you."

He made the noise again while giving her a hard stare. What was his problem? Oh crap, surely he didn't think...

"Don't tell me you thought I meant I'm leaving you?"

He gave her a slight nod of his massive head. Lifting her butt of her heels, she rose enough to get up to his face level. Taking his head in her hands, she threaded her fingers through the thick fur around his jaw before she planted a firm kiss between his eyes.

"Never, my chaton, *I'd never leave you or this place we have. I'm leaving my home, the one I shared with my* Maman. *The memories are too much for me. I need to start over and now I've finished with University I need to find a job. There are a few in Tasmania that would be perfect—"*

He licked up her cheek and gave a loud purr.

"Well, I guess that answers the question of whether or not you approve of my decision, then."

Relieved by his easy acceptance, she chuckled as she wiped her cheek dry on her shoulder.

"That tongue of yours tickles something fierce, you know that?"

He dipped his head and licked up her neck then nuzzled her.

"Cheeky,"she stated, shaking her head as she rubbed his ears just how he liked it.

Relaxing into his seat, Jake watched his team enjoy their New Year's Eve. It had been twelve years since the Government panicked, thinking the dreaded "Y2K bug" would blow up all the country's computers or some such garbage. In their panic, they'd demanded all fire stations be manned for the entire night of NYE 1999. Totally stupid really, as nothing came of it of course. Aside from a few thousand computers crapping out because they couldn't cope with the new year not having a "19" at the beginning. Certainly, nothing blew up, to many a Firie's disappointment. However, a tradition was created. Every NYE the Rosebery fire station was party central for his team, their friends, and family, and he liked nothing better than to sit back and watch the festivities.

A grin spread over his face when he caught sight of the twins. They were out front setting up their fireworks. Apparently, they'd had too much spare time and decided learning how to blow stuff up while making it look pretty was a good investment of their time. Not that Jake minded. It was one hell of a lot cheaper than buying the things in, plus there was the added entertainment of watching Joel and Jordan, who were identical six foot three muscle-bound firemen, finishing each other's sentences and rushing around like excited five-year-olds on Christmas morning.

Just as he finished his can of lemonade, his eldest son, Dominic, brought him another one. NYE at the station was a family friendly event. They didn't need alcohol to have a great time, and if they did get a call-out they would be fine to go deal with it.

"You're looking pretty happy there, son. Anything you want to share with your old man?"

Jake was pleased to see the huge grin that spread across Dominic's face until it reached his eyes and made the sparkle with true happiness. He'd been worried about his eldest since before he confessed he'd stated dreaming of his mate. Poor bloke had been dreaming of his mate for just over four years and had yet to meet her. Every year Jake's heart ached a little more as Dominic sunk a little further into sorrow. His happy laid-back son had been replaced by a somber man who smiled little and laughed even less. It was heartbreaking for a father to watch.

"Hell yeah I'm happy, you would be too. My mate not only pulled me into her dream last night, but she told me that today she was catching the ferry over here to look for work and a fresh start."

Joy heated Jake's blood as he slapped his son on the back before pulling him in for a quick hug.

"That does sound promising, son. Good to hear the new year is looking up for you."

"Yeah, it is. I hope it doesn't take too long for her to

find her way to Rosebery. Tassie's a big place and I can't wait to meet her for real."

Jake chuckled at his son's enthusiasm. Oh, to be young again!

"It shouldn't take too long now. Once she starts toward you she'll be drawn closer. The feeling will get stronger and the pull more insistent until she gets here. Just watch yourself when you do meet her. You need to remember you aren't meant to know what she's told you in your dreams."

"Yeah, that could be fun to explain. Especially since she already has issues with men."

Jake smiled at his son before taking a drink. His skin tingled with excitement. It was going to be fun watching Dominic win over his mate. He just knew it.

Adele sat outside a divine little cafe, sipping her coffee after having eaten her breakfast and looked out over the ocean toward where Melbourne hid beyond the horizon. She'd arrived at six the night before last and crashed at a budget motel here in Devonport to rest after the craziness of packing and moving. Now freshly showered and eager to start her new life, she looked down at the map in front of her. Nerves and excitement had her struggling to sit still. Her interview at the Devonport Hospital was in an hour's time. After that, she had a couple of days to find her way south to her other interviews.

Adele closed her eyes in bliss as she took a draw of

her flat white. Despite growing up in Melbourne, she had simple tastes and didn't go for the fancy coffees. A good hot cup of old-fashioned plain coffee with a dash of milk and a spoon full of sugar made her one happy lady. Licking her lips, she refocused on the map. What was the best way to go? She mapped out a couple of options in her mind, and decided to follow her instincts on which way to go as she drove. She had plenty of time.

Two hours later Adele was enjoying the Tasmanian scenery as she drove down the highway. The interview had been short and sweet. They were eager to have her on board but were happy to give her two weeks to attend the other interviews before she gave them her answer. They had a good set up with four teams that rotated shifts. She was a little concerned about the large area that the hospital was responsible for. However, the manager had assured her, with the four teams in place, the hospital handled the load just fine.

Taking a deep breath, she let go of work worries and relaxed. She started to tap her fingers against the steering wheel to the radio. Gwen Stefani's "If I was a Rich Girl" came on and Adele chuckled. *Couldn't agree more, Gwen.* The countryside of Tasmania was beautiful. She would have loved to have had enough money saved so she could simply explore for a few weeks before having to focus on her job hunt. Unfortunately, the small nest egg her mother had managed to save over the years disappeared quickly with medical bills and funeral costs. Adele hadn't been able to save much while she was at University, even after dropping back to part time so she could work more hours. The small amount she had managed to put away wouldn't keep her going longer than a week or two at the most. Finding a job would sadly remain her top priority, not relaxing and exploring her new island home like she truly wanted to do.

Pushing aside her financial worries she focused on the upcoming fork in the road. Decision time. Turn left and continue on the highway, or detour closer to the coast on smaller roads. The sign said "Rosebery" so she guessed she could check out the town on the way down, then come back this way after her interview at Strahan. Maybe she could stop there for lunch and get a feel of the place.

As she flicked on her indicator and began turning, the next song was introduced, Rob Thomas's "Lonely No More." She frowned down at her radio. Was the damn thing possessed? Each song that came on seemed to hit just a little too close to where her head was at. Maybe she should paint her Corolla yellow and black and start calling it "Bumblebee."

Humming the Transformers theme song, which was now stuck in her head, she shifted her focus back to the road. Her heart instantly pounding hard, she gasped and slammed her foot down on the brake pedal. Praying she stopped before she hit the mess in the middle of the road.

Her Corolla pulled up with a screech before hitting anything. Taking a few deep breaths, she continued to hold the steering wheel with a tight grip, taking in the damage. Damn, Tassie had bloody huge logging trucks, which apparently created an equally huge mess when they fell over. There were logs all over the place and when she saw the crumpled cab of the truck, her instincts took over. Clear-minded and running through what she was likely to find, she grabbed her first aid kit. She noticed a fire truck pulling up on the other side of the accident but she didn't stop to wait for them. She had no idea how long that driver had been stuck in the wreckage, if they were in fact stuck at all. She ignored the Firies and stayed focused on her destination.

Dominic's spectacular mood was unbreakable. Even this logging truck accident they were heading to would not dampen his spirits. His mate was coming to him.

"Are you going to be able to focus on the task at hand, Dominic?" Xander asked in a quiet voice.

Xander had his full attention on the road as he drove the truck with precision of long practice. Dominic's father was with them in the cab and Dominic could see him trying hard not to laugh. Fortunately for him, Nick and Kit were in the Rescue Vehicle behind them. Those two would not be as polite as Xander.

"I'll be fine, Xander. You watch, I'm going to be the epitome of professional firefighter today."

Dominic was still riding high from knowing his mate

was coming closer to him, he'd never allow it to impede a job. As they pulled up at the scene, he winced at the sight of the crumpled cab. He hoped the driver wasn't too badly injured. Rosebery was currently short a paramedic. Their remaining one and only ambo was otherwise occupied today so they were it for emergency call-outs.

There was more than one reason his father chose firefighting and not medicine. Jake was one of the few shifters who had a special ability. His was heightened empathy. Dominic didn't envy his dad that talent one bit. He was fairly proficient at blocking out most emotions. But an accident where they were really high, the levels would make him sick very quickly.

Xander pulled the truck up as close to the wrecked cab as possible. Nick and Kit pulled up behind them and without needed to see, he knew they were already rushing to get the Jaws of Life, stretcher, and first aid case out the back of the Rescue Vehicle.

While those two got the equipment, Dominic grabbed his helmet and jumped out the cab. As soon as his feet hit the road, his head snapped up as his instincts went nuts. There was a familiar scent in the air.

He stumbled forward when his father jumped out the truck and all but landed on top of him.

"What the hell, Dominic? You told us you were fine, so get moving, boy. Times-a-wasting."

"It's her, Dad."

He took a deep inhale and knew without a doubt that

his mate was here. Fear gripped him. She wasn't inside the truck cab, was she? He glanced around and relief flowed through him when he spotted her trying to get to the truck. He couldn't believe it; her first day on the island and she'd come straight to him! Shocked, he stood in a trance-like state as she all but danced around the fallen logs. She was clutching a first aid kit and was obviously trying to get to the cab. A thump to his shoulder knocked him back to reality.

"Head out the clouds, son, you can see to her later. We got a victim to help and a job to do first."

Dominic shook his head to clear it and settled his helmet in place as his father strode a few steps away before turning back to him.

"Remember, son, she doesn't know you and you can not let her know that you know her. She'll freak out and run and then you'll really have your work cut out for you."

Dominic winced. He was going to have to be extremely careful over what he said. He knew so much about her after four years of being her confident. Wetting his lips, he pushed it all down and focused on the task at hand. They had a truckie to save.

He followed the rest of the team to the wreaked cab. Kit and Nick were already cutting the driver from the wreck. He watched as Kit leaned in the broken window to check for a pulse on the unconscious man. Dominic gave a sigh of relief when she gave them the thumbs up to indicate he was still breathing.

It would take a few minutes for them to cut the cab apart enough to remove the driver so he moved his focus to his mate, watching her come closer to them. She was completely focused on her feet as she continued to make her way through the maze of logs. She looked up as she reached the cab and stumbled backwards with a gasp. Dominic caught her elbow before she went over and relished the jolt of awareness that spread up his arm.

"Easy there, beautiful. We don't need to go adding any more injuries to this accident."

He cleared his throat after he spoke. His voice had sounded deeper, smoother than it normally did. Strange. However, he very much liked the shiver he'd felt run through her while he'd spoken.

She was fast to find her balance and reluctantly, Dominic released his hold on her. She turned to him with a slight smile in place. Then her eyes popped wide open and she scanned him from head to foot. She frowned slightly as she focused on his eyes, no doubt she thought they looked familiar. After all, she'd been seeing them for the last four years in her sleep. She closed her eyes and took a deep breath before she opened them.

"Thanks for the save. I saw the accident and thought I could help. I've just finished my degree in para-medicine and have been a St Johns volunteer for the last nine years so I thought you might like help with the driver, you know, only if you need it. I don't want to tread on anyone's toes."

She sounded nervous, but even so, her voice was so sweet it sent shivers up his spine, turning his brain to mush. Thankfully his father's brain still functioned and he stepped in to save the day.

"That sounds great. We could certainly use a hand in that department. I'm Jake White by the way. The captain of the TFS here in Rosebery. The man that caught you would be my son, Dominic. The one by the gear is Xander. The two over at the cab are Nick and Kit. What's your name?"

Dominic liked how she took a firm grip of his father's hand when she shook it. Like in her dreams, she was no wilting flower.

"Pleased to meet you, Jake, my name's Adele."

Adele. Dominic rolled the name around his head, finally after four years he knew her name. It was as beautiful as her.

"Well, Adele. Let's get this job done, shall we?"

His dad led the way to the wreck that Kit and Nick had now finished opening up.

Five long hours later Adele was completely exhausted. Her body was crying out for rest but she was having such a wonderful time in the local pub. Everyone who'd helped out at the accident was here having dinner together. She grinned at the owners of the place; they sat with Jake and his wife Sophie, laughing and enjoying themselves. Apparently after any big incident, Tom and Jo would have everyone who'd helped in for a meal on the house. Which was both sweet and extremely generous of them.

Rosebery was a large mining town but it seemed to have managed to keep a small town feel to it. Everybody knew each other here. It also appeared to be mostly populated by men given the fact there were only a handful of women here at the pub. Adele guessed it was due to the mine. She was rather grateful that Kit had chosen to sit with her. One thing her single mother had taught her well was to stay clear of men and she agreed with her. She did not need, or want, a man in her life.

Adele was enjoying getting to know Kit though. The woman was totally different from her. When Adele had first met her out at the accident, Kit had scared the hell out of her. She'd been so serious and larger than life. Now she was off the clock, she'd become friendly and made sure Adele knew everyone's names and who they were.

Kit had to be over six feet tall and out of her turnout gear, Adele could see she was built slim but muscular. The way she'd pulled her flame red hair back in a high ponytail made her stunning green eyes stand out. They looked almost feline with their slight angle; she was flat out gorgeous and Adele had trouble believing the woman was single. In a mining town of mostly men, she'd thought a woman like Kit would be snapped up in no time. Kit had an air about her that said loud and clear she didn't take shit from anyone, even while relaxed. A pang of envy coiled in Adele's gut. Kit seemed like she knew her place in the world and was happy with it. Which was pretty much all Adele had ever wanted.

The smoothest voice she had ever heard pulled her out of her thoughts and had her skin tingling.

"So, Adele, noticed the Victorian plates on your car. You visiting our fair island for a holiday?"

Dominic White. The man was already testing her commitment to no men. She needed to be careful and keep her distance from him if she was going to stay in this part of Tassie.

"Nope, no holidaying for me. I guess you could say I'm embarking on a sea-change."

The moment she finished speaking, a shiver ran down her spine. The people in their sitting area grew quiet as everyone's attention was now firmly on her. Adele lowered her gaze and wiped her sweaty palms on her jeans. She really didn't like being the center of attention.

Kit grabbed hold of her arm, like she thought Adele was going to run away. Which proved how observant the woman was because that was precisely what she was thinking of doing.

"You looking to stay around here? You may have noticed we're kind of short on paramedics as we only have one so whenever he's off duty, like today, us Firies get stuck with the job and I, for one, am getting sick of cleaning up after Jake. The damn man pukes whenever we have to deal with blood and gore."

Kit winked over at the captain who was shaking his head at her like he wanted to reprimand her. The man's sly grin and the spark of amusement in his eyes gave away how much he was enjoying her ribbing. Adele really liked how they all carried on together. They were more like a big family, rather than workmates. Could she have that if she stayed here? A family of friends?

"Funny you should mention that, Kit. I actually knew about the shortage before today's accident. That's why I'm here. I'm looking for work as a paramedic. I had an interview this morning in Devonport, one tomorrow in Strahan, one here on Wednesday. Then another in Hobart on Friday."

As Adele nervously glanced around, she caught Dominic giving the doctor a strange look. After a moment, Dominic seemed to sense she was looking at him as his expression smoothed over to a smile so quickly she couldn't work out what he was trying to tell the doctor.

"Well, Adele, with all the craziness around the accident we didn't get to officially be introduced. I'm Dr Clint Maynard, the one you have an interview with on Wednesday. I can safely say the job is all yours if you want it. You more than proved yourself out in the field and at the hospital today. I'm certainly convinced you know what you're doing. You've struck up friendships with most of the town's emergency response teams already, so I know you're going to get along here in Rosebery just fine. How would you like to blow off those other interviews and hang around Rosebery with us?"

Adele coughed as she nearly choked on her drink in shock. Clint was the Dr Maynard she was booked in to meet on Wednesday? She'd planned on attending all the interviews before making a decision about which position to take. This was going to be her first real job and she wanted to be careful she chose well.

Clearing her throat, she snuck a sideways peek at Dominic while she sipped from her drink to calm herself. He really was handsome, not that she wanted a man, but if she did...he would be a spectacular choice. She closed her eyes a moment to think. Aside from Dominic, there was something about this town that pulled at her to stay. Before she changed her mind, she put her drink down, swallowed her mouthful, looked up into Clint's face, and made one of the biggest decisions of her life.

"Dr Maynard, I think I may do just that. I'd like nothing better than to hang around here and be your ambo. *Merci.*"

She ducked her head as heat crept over her cheeks. She often slipped a French word or two in when she was excited or overemotional. She hadn't meant to do it in front of so many people.

"The pleasure is all ours, Adele. Like Kit, I too am sick of cleaning up after Jake and his reactions."

He flashed a huge grin along with a wink that had

her feeling less self-conscious. Maybe they hadn't noticed her little French slip up.

"Now, since we're going to be working together, please call me Clint. I'm only Dr Maynard in front of patients. *Merci* is French, right? Are you French? You don't speak with an accent so I'd never have guessed."

"My mother emigrated from France when she was pregnant with me. We always spoke French to each other. I like to think it helped her with her homesickness. Every now and then I accidentally say a word or two in French but I assure you, I'm as Aussie as Mick Dundee."

She put on a thick Aussie accent for those last few words, hoping it would cover the grief currently tearing up her insides from thinking of her mother. Thankfully, it worked. The twins took her words and ran with it. Joel and Jordan grabbed their butter knives and with his own exaggerated Aussie accent, Joel started off with, "That's not a knife, *that*'s a knife."

For the next twenty minutes the men all took turns doing various impersonations of Mick Dundee until they were all laughing so much tears ran down their cheeks. Adele couldn't remember a time when she'd ever laughed so hard. It felt good to be happy and share joy with these people.

A flutter of hope pulsed through Alex as he hung up the phone. James, the foreman down at the Strahan Docks, was more than happy to allow the Police to use their next random drug test to collect DNA. Understandably, James had not been happy to learn that a serial rapist and killer may be working for him. Alex was still waiting on the Court Order but with James's permission, they could get the ball rolling on testing.

Even better, the next test was scheduled for Friday. If their profiler was correct, they could have a name and arrest warrant by Monday, if not sooner. Alex couldn't wait to get this particular bastard off the streets. This killer was particularly viscous and had gotten worse over the years. Alex rather dreaded finding his next victim and hoped like hell he could catch him before there was another one. Although, considering the break between the last body and now, it was more likely they just hadn't found the body yet. There might even be more than one body out in the national park somewhere. It wasn't a huge stretch to think he'd stop dumping bodies in the waterways at some point. He had to know the bodies had been found and the police were looking into them. Was that why there'd been six months since the last body turned up? Terror cooled his blood. Had the killer moved on from Strahan? He hoped not. He was so close to catching this bastard.

He quickly checked the system for any bodies found statewide. When the computer came up with nothing, he slumped back into his chair. The profiler had been quite sure this perpetrator would never stop. So, if he had moved on, there'd be a body trail to show it.

With a heavy heart, he shut down his computer and

gathered his things to go home. Unfortunately, there was nothing he could do until he got the results from the DNA tests. Considering it was Monday, he hoped like hell the killer didn't finish off another victim between now and then.

Adele had assumed she would end up staying at Top Pub, but Kit had insisted her spare room was more comfortable. Until her first pay came in, she couldn't really afford to be staying at a hotel, so she'd accepted Kit's offer. Now, Adele lay in the comfortable single bed in Kit's spacious spare room drifting off to sleep. With a sense of contentment, she thought back over her day. She couldn't believe all she'd accomplished in twenty-four hours. She'd gone from being completely alone, homeless, and jobless, to having a whole group of people who seemed to genuinely like her, a temporary home. Kit had told her she would help her find a place as soon as she had the money, and tomorrow morning she was starting her new job. As a paramedic. Excitement bubbled through her. Her first real job. She couldn't wait to tell her *chaton* about all of it...including the man she was going to have to be very, very careful around—Dominic White.

As soon as Adele arrived in their field, she began searching for her chaton. *She had so much to tell him, she didn't want to waste a moment. A glance over her shoulder revealed his presence behind her. His sleek body was low to the ground as he stalked toward her.*

Her heart started racing. He'd never attacked her before, why would he do so now? When she heard his loud purr she instantly relaxed. He only wanted a game.

She smiled slyly at him, her playful chaton. *She'd give him a game. Chuckling, she sprinted away from him across the field toward the trees. As she'd expected, she only got half a dozen steps in before he caught her. Laughing, she clung to him as he lowered her down to the soft grass. With her spine against the earth, she stared up at her huge guardian as he stood over her. His soft fur made her fingers tingle as she stroked his neck and chest. The cheeky thing had his back paws on either side of her knees so when he swished his thick tail back and forth it tickled her ankles. When she attempted to shove him off her, he lowered his head into her neck. She shivered at the feel of his whiskers and fur against her sensitive skin. When she gasped, the cheeky thing gave her a lick across the side of her neck before he bounded off her. The sensation of his rough tongue had her giggling like a schoolgirl. When she finally managed to calm down enough to sit up, she found him waiting for her. Sitting with his head cocked to the side as he watched her.*

"You want to know why I'm so happy, my chaton?*"*

When he gave her one of his little nods, she proceeded to tell him about her life-altering day.

"So, I've found my new start." She sighed. "But I'm worried. There's a man. Dominic White. He is so handsome and the way he looks at me, the way his deep,

smooth voice slides up my spine. It makes me shiver..."
She sighed again, then shook her head. "I can't give
in."

He cocked his head to the other side.
"You want to know why?"
Another nod of his massive head had her answering.
"Because of what happened to my mother. You see,
she got pregnant with me when she was quite young and
when she told her boyfriend he ran for the hills.
According to my mother, he ran fast enough to leave a
vapor trail behind him. He broke her heart. She never
recovered. Never moved on. To make it even worse, her
parents' response to the pregnancy was to send her
away. They shipped her off from the only home she had
ever known in Lyon, France, to live with an elderly
relative she had never even met before in Melbourne
without a backward glance."

She took a deep breath before continuing.
"I am twenty-five years old and have never met
either my father or my grandparents. My mother died
having not seen her parents for over twenty years. So
you understand? I can't let a man get close. I can't
stand to be hurt like my Maman *was hurt. My heart*
simply isn't strong enough to survive that kind of pain.
Especially when it's still healing from losing Maman."
She licked her lips. "It doesn't matter. I'll be fine on my
own. I don't need a man."

He nuzzled her cheek and she felt the wetness there.
Adele hadn't realized she'd began crying as she spoke.

Instinctively, she wrapped her arms around his neck sinking her fingers into his thick coat as she laid her head against his. Eyes closed, she allowed the vibrations of his purring to soothe her.

Chapter Three

Damn it! Cole had lost himself. He'd gotten so caught up in the moment he'd pushed her too far. So intent on releasing his anger, he hadn't paid attention like he should have. If only he'd been able to find a whore to pick up tonight. He didn't get this worked up often, but when he did, he didn't risk killing the slave. He'd go out and find some hapless lonely female and take her out into the thickest part of the national park, far away from anywhere tourists went and work her over.

It had been six months since he'd needed this level of release and tonight, when he'd been desperate for it, the weather had foiled any chance he had. A storm had passed through. The heavy rain keeping everyone indoors. He'd driven around for an hour searching but in the end his need to vent became too much so he'd come home and brought the slave down here.

He began pacing back and forth across the stained concrete floor, running his hands through his hair and pulling at it. The slave was dead. His lousy day just kept getting better and better. Thanks to a massive fuck up with paperwork at the docks, he'd spent his day unloading and reloading a boatload of logs. All while putting up with the ship's captain and dock foreman fighting over whose fault it was and who was going to pay for it every step of the bloody way. His heart racing and his body tense, he'd really needed to work off his anger and frustration tonight. But she hadn't lasted long enough for him to find his calm.

His need had been so high, he didn't even bother playing his usual mind games with her tonight. As soon as he'd walked in the door, he'd simply grabbed her and gotten straight to it. A groan escaped him as he recalled how he'd tied her up before whipping her raw and fucking her hard. The experience had been a thing of beauty, near perfection. The way she'd screamed so nicely for him, and the way that woman bled...got him hard every time.

He stopped pacing and rubbed his hands over his face before he turned to examine her limp body hanging from the ceiling hook. Her head hung forward, spilling her long dark hair over her tits and soaking up the blood from the welts he'd put there. Her arms where stretched straight as the full dead weight of her body pulled on them, her knees had bent a little and blood was slowly dripping from her knees. Damn, she made a fucking sexy sight, that's for sure.

If only she were still breathing.

He cursed and screamed out loud to vent some of the frustration he had building up inside. How was he going to bring himself down now? To top it off, he now had to deal with the body. He'd dumped the others over a cliff into the ocean. The water soaked away any evidence that would tie him to them and the current took them far enough away the cops didn't know where to start looking. Hopefully. This would be the ninth body he'd disposed of up there. Maybe he should try something different this time. Then again, it had been six months since his last one. Surely the cops would have given up on that last one by now. And the storm was still raging outside. He didn't want to be out in the rain any longer than absolutely necessary so he'd stick with what he knew worked.

Before he got stuck into the messy job he needed a stiff drink. Rolling his shoulders, he headed up the stairs to the kitchen. As he poured himself some Jim Beam in a glass tumbler he heard a noise, the quiet snick of a door closing. His body lit up and he felt a grin spread over his face before he threw back the cheap alcohol, enjoying the burn it left in its wake on the way down. The brat. He still had her to ease his needs. With renewed vigor, he headed back down the stairs while he planned what he needed to do.

First, he needed to wrap the body up with a few garbage bags and tie it up good and tight. He didn't want any mess to be left in his pride and joy when he put her in the tray of his jet black 2009 Holden VE SV6 Commodore Ute. With the hard cover closed the rain wouldn't spread the blood and there was no risk of anyone seeing it when he took it away later.

He intended to handle the brat before he dealt with the body. Good thing he had a garage. No one would see a thing. After he finished with the brat, he'd take the slave up to the cliffs and dump her over into the ocean. He'd hose out the tray with the high-pressure hose at work early tomorrow before his shift started. No one would ever know, just like the last time, and the time before that. Oh, tonight was starting to look up after all.

Kelly let her body sag against the door as she heard him go back down the stairs. Something was wrong, different than normal. He'd been in a worse mood than usual when he'd come home. As soon as he'd stalked through the front door he'd been on her mother, dragged her down the stairs by her hair. Kelly had never witnessed that part before. She'd always had a precious few seconds to dash into her room.

Her body shuddered with revulsion. She'd ran for her room and stayed there, leaving her door open just a crack as she always did so she would know when they returned and she'd need to go help her mother.

But her mother hadn't returned.

Her screams had stopped suddenly a few short minutes before he'd stormed up the stairs wearing just an old pair of jeans. Denim that was splattered with fresh blood. His bare chest was also wet with it in places. Her own blood turned to ice in her veins as he prowled over to the kitchen and poured himself a drink. Something he normally had her mother do for him.

She'd thought him incapable of getting anything for himself aside from beer. That was when Kelly had closed her door and struggled to breathe through the dread and fear.

All she could hear was the sound of her heartbeat in her ears as the realization washed over her that her mother must be dead. The bastard must have finally pushed too far and killed her. She sobbed as grief overwhelmed her. While her body shook from the force of her grief, a more frightening thought entered her mind. Her mother was gone, no longer useful to him, but she was still here. Kelly held no delusions about the fact he would happily begin to use her. She sobbed harder, for herself and for her mother, as she curled up on her bed. She knew, deep in her soul, her already crappy life was about to take a drastic turn straight over a cliff.

Kelly jumped in fright, before quickly huddling into a tighter ball. She pushed her back against the wall as he crashed through her bedroom door so hard the thing must have come off its hinges. She risked a peek at him through her fingers and bile rose up her throat. He was stalking toward her while grinning a horrible sinister looking smile she knew meant evil bad things would be happening to her soon. If the grin didn't give his intent away, the glint in his cold hazel eyes certainly did. She swallowed against the urge to puke and cringed when he ran his hand gently through her black curls. Suddenly the hold turned nasty and she whimpered. He roughly grabbed a handful of her hair, using it to yank her off the bed to her feet. As she stood in shock and gasping at the pain that continued to light up her skull, he grabbed the front of her thin shirt in his other fist and tore it from her body. He repeated the action with her cotton shorts and knickers.

"You won't need them where you're going."

His voice was hard, dripping with venom. Kelly shuddered as through her tears she watched him look over her body, making her feel dirty and violated.

Her heart was pounding louder than ever when he dragged her out of her room and toward the stairs. She struggled to breathe through her fear. She tripped but didn't fall as he held tight onto her hair. Another whimper slipped past her lips as she fought to get her feet beneath her again.

At the bottom of the stairs, he thrust her into one of the rooms. She stopped short, frozen in horror. Oh dear God, the blood. So much blood. It was splattered all over the wall and had pooled on the floor. There were older dark brown stains and fresh bright red ones. Any hope she had her mother was alive fled. She had to be dead, surely no one could lose that much blood and survive. While she stood there frozen, he let go of her and moved away for a minute. Just as she was thinking that she should turn and run while he wasn't looking, he returned to stand in front of her with the collar she'd seen her mother wearing for the past five years. It was heavily stained with blood. Bile rose once more and she swallowed it down, instinctively knowing he'd not react well to her puking on him. The bastard was going to make her wear her dead mother's blood.

"You are mine now, little brat. I am going to train you to be the best slave I've ever had. You'll be perfect and strong and you will never leave me."

Kelly felt all her blood drain from her head while her mind spun out of control. Her life was over. She would no doubt die in this room just like her mother. No longer caring what he thought of the weakness, she fell to her knees and welcomed the darkness that overtook her vision as she processed the horror of his words.

Satisfaction coiled through Cole while he chuckled and looked over his newest slave passed out at his feet. Kneeling beside her, he wrapped the collar around her neck and locked it with a padlock so there was no way for her to get it off. He grabbed the leather cuffs and used them to bind her wrists together before he lifted her up to hang her from the new hook on the wall. Realizing she'd been too short to hang from the ceiling one, he'd added this hook just for her.

Once she was in place, he stood back to inspect her fully. She couldn't be much more than eleven or twelve years old. Her skin perfectly unmarred at the moment. Her pale skin would mark up so beautifully under his care. Her hair was a mess of glossy black curls that hung down over her shoulders past her chest down to her navel. He couldn't see her face as it hung forward, but he knew she had big round grey eyes. Eyes that had looked so good widened in fear of him earlier.

She didn't have any hair on her body yet, nothing to obstruct his view. Her legs were long and lean, while her feet were perfectly delicate. Her chest was basically flat. He could see her nipples standing out through her hair, so she was starting to get tits. He smiled. She was too young and small for his sexual tastes but in a couple of years she'd be fucking perfect, and by then he'd have her trained just right. Until then, he had himself a virginal Slave to play with. One he was going to beat and make bleed to ease his dark soul. He left her hanging while he went and got some cold water to throw on her to wake her up. He couldn't wait any longer to hear how well she would scream for him.

Chapter Four

Dominic showered and dressed as fast as he could. He needed to get to Adele before she left work for the day. He'd gone around on Tuesday night to ask her out to celebrate her first day of work but she'd politely turned him down with a smile. It was her smile that gave him hope. Now that it was Friday night, the end of her shift, and he knew she had the weekend off, he had high hopes. Kit, bless her, had been feeding him information. With that knowledge, he wasn't going to allow her to brush him off tonight. He wouldn't accept anything else but her saying yes. Adele was his mate. He knew from their dreams that she could feel the connection between them and if only she would stop fighting it they could get somewhere.

He'd been waiting four long years for her and he really didn't want to wait anymore. Not when she was so close. Tonight she would be tired, worn out and hopefully not in the mood to cook tea—or to fight the attraction between them. He was sure of it. He bolted out of the locker room in a rush to the soundtrack of the rest of the crew laughing and catcalling. He figured his face must look like he felt, like a cat that finally caught the canary. Not that he cared. He was off to catch his mate.

Dominic stood silently by the door, watching Adele. She was so graceful; she glided around the office as she readied things to leave. His heart ached a little when she flopped exhausted into her chair with a sigh then scrubbed her hands over her face. Damn, she looked totally worn out. Anticipation had his stomach tightening. His plan would definitely work. There was no way she'd feel like cooking dinner tonight. From the looks of things, she didn't look up to driving home, let alone function well enough to cook. When she leaned back in the chair with her eyes closed like she was going to take a nap, Dominic's instincts came roaring to life. The need to care for his mate had him knocking on the doorframe before he was aware that he had moved.

Adele's eyes opened slowly, without her head moving. After a moment, her mouth twitched before a wide grin bloomed over her face. His heart swelled, her beautiful brown eyes sparkled with happiness to see him. That simple gesture had him feeling like he was ten feet tall. His presence alone was enough to make his little mate instantly so happy, even when she was clearly bone-tired.

"To what do I owe this pleasure, Dominic?" she asked sweetly, her voice only giving away a hint of her tiredness.

"Well, I thought I would take you to dinner down the pub to celebrate you surviving your first week here. I know how by the end of the week, cooking just isn't high on anyone's list of priorities. What do you say? Want to join me?"

Dominic was surprised at how confident and strong his voice sounded as he didn't feel either of those things. The way Adele's gaze softened made him nervous. Had she picked up on his fear that she would again reject him?

"I see that look in your eyes, Dominic. I'm not going to get out of it tonight no matter what I say, am I?"

Adele spoke softly. Her tone gentle with a little humor laced through it. He loved that even tired, she let her sense of humor shine through.

"Well, I wasn't planning on hog-tying you and dragging you along if you truly don't want to come...but yeah, I really want to have dinner with you, Adele. Get to know you better."

He followed that comment up with a lopsided grin. He'd seen how she melted when he did it and hoped it prevented her from voicing any argument her mind was currently thinking up.

"Okay, I give in. I was about to leave anyway, so let's go have some dinner."

Satisfaction had him smiling as he waited by the door for her to finish packing up and grab her bag. He couldn't resist the temptation of placing his hand on her lower back to guide her out of the building to the car park. He loved how his touch made her shiver slightly as she felt the connection between them. He could feel the sparks all the way up his arm.

Adele snuck a glance at Dominic as he guided her over to a small table in a quiet back corner. She suspected he'd planned this and arranged this table to be left vacant. How sweet was he? Every table was occupied except that one. On a Friday night, most places would get too rowdy to be able to carry on a conversation but this out-of-the-way table would stay fairly quiet she imagined.

She lowered herself into the chair Dominic held out for her before tucking her bag under the table. She couldn't look away as Dominic smoothly lowered his large frame into the seat opposite her. He gave her a cheeky grin and a wink when he busted her watching him. Heat flamed over her cheeks as she quickly lowered her gaze to her hands resting on the table. Silently she repeated her mantra "I do not need a man" over and over in her head. Maybe if she said it often enough she might believe it, because she hadn't even been in Rosebery a full week and she was already struggling to stay away from Dominic. She let out a small huff. For some reason she just melted whenever he was near, and the effect his voice had on her was lethal. How strange that she'd never felt this way around any other man before. Dominic rapped his knuckles quickly on the table, as if he'd known she'd gotten lost inside her mind.

"Sorry, Dominic, I was a million miles away. Did

you say something?"

"No, beautiful, I was just pulling you back to me and away from wherever your mind just went."

"Oh, yeah, when I'm tired I tend to vague out a bit, sorry. How about we grab some drinks?"

"I think since it's the end of the week and all, we should splash out. Would you like some wine?"

Adele looked up into his face as her mind finished the climb out of the hole it'd fallen in.

"The end of this week definitely deserves a splash out. But I have a confession. I've never really drunk wine before. Could you pick something for me? Only if you don't mind."

"I don't mind one bit. It'd be my pleasure to introduce you to one of the finer things in life."

Adele contemplated the look on Dominic's face; as if he was proud to be able to select her drink. He seemed so possessive around her. She would have thought she'd hate it. But she loved it, loved how she felt claimed when she was with him. She mentally shook her head. She needed to remember that she did not need a man and most certainly didn't need to be claimed by one.

While Dominic headed to the bar, Adele took her jacket off and slung it over the back of her chair before she settled in. Weariness flowed over her and she closed her eyes for a moment. She was definitely going to sleep well tonight. A yawn escaped and she rubbed her eyes with her thumb and forefinger. She couldn't believe how draining full-time work was compared to

High School, or even University.

"Are you okay, beautiful?"

Dominic set her drink in front of her. A shiver ran through her as he ran his palm up her arm and over her shoulder. Her breath caught in her throat when, for just a few moments, his hand wrapped around the back of her neck in a possessive hold. She gulped in air trying to calm her body down when he moved over to his seat.

"Yeah, I'm fine. Just worn out is all. I only finished University last year, so this is my first full-time job. I think it's going to take me a bit to get used to the hours."

"That it does, I remember it well. Try spending that week with your dad as your boss, pushing you around while your little brother's under your feet trying to help."

Dominic's grin grew larger as he spoke, but as her gaze blurred with unshed tears, his face lost all humor and he winced.

"Oh hell, Adele. I'm sorry. I didn't mean to upset you. This is meant to be a celebration. Here, have a drink and I'll go order us some dinner. Daily special okay?"

All Adele could manage was a nod as she desperately tried to hold on to her emotions. She sighed when Dominic headed up to the bar and left her alone for a few moments. That man seemed so in tune with what she needed.

She covered her face with both palms and took

several deep breaths. Damn, she hadn't expected that reaction and now she felt like a fool. If every time she heard someone talk about their parents she freaked out, it was going to be hard to make friends. She took another deep breath and wiped away the stray tears. She needed to get herself under control. Not the easiest thing to do when she was so damn tired.

She blinked and felt another tear slip down her cheek. She brushed it away. Damn it. Maybe she should have said no to dinner and gone straight home. Dominic returned and she gave him a weak smile as he pulled his chair next to hers. His scent enveloped her and she drew it deep into her lungs, allowing it to soothe her as he started stroking her back in lazy circles with his large hand.

"I'm so sorry, beautiful. I didn't mean to upset you."

"It's all right, Dominic, you couldn't have known. It's just that my mother passed away four years ago. I've been on my own ever since. She was all the family I ever had. You talking about your family just pricked a nerve. Honestly, I didn't expect the reaction either. I'm sure if I wasn't so tired it wouldn't have affected me. I'm okay now, really. Can we please just talk about something else?"

Dominic was grateful Jenny picked that perfect moment to bring their meals out. Today's special was his favorite, beer battered butterfish with chips and salad. He couldn't help it, all cats love their fish. He was curious to whether Adele liked seafood. A grin pulled at his lips, basically, he was curious about everything to do with Adele. Looked like Conner was right; Dominic was totally acting like a lovesick kitten.

"Oh, great. I love fish." Adele chuckled. "I didn't even look at the specials board on the way in. I could have ended up with anything!"

"You're pretty safe here. Generally the special is either battered fish or chicken schnitzels, sometimes soup in winter."

Dominic gave her a gentle smile. The tension eased from his muscles now he had her happy and giggling. He loved the sound of her laughter. It was so carefree and relaxed. The fact she was drinking wine he'd selected and food he'd ordered for her, made him want to purr in satisfaction.

They both proceeded to eat in comfortable silence until they were just picking over the last few chips on their plates.

"Well, that certainly feels better. I've never eaten as much as I have this week, at least with all the running around I'm doing I won't gain any weight."

Adele leaned back in her chair and rested a hand over her tummy while she took sips of her wine.

"You would still be beautiful."

Dominic kept his voice low. His mate was stunning, the perfect hourglass shape with curves in all the right places. He didn't want her fussing about her weight. If she gained or lost weight, it wouldn't matter to him.

He'd adore her no matter her size.

Adele's gaze flicked up to his and he could clearly see she was shocked. Guess she'd heard his comment but was having difficulty believing it. He knew his eyes must be showing his emotions when a look of panic crossed her face. Taking a deep breath, he forced the emotion from his expression. He needed to change the topic, pretend like he didn't say anything about her being beautiful. He wasn't ready for the evening to be over just yet and she looked ready to bolt on him.

"Kit mentioned you're going to start keeping an eye out for your own place here in town. Does that mean you like it here and you're going to stay on?"

Dominic smiled innocently at Adele, waiting for her to register the change of topic, to what was hopefully a safer one. One that would extend their night a little longer.

"Um, yeah, I'm just going to keep an eye out in the local paper and check out the agents down Main Street. I won't be able to afford to move for at least another few weeks. I love staying with Kit but I've always been independent and I don't want to overstay my welcome."

"I doubt you'd ever wear out your welcome, especially with Kit. But I certainly understand the need for some personal space. How do you like the job? I mean, apart from the long hours, are you enjoying it?"

"I love my new job. I've always liked helping people, it soothes me. I've been volunteering for years and it's great to finally be able to do it professionally."

"Yeah, I understand. I like being able to help people and I also love the thrill of chasing down a fire so firefighting was the natural choice for me. As Dad's the captain, I knew when there were job vacancies so that helped make the choice even easier."

They chatted for a while longer about their jobs and the week they'd each had when Adele yawned.

"I'm sorry, Dominic, but I really must head home. I'm about to fall asleep at the table."

His heart clenched when another yawn cut her off from saying anything else.

"Ah well, we can't have that now can we? How about I drive your car back to Kit's? I don't live far from her place so I can walk home afterwards."

Adele meant to brush him off, she meant to say "no thanks, I'll be right" but apparently her mouth didn't get that message and ran off on its own.

"That would be nice, thanks, Dominic."

She rose and grabbed her jacket before she led Dominic out toward her Corolla.

"What about your car?"

His Rav 4 sat next to her car.

"Don't worry about it, beautiful. I'll get a lift with Conner tomorrow morning and come get it."

Adele hated being a burden, but she was so damn tired she knew she'd be a danger on the road if she drove. She unlocked the car then handed her keys to Dominic before she hopped in. They drove back to Kit's place in comfortable silence. Adele allowed herself to simply relax.

Dominic pulled her car into Kit's driveway and hopped out. He was around her side opening the door before she could do it herself. Damn he was fast! When he held his hand out for hers, she slid her palm into it without a moment's hesitation. He gently pulled her out of the car and straight into his arms. His hands moved so they rested on her waist, thumbs around the front, fingers splayed across her lower back. Again, his actions screamed of possessiveness, like he was laying his claim on her. She could feel his heat searing through her clothes, sending shivers up and down her spine.

"I had a great night, Adele, thank you."

His voice was low, deep, and so damn sexy. Adele raised her head to look into his eyes to voice a response but didn't get the chance. Before she could let a sound out, his mouth covered hers.

Oh, wow. Despite never having been kissed before, she knew this was way beyond a normal kiss. Butterflies fluttered in her belly and every ounce of tension left her body. Slowly, she put her hands on his solid chest and ran them up until she had her arms wrapped around his neck. He was so strong. His whole body hard with muscle, except his lips. Those were soft. His mouth was wooing her with seductive gentleness.

For the first time in her life, her body came alive. Arousal coursed through her and settled low in her torso. He traced his tongue along the seam of her lips, pulling a gasp from her. Making the most of her parted lips, he delved into her mouth, drugging her with lust, pulling her further under his spell.

When the need to breathe became more than she could ignore, she pulled back. Her chest heaved with rapid breaths as she tried to return to earth. Dominic rested his forehead against hers and she stared into his hooded and smoldering gaze. In that moment, she desperately wished she already had her own place so he could come inside with her and continue with his seduction.

"Wh-what are you doing to me?"

Adele winced at her hoarse voice. She lowered her arms, placing her palms against his very well-defined pectoral muscles; his rapid heartbeat and the muscles twitching beneath her palms had a giddy feeling rush through her. He was as affected as she was by their kiss.

"I was kissing you, beautiful. I like you, Adele, really like you. I simply thought I'd show you."

He was so close to her, she felt his breath on her cheek as he spoke. A whimper escaped her as she struggled with what to say. When he pressed his lips against hers again, she melted against him. A shiver passed through her when he trailed his fingers down her cheek to hold her chin while he brushed his thumb over her sensitive lower lip.

"Good night, my beautiful Adele. Sweet dreams."

Her mind still fogged with arousal and his scent, she didn't move when he released his hold on her and pressed her keys into her palm.

Dominic left Adele leaning against her car in a daze. He didn't like leaving her out in the open but if he hadn't left, he would be inside her and he knew it was too soon for that. Instinct told him if he'd gone that far tonight, she would run from him. He wasn't sure he'd ever win her heart if that happened.

He forced his stiff body to move and jogged across the road out of her sight before he stopped. He rubbed over his aching erection with the heel of his palm in a vain attempt to ease it. Across the road, his mate was slowly returning to earth from their kiss. She looked down at her hand a moment before using her keys to lock her car. He ached to go to her as she slowly walked up to the front door. He'd give anything to be able to enter behind her, to have the right to lay down beside her and hold her close all night long.

Satisfaction seeped through him as she kept touching her lips in a way that made Dominic certain that it had been her first kiss. The tentative way she responded to him had made him wonder, but watching her now, he was certain of it. The thought that no other man had touched what was fated to be his made him purr out loud with pride and delight.

The moment she was safely inside, he stripped down, and after folding his clothes into a pile he could grab in his mouth, he shifted to his leopard form. He needed to burn off his energy and a nice long run along the riverbank would do the trick, he was sure. With the world looking a little brighter than it had earlier, he took off.

Chapter Five

Jake listened to the details of this latest job in shock. After he hung up the phone, he pushed all emotion behind a thick wall in his mind as he slammed his hand on the station house siren. The team on deck included Dominic, Conner, Kit, Joel, and Jordan. Jake was grateful so many of his senior firefighters were going with him on this one.

Ten minutes later, Jake jumped behind the wheel of one of their two trucks, while Dominic drove the other. In quick order, Jake hit the door opener and started the vehicle up before he headed out with Dominic following him.

"What have we got, boss?" Joel asked him as they took off.

"It's a nasty one. A fire down at the Strahan Docks. A bloody logging ship's gone up and all the timber's alight. From the sound of it, the ship's going to be a goner. The report I received was that it's burning pretty hot. They've called in both us and Queenstown to back up Strahan's units, so that should give you an idea how big this thing is predicted to grow."

Once a logging ship full of timber got going, there

wasn't much they could do for the vessel. Jake was certain their main focus would be to stop the fire spreading to any of the other ships or the wharf itself.

"Any casualties?" Kit asked over the radio from the other truck.

"As far as the manager knew, everyone was accounted for, so hopefully we won't find any nasty surprises," Jake responded through the radio.

Jake hoped that was true. Being burned to death was not a pleasant way to go and not something he enjoyed having to deal with. Deaths didn't make him ill like injuries did, but even so. He could clearly remember each and every body he'd ever seen. He didn't need to add more to the lineup today.

Keeping his focus on the road, he let silence fill the cab as they all mentally prepared for the day ahead of them. Fighting fires was draining both mentally and physically. They needed to conserve all the energy they could as once they arrived on scene it would be all systems go until they got it contained.

Jake looked at his watch, feeling proud. He'd made it down to Strahan in under an hour—record time. He'd seen the red glow for some distance before they arrived, so he wasn't surprised when they arrived to find the entire ship was well and truly alight and burning. Unfortunately, it looked like the ship had only been half loaded when it went up, so there was still several lots of logs piled on the dock. The fire had already spread to the pile closest to the ship. They definitely had their work cut out for them today.

Jake backed the truck up as close to the logs as was safe. Within five minutes he'd radioed through and received their orders.

"Right. My team will focus on putting out the burning logs while Dominic's team wets down the other logs to prevent the spread. Queenstown will assist Strahan with the ship when they get here."

In moments, his team had the hoses going, pumping water on to the burning logs. Dominic's team was equally efficient with wetting down the other unburnt piles. Jake climbed up on the truck to add the foam into the water. On a big fire like this, foam helped to smother the flames and prevented hot spots from flaring back up once they'd moved on to a different area. He could see the dock workers had their skates on, moving as much of the timber away from the site as they could.

Several hours later Jake was more than ready to have this day end. Finally, they had the fire completely out and mopped up. He lifted his bottle of water and took a deep drink. While he swallowed, he glanced around the Strahan station house where they'd all returned to. There were easily fifty men and ladies here, each one of them having helped to put the fire out and now they were being debriefed while they rehydrated. The investigators were back at the site trying to identify the cause of the fire, but that could take days. Weariness pulled at him and he started to wonder how long he could keep up being captain. He wasn't getting any younger and Dominic was more than capable of taking over. He glanced at his eldest son. He was going to be the next Alpha of their Leap too. Jake really needed to start training him for both the captaincy and the Alpha work. Once the debriefing was over, Jake quickly gathered his team and headed back to the trucks so they could all go home and get some well-deserved rest.

Cole had stood back to enjoy watching all the action unfold. That will give that damn captain something to think about for a while. Bastard had been giving Cole crap for months. Never bloody happy no matter what happened. So while everyone was off on their lunch break and the coast was clear, Cole snuck on board and doused the crew's bunkroom in petrol. He'd soaked those mattresses good, then grabbed one of the soaked sheets to use as a wick to trail out the door. Yeah, he'd had to be damn careful, getting himself lit up or burnt was not part of his plan.

When he'd lit that sheet, it had flared up quicker than he'd imagined it would. He ran his thumb over his singed fingertips, remembering the sting of pain as they'd been injured. In seconds, the bunkroom was engulfed in flames and he'd turned tail and run like hell to get off the damn boat before he was spotted. Once he got above deck, he slowed down his pace to sneak off the ship and return to his duties. He was certain no one had seen him.

Elation had him wanting to cheer when the fire

spread to the logs still on the dock. Bloody beautiful and so much better than anything he had planned for. Even better, the docks would be shut down while the investigation was going on so he was going to have a few days off to spend some quality time training his slave. Now that was something worth smiling about. When the last of the fire trucks had headed out of the yard, he went over to his ute, barely resisting the urge to whistle and started for home.

Coldness coated Kelly despite curling up on the couch and gently rubbing her palms over her arms and legs. She was so sore but she was used to hurting now. In the months since her mother had died, she'd been at the receiving end of his attention on a daily basis and was always in pain.

Funny, she'd already thought her life had been pretty crappy, but she'd been wrong. Even before her mother's body had time to cool, he had come for her. Sending her world straight to a hell she couldn't have imagined. Week after endless week of being tied up and beaten, physically abused beyond anything she could have ever imagined before. However, he still hadn't raped her. He often called her his *virgin slave*. But she wasn't sure how long that would last. She knew full well he used her mother in that way. Thoughts of her mother had her remembering how she'd help her clean up after the abuse. Of the times she'd snuck out and stolen clothes for them both. A tear slipped down her cheek. How she wished someone would do those things for her. It felt like forever since she'd had clothes to wear; he'd ripped all she had within the first few days.

Now she had nothing.

She *was* nothing.

Naked and collared.

More like a pet than a person.

Without thought, her hand went to her neck to grip and tug on the collar locked around her neck. She really did feel like a dog, kept on a leash by her master. Left to sit and await his return. She glanced up at the clock, three o'clock. She had another two and half, maybe three hours before he would be back. She spent her days cleaning, cooking, and watching TV. Those precious hours where she got to watch others live lives she'd never get to were her only escape now. She was chained up so there was no way to sneak out like she used to. He only ever unchained her when he took her downstairs. How she wished she had run away before her mother had died, but she couldn't do it. She hadn't been able to abandon her mother like that, and back then she hadn't known where she would go if she'd left. She'd been too afraid of the unknown out in the world.

She'd spent the first two days of her new hell trying to pick the lock on her collar and the one on the end of chain where it locked into a bolt cemented into the kitchen floor. She'd spent every spare minute desperately trying to get free, but she couldn't pick the locks no matter how hard she tried. She wasn't sure what made her think she could. She'd watched her mother try the same thing over and over again for years. So now her only escape was to watch TV, watch what the rest of world did with their days, all those lucky people that had the simple pleasure of freedom.

A car pulling into the drive had her cringing with terror. The garage door rattled as it lifted and her heart rate tripled. He was home early. That was never a good thing. He would be in a mood, which meant her beating would be extra harsh. She closed her eyes and took a deep breath. It was going to be a long afternoon and an even longer night. She was going to need all her strength to get through it.

She leaped from the couch and ran for her room. She wasn't sure why she tried to hide from him, it had never worked. But she had to try. Her mind wouldn't allow her to simply hand herself over to the monster. Even though she knew he'd find her, that it was impossible to hide.

She'd made it to the back wall, only a few steps from her room, when she heard the rasp of the key in the lock and the handle turn. Eyes wide in fear she pressed herself against the wall. She knew he would open the door in a rush any second. He seemed to like the mind games as much as the physical ones. He knew not knowing what he was going to do drove her crazy. Just like she knew he needed to see her reactions to him, hence he would open the door quickly so he could see her freak out.

Shaking in fear, her legs refused to hold her up and she cowered down on the ground when the door finally opened. He looked calm, totally in control on the outside. Which meant on the inside there was a storm brewing, a storm that would crash right through her. She heard the door close, the lock click into place. He didn't take his gaze off her as he prowled farther into the room, stopping halfway to her.

"You trying to hide again, slave? How sweet." He chuckled, the evil sound sending a shudder through her on a bone deep level.

"Come to me, my slave. Do *not* make me come and get you. You know you won't like the consequences if I have to." His deep icy voice was enough to give her nightmares all on its own.

Blood rushing in her ears, she scrambled up to her feet, rushing over to him. It was never in her best interest to annoy him, especially when he was in a mood. The one time she decided to push her luck and make a stand, he had beaten her so badly she was sure he'd cracked at least a couple of ribs. She learned her lesson.

When she got to him she lowered her head, focusing on the floor, her hands behind her back. Just the way he'd *trained* her to do. Hell, she really was a pet, a well-trained one.

Her breath hitched as he grabbed a fistful of her curls, tilting her head back. She cringed when she saw his smirk. This was going to hurt.

"Very good, but you have still forgotten something."

Forgotten? Damn, what did she not do this time? And how bad would the punishment be? He only gave her a moment before he pulled on her hair to get her to lower to her knees.

"You need to be on your knees, slave."

Of course, her knees. How could she have forgotten that? She prayed silently that he wouldn't punish her too harshly for the error. Not that it mattered, he was going to beat the crap out of her anyhow. She prayed he didn't break any bones.

He pulled the key-chain that hung around his neck from under his shirt and proceeded to unlock the collar around her neck. She did her best not to shudder as he ran his fingers down her cheek, over her neck and collarbone to her shoulder. He pushed firmly at a bruise on her shoulder with his thumb until her shoulder gave out. She groaned in pain until he released the pressure, but even then it continued to sting.

"Hmm, your skin looks so bloody good with my marks on it, slave. Me and you are in for some good times. I've got me a couple of days off work. So we need to get downstairs and get to work. You need some more marks, don't you think?"

Kelly started shaking before he even finished talking. Oh double damn. This was worse than she had thought. A bad mood was one thing, a couple of days of continuous abuse was an entirely different level of hell. She took a deep breath, tried to seal herself for what was to come as he pulled her from the floor and led her down the stairs to her very own personal living nightmare. She couldn't stop the tears that silently ran down her cheeks and dripped to the floor. These were going to be the longest days of life so far, and she wasn't sure if she should pray he didn't kill her, or for him to kill her quickly.

"What the hell? Arson? Are you serious?"

Dominic's body all but vibrated with anger. People could have easily been hurt or killed on that ship. As it was, a lot of logs were burned beyond saving. Trees took decades to grow so their timber should be put to good use, cherished for the precious gift it was, not wasted like it doesn't have any value.

No matter how many fires he attended that had been purposely lit, he just couldn't wrap his mind around why people did it. Fire was unique in its ability to completely wipe out lives and property from the face of the earth, certainly not something to be taken lightly.

"Have the investigators worked out how it was started yet?"

"The investigator said the point of origin was definitely in the sleeping cabin. The mattresses and beddings had been soaked in accelerant then set alight. The captain reported smelling petrol as he approached his ship just before he noticed the smoke and raised the alarm."

The look on his dad's face as he shook his head

showed he felt the same way Dominic did.

"Do they have any suspects?"

Dominic really wanted this guy caught. What they didn't need in the heart of summer was a hyped up firebug with a jerry-can of petrol and a lighter running around the place.

"Well, they are pretty sure it's someone who is familiar with the docks. They're having a close look at a few of the workers. Apparently the captain of that particular ship has been taking out his frustrations on a couple of them for a while now. Guess one or more of them decided to get him back with their own style of justice."

"Do they think they'll be able to lay charges for it?"

Dominic knew full well, just because they *knew* who did it, didn't mean they could charge the bastard for it.

"Nah, he doesn't think they'll be able to get enough evidence to charge anyone, but the foreman down there is planning on sacking the two workers who are implicated the most. From what I heard, they've been singled out for other crimes around the area too. The foreman doesn't want to risk any more ship fires, or for the docks to be linked to criminals in any way."

Frustration was thick in his dad's tone, a feeling Dominic could relate to one hundred percent.

"I know how you feel, Dad. I hate that these bastards get away with it so often, leaving them free to do it again."

Dominic scrubbed his face as he sighed. There was

no point in getting all worked up over it. There wasn't anything he could do to change the situation.

"You know I feel the same. Sadly, nothing we can do about it. Now, son, onto a different matter. I want you to start sitting in on the monthly Council of Alphas meetings with me. That means you need to learn who all the members of the Council of Alphas are."

His dad leaned back in his chair, looking like he was settling in for a long talk.

"What? Why?" Confusion had Dominic frowning at his father. What was he on about?

"You are the future, son. When it's time for me to step aside as Alpha, you will not only be Alpha of the Leap here in Rosebery but of the Continental Leap. You will be our representative on the Council of Alphas."

Dominic sat hard into a chair in shock. His father had previously told him that as his eldest son, he would be the next Alpha of the Leap here in Rosebery, but he'd never drawn the now obvious conclusion that he would also be their representative on the Council. Dumbfounded, he watched as his father pulled out a note pad and tossed it toward him along with a pen.

"You'd better take notes. It will take you a while to get everyone's names straight."

Curiosity beat back the shock. Just like with the stuff about mating, Dominic was eager to learn about all things Alpha, had been for years. After leaning forward to snatch the pen and paper from the edge of the desk, he settled in for his first lesson.

"Okay, let's start at the top. You know Choden Sangye, but I'll refresh your memory on his history. He is the original shifter, the first of our kind. Created in 1759 when he was fifteen. He is the only one of us that is immortal. He also has a boatload of other tricks. Don't ever be surprised when he knows things he shouldn't or turns up in places you wouldn't expect. Don't bother trying to work him out either, you won't be able to, so save your energy. He will always be the Head Alpha of the Council and all shifters. Any problem you have that you need advice on, you can call him for help.

"As for the others, there are seven Council members, one for each continent, plus Choden. I'll only give you a brief rundown of who and where for now. I'll give you a more in-depth profile on each of them next time. You'll never remember any of it if I dump all of it on you now. Let's start with North America. Maddix Torres is their Alpha, he lives in Maple Ridge, Canada—"

"Hang on, Dad, you're going to have to spell these names for me. I want to make sure I get them right from the start."

"Fair enough and a good point. Some of them are a mouthful. So, Maddix is M-A-D-D-I-X and Torres is T-O-R-R-E-S. You got that one?"

"Yep, all good. Who else?"

"South America's is Fernando Molina, that's F-E-R-N-A-N-D-O, M-O-L-I-N-A. His Leap is based in Arica, Chile. Asia's representative is the newest on board.

Dishi Wee, D-I-S-H-I, W-E-E. He's in the Himalayas, India. Europe's is Tristian Laprise, T-R-I-S-T-I-A-N, L-A-P-R-I-S-E. He's in France, the Besancon region. I believe that's a little east of where Adele's mother was raised, near the Swiss border. Now, who haven't I covered?"

"You've covered North and South America, Asia, and Europe."

"Ah, okay, so Africa would be Obi Traore, O-B-I, T-R-A-O-R-E. He's in Springbok, South Africa. And last but not least, Antarctica. Joe Fairley, Joe with an 'e', Fairley is F-A-I-R-L-E-Y. He lives on the Mawson compound down there. His is by far the smallest Leap in number, even leopards find the cold down there a little harsh."

Dominic looked over the list. He was sure he'd have the names and their locations sorted in no time, although being able to spell half of them might take a while longer.

"How soon do you want me to join in on the meetings?"

"We might leave it until you get things settled with Adele, your mind won't be fully on board until you complete the mating. I just figured I'd start off your lessons a little earlier, give you time to be able to remember everything by going slowly through it all."

"Thanks, Dad, you mind if I head out? Conner wanted to go for a run this afternoon."

"Sure, you boys have fun. Just wish I could join you

but I have way too much here that needs doing."

Dominic ripped the page from the pad and tucked it into his pocket, a grin on his face as he left his dad's office. He and Conner always had fun on their runs. With all the stress of trying to find ways to win over Adele, he really needed the stress relief of a nice long run.

Chapter Six

Cole slammed his ute door shut in anger. Fired. Bloody hell. He'd been careful, made sure he left no proof. No one could prove he was the one who'd lit the damn fire but because he and Ben were seen arguing with the captain they both got sacked.

He was so damn mad he wasn't tracking and got home in record time. He stormed up to his front door, unlocked it, and slammed it behind him. Out of habit his eyes instantly searched for his slave. She stood in the middle of the room, still as a statue with her eyes wide in shock. He took a moment to admire how the color drained from her face. She started to shake as she obviously read the mood he was in. *That's right, slave, you and me are going to go a few rounds tonight.*

As it was only eleven in the morning, he knew she'd not been expecting him for hours. He also knew she could read him well enough to know she was in for one hell of a night. He stalked up to her, unlocked the collar, grabbed her arm, and dragged her downstairs. He didn't have the patience to wait for her to greet him properly today. Or even to hang up the chain properly. He needed to vent, calm down, get his focus back, and she was the perfect tool for him to do it. Silently, she stumbled along after him down the stairs into the basement. He shoved her ahead of him into the room. He didn't draw things out like he normally did. Normally he took his time, enjoying her shaking in fear of what was to come.

Not today.

Today he needed his release too badly.

He quickly got her wrists in the cuffs and hung her on the hook in the wall. He stood back a moment to look her over. So fucking beautiful. He'd only been training her for a few months, yet she was already on the verge of becoming a woman. She must be older than he'd originally thought. Sometimes being wrong could be a good thing. Her breasts had grown since he first inspected her. They still had a long way to go but they were definitely getting there. She still didn't have any hair but that suited him. He liked to be able to see all of her. She could hide nothing from him.

"Look at you, slave. You're becoming a woman so quickly. I don't have the patience to deflower you tonight but tomorrow I think. Yeah, definitely tomorrow I'll be up for taking you. Up your training, make you completely mine, that's what I'll do. What do you think about that, slave? Ready to be mine, completely, forever?"

He watched her eyes as they dulled and lost focus, almost like a piece of her just died. Good, she was accepting her place. When he saw her tears start, he smiled evilly. He had just about broken her spirit, once that happened she would truly be wholly his. Mind, body, soul—completely his.

There were many responsibilities involved with being the Continental Alpha. Currently, Jake was focused on the Search. Every time Halley's Comet passed over the Earth, fourteen new shifters were conceived. A fated pair on each continent. Fifteen years after the last comet passing was 2001. In that year, those fourteen shifters would have changed into snow leopards for the first time when the moon rose on their birthdays.

They called finding those pairs the Search. In the past, the Search was always limited to each continent's new shifter pair, but in the last year the Council of Alphas had decided to start searching for other lost shifters too. Ones who'd been orphaned, adopted, or simply lost track of. They were all lost in a world that didn't understand them.

The Alpha of each Leap would watch news reports daily and search online for strange sightings and the like regularly. When they found something relevant, they would go in, or send someone on their behalf to go in and find them. The Lost Ones would then either be brought into the closest Leap or time would be spent educating them so they could safely stay where they were. They couldn't waste time, their enemies were watching the same reports and going after the same shifters they were. And if Trigger got them first, they had no chance. Trigger murdered any shifter if found. No questions asked.

The Search had always been a big job, add in the Lost Ones and it was a massive task. They'd each started by drawing up Leap family trees, writing a list of known missing shifters and whether they would be an adult or child. The next step was to consolidate the lists so if they had moved continent they could still be found. It was these lists that Jake was currently going through.

A knock on the doorframe had Jake glancing up from his work to see Dominic walk in. His eldest boy had grown into such a good strong man. Despite his strength, he was not violent in the least. He'd always exuded a calm aura that radiated to those around him. He very rarely lost his cool no matter what happened. He was a man that Jake was proud to call his son. He knew he would make an excellent Alpha when his time came.

"Heard you were looking for me," Dominic said, taking a seat opposite him.

"That I was. I'm sure you've noticed I've been getting more and more involved with the Search and other Alpha matters of late and it's beginning to take up a considerable amount of my time."

"Yeah, I know. You're doing a great job. There's got to be so many lost shifters out there struggling."

The edge of pain was obvious in Dominic's voice. Compassion was another trait his son had in spades.

"Thanks, son. Well, the problem is your mother

would like to see me every now and again." He quietly chuckled at Dominic's wince. "So, I've decided I'm going to step down as captain here at the station. I just don't have the time. I recommended that you be promoted to captain and the State Office has agreed—so long as you want it, that is. So, from now on when you're not out in the field, you'll be working in here learning from me so I can show you the ropes and get you settled."

Jake did his best to hold off his laugh but Dominic frozen in shock, was funny as hell. After a moment or two, Dominic shook his head and frowned.

"You sure, Dad? You won't miss it?"

"Hell yeah, I'll miss it, but I'll still hang around to volunteer and help out when I can; you won't be rid of me that easy."

"When will it be official? Who knows about it?"

"As soon as you say yes, it will be official. And I haven't told anyone yet, except your mother of course. Thought you would like the pleasure of that task. Perhaps dinner down at Top Pub? Maybe you could convince your lovely little mate to stop ignoring you for the night?"

Jake chuckled. The last couple of weeks had been highly entertaining watching Dominic attempt to get Adele's attention and Adele trying to avoid Dominic's. Jake wasn't worried though, they were mates so sooner or later Adele wouldn't be able to resist and would cave in to Dominic.

"I wish, Dad. She's still ignoring me. When I got an amazing kiss three weeks ago, I thought we were set. But the next day she'd closed me out again. Tighter than before."

"Talk to Kit, she'll be able to convince her to come along with her. Adele is still living with her, isn't she?"

"Yeah, she is. Do you need me for anything right now or can I go start planning for tonight?"

"You're good to go, son, enjoy your freedom while you can."

Jake gave him a wink and laughed when the boy all but ran from the room.

As Adele stood in front of Top Pub, she wondered how the hell she'd let Kit talk her into this one. Oh yeah, that's right, she was half in love with Dominic after their one and only—albeit toe-curling—kiss three weeks ago and couldn't seem to keep herself away from him. Kit nudged her toward the door while whispering in her ear.

"C'mon, Adele, you know what you really want to do. And I can assure you, it isn't hanging out here on your own."

Adele glanced over her shoulder glaring at Kit, her new best friend, as she raised her hand to open the door. Since she was living with Kit, they'd had lots of time to bond. Adele saw Kit as a sister, the one person she could open up to without fear of judgement or rejection. Even if she was rather annoying in her perceptiveness.

Regardless, she knew Kit would keep her secrets. The woman didn't even freak out when Adele had confessed to her about her dreams of snow leopards.

"That's what scares me, Kit," she ground out. "I shouldn't want what I want."

Kit gave her a wide grin and a wink.

"The best things in life are the unexpected ones, Adele. Your mother wouldn't want you to be alone all your life. Why not give Dominic a chance? I've known him since I was a teenager and I assure you he doesn't have a mean bone in his body, nor is he a player. You can trust him with your heart."

Adele couldn't respond. She didn't have the words. She knew Kit was right about her mother. There was no way she'd have wanted her daughter to be alone all her life. But surely she could have friends to not be alone. She licked her lips as she entered. Even she knew she was lying to herself. She'd seen enough of Jake and Sophie and a few other couples around Rosebery alone to see that a bond between man and wife was something beyond what friendship could provide. The pub was at full capacity for Dominic's promotion celebration and thankfully the noise of it all clogged her mind and stopped her thinking too hard.

Dominic knew the moment Adele entered the pub; he'd felt her presence long before he managed to catch sight of her. After about ten minutes of watching her mingle with the others, he couldn't wait any longer. He headed toward her. There was no way she could avoid him at his own damn party, that's for sure.

He came up behind her and inhaled deeply, shivering as he allowed her scent to seep into him. She gasped, spinning around to face him with wide eyes. Hmm, good to know she could feel his presence too. Kit was standing behind Adele so she didn't see when Kit winked at him. What the hell was that about? He'd have to ask her later. He was too busy enjoying his mate's sweet smell. Natural woman with just a hint of vanilla, so subtle it couldn't be a perfume. No shifter liked his nose offended by heavy perfume on his mate, especially when her natural scent was so damn irresistible.

"Congratulations, Dominic, our new captain." Adele's sweet voice was like a gentle caress over his skin.

He couldn't move when she stood on her tiptoes and placed her hands on his pectorals. His heart rate sped up as she leaned in and chastely kissed his cheek. A groan left his throat and he wrapped an arm firmly around her waist to capture her. He pulled her in close so they were touching from chest to hip, his other hand wrapped possessively around her neck before he splayed his fingers into her hair. He put his mouth near her ear and whispered quietly so only she would hear him.

"Please, Adele, stop fighting against us. I promise I will *never* hurt you. Please come out with me on Saturday? Nothing big, I promise. We'll just go for a hike up near the lake and I'll bring a picnic for lunch.

We'll keep it nice and casual."

He could hear the edge of desperation in his voice but he didn't care, he needed his mate in his arms, needed to claim her. Dominic turned her face as he nibbled his way from her ear to her mouth where he gave her a quick but passionate kiss that he was sure they both felt down to their souls.

"Okay." Adele breathed out once he released her lips.

Elation had Dominic grinning like a fool. She said yes.

"I'll pick you up at ten Saturday morning. Make sure you wear your hiking boots."

He gave her another quick kiss before he reluctantly released her from his arms. His gaze stayed locked on her as she wondered over to the bar to get herself a drink. Kit place both hands on his shoulder before resting her cheek on them.

"So, she's finally weakening to your charms, Dominic, where are you taking her?"

He'd known that with her shifter hearing, Kit heard what he'd said to Adele. However, Adele didn't know she'd heard and that was the point. He'd wanted her to know it was meant to be just between them.

"I'm taking her to the field up by the lake. I'm hoping when she sees it she'll recognize it from our dreams and feel more like everything that is happening between us is meant to be."

"You plan on telling her everything? Because, this plan of yours could backfire big time. What you going to do if she freaks out and runs off on you?"

He winced. He had briefly considered that she might react badly, but he was getting desperate.

"Yeah, I know. I'll see how she reacts before I go telling her anything. I can't wait much longer, Kit. She's my mate. I can't stand having her so close but not in my arms and in my life. She's as vital to me as air."

"Wow, that's some powerful stuff there, Dominic. Well, let me know if I can help you out at all."

"You already have, Kit. Letting her move in with you, I know you'll keep her protected. If you hadn't done that, I'm not sure what I would have done to make sure she was safe. Probably would have blown any chance I had with her, that's for sure. Then tonight, you dragged her in here."

Kit lifted her head and hands before lightly punching him in the arm.

"Oh no you don't, Dominic. Don't go all mushy on me. Save that shit for your mate who might just appreciate it. And you know full well you'd do the same for me. We're family, that's what we do."

Dominic wrapped his arm around Kit's shoulders for a quick side hug before nodding and releasing her. Yeah, they were family, all right. She might not be his sister by birth, but she was his sister of the heart.

Chapter Seven

Kelly's mind was fuzzy as she hovered between consciousness and unconsciousness. She vaguely heard him grab the towel, wipe his face and chest. From experience, she knew he'd then tuck it into his back pocket. When he lifted her down off the hook, a hellish wave of pain made her gasp before she was knocked firmly into the land of unconsciousness.

The sound of his boots hitting the floor upstairs brought her back to the land of the living. *Unfortunately.* Everywhere hurt, except between her legs and that was going to hurt most of all in the morning. Unable to move, she lay in a broken heap on the floor, in a pool of her own blood where he'd left her like yesterday's garbage. Inside she sobbed; she didn't have the energy to do it out loud, and she knew from experience the movement would cause her injuries to hurt even more.

As her brain began to come more fully back online, it registered that she was still unchained. He never left her down here after a session, no matter how brutal. He always dragged her upstairs, chained her, and left her in the bathroom to clean up.

He must have assumed she wouldn't be able to move for days after all he'd done to her, so he'd left her on the stone cold floor to absorb her pain and ponder what her future would hold. *Sadistic bastard.* What he didn't take into account was that with the knowledge he planned on raping her repeatedly from tomorrow, she had all the motivation she needed to push past her pain. He was always telling her how strong she was, but he had no bloody idea just how strong she could be. He would. She vowed to herself that she would escape or die trying. He would never have all of her.

Decision made, she attempted to get her body on board with the plan. It took what seemed like forever— but she hoped it was only half an hour or so—to get her body to listen to her mind's commands but eventually she was able to shift her limbs. Kelly knew she had to get out now, while he thought she was too weak to move. Her time was very limited. Without a doubt, as soon as he woke up, she'd be back in chains. She knew with all her soul that if she didn't get out now, she never would. Taking as deep a breath as she dared, she slowly pulled herself over to his discarded T-shirt and carefully put it on. He'd worked up quite a sweat beating her, so he'd taken it off, obviously forgetting about it.

Slowly but surely, she dragged her aching broken body over to the door, before continuing her journey up the stairs. Every movement, no matter how small, hurt like hell, even breathing hurt and she suspected he'd cracked her ribs again. Her body began to tremble. She was so cold. The T-shirt wasn't much to cover her but she didn't have any clothes left and it would have to do.

She made it to the top of the stairs, sighing in relief. As she took a moment to catch her breath, she listened for any sign of him. She sagged against the floor when she heard a soft snore coming from his room. Bastard had worn himself out beating her. On the upside, the sound of his snoring should cover any noise she might make getting out. Normally, she was very skilled at moving without making a sound but injured like she was, she wasn't so confident of her skills.

Clenching her jaw so she wouldn't cry out in pain, she crawled over to the front door on all fours. Seeing his shoes by the door, she decided it was worth the risk to take the time to put them on. They were way too big for her but she did the laces up as tight as she could, hoping she wouldn't blister too badly. She knew she wouldn't get far barefoot. Her adrenaline was well and truly pumping now that she was nearly out. Gritting her teeth, she used the doorframe to drag herself to her feet. Her vision clouded for a moment, and the second it cleared, she opened the door and staggered out. Holding her breath, she closed the door as softy as she could. She couldn't risk the cool night air waking him up. Heart pounding, she took her first steps into freedom. Elation had her smiling and her heart racing when she made it to the end of the drive. She'd done it and got free of that house. Refusing to allow herself to stop yet, she started walking as fast as she could downhill. As battered as she was, it was slow going. One baby step in front of the other, but it was enough to take her to freedom from her living nightmare.

The longer she walked the easier it was to block out the aches in her body. The reward of freedom was worth every moment of pushing herself. It was late at night and dark enough that she was confident no one could see her as she moved silently through the streets. She headed to the clothing bin she used to raid for her and her mother. She moaned in relief when she saw there were bags sitting in front of it. She wasn't sure she had the energy, or the time, to break into the thing. She sent a thank you to the heavens as she began pawing through the bags until she had a jumper, track pants, and socks added to her body. She didn't risk taking longer to look for shoes that fit. He could wake at any moment and come looking for her. She may have gotten out of the house, but she was not free yet.

With only the thought to get as far away from him as possible, she headed to the main road, and sticking to the trees off to the side of it, just kept walking. As she was heading out of town, she saw a big green sign saying "Rosebery 67km." She liked roses, they smelled nice and looked pretty. Her heart feeling lighter with each step, she kept walking. She was finally free.

"I cannot believe I caved in," Adele grumbled as she tugged on her hiking boots.

Kit chuckled. "You've given that man the slip for

how long now? You've done well to last this long without caving in to that man's charms, doll."

"You're not helping, Kit, you know why I can't give in."

"Adele, your mother wouldn't want you hiding away from life because of the choices she made and were made for her. She would want you to *live*." Kit wrapped Adele in a hug as she continued speaking. "I know where you're going today, keep your phone close, if you feel threatened at all, call me and I'll come running. You know I will."

Adele continued to hug her friend while she blinked back her tears.

"I know, Kit. Thanks, what would I do without you?" She was so grateful for everything Kit did for her.

"Let's see, you'd be staying home getting bored out of your mind because I wouldn't be pushing you to accept the attention of a hot man who's chasing you down?"

Adele couldn't help but laugh at Kit's cheeky response.

"You're totally insane, Kit, but you know I love you for it, right?"

"Oh, don't go getting mushy on me, doll. You know I love you like a sister and let's leave it at that."

Adele was grateful when their sisterly bonding moment was broken by the sound of the doorbell. She hadn't known how to respond.

Adele headed to the door to greet Dominic. He had

been avoiding her for the last three days. She was certain it was because he didn't want to give her a chance to back out, but she'd discovered she missed not seeing him every day. From her first day in Rosebery, he'd always found ways to see her during the day. He really was very sweet and attentive toward her.

She opened the door and drunk in the beauty that was Dominic—his lean waist and broad shoulders to his ice-blue eyes and cheeky grin. Heat flared in her face as Adele realized she'd been busted staring. She felt his warmth seep into her as he stepped in close to her and wrapped one arm around her waist while he lowered his head to put his mouth near her ear.

"Good morning, beautiful. You look absolutely radiant this morning."

He kissed her cheek, which she was certain still showed her blush. He pulled back, slightly loosening his hold so he could look down at her face. Adele gazed wide-eyed up at Dominic. She was going up in flames from his kiss and his touch. Why did this man affect her so when no man had ever caught her eye? Dominic's arm was still wrapped around her waist and her neck was tingling from where his hot breath had caressed her as he'd whispered.

He'd told her she looked "radiant" but she wasn't sure he was being honest. No one had ever called her that before. She was average height, had average brown hair and a slightly larger than average body—nothing she'd thought a man would find appealing. Kit thankfully saved the day by coming up behind her to hand her the small backpack she'd readied this morning.

"Here you go, doll. Don't let him whisk you away without your bag. Hi, Dominic." Without taking his gaze from hers, he reached out and took her bag from Kit. Had he missed her over the past days too?

"Hey, Kit. How are you doing?"

"I'm doing okay. I think I'll leave you two be so you can get going. Catch you both later."

Kit walked back into the house chuckling, leaving Adele alone with Dominic.

"I've got everything covered for today, beautiful, you don't need to bring anything but yourself."

"It's just habit I guess. I always take a first aid kit and water with me everywhere. It's kind of like a security blanket."

Adele felt her face heat further with embarrassment. Dominic seemed to pick up on it and thankfully let the topic go, slinging her bag over his shoulder.

"Okay, so we're all set. Let's get moving. It's going to be a hot one later this afternoon so the earlier we get there the better."

His arm still firmly around Adele's waist, he led her down the drive to his metallic blue Toyota Rav 4.

"I'll be able to get fairly close to where we're going in the Rav so we won't have too far to walk later when it gets hotter."

Her heart fluttered when he opened her door for her.

Such a gentleman. As he drove the windy roads to their destination, Adele kept her gaze fixed out the window. She loved Tasmania. All the lush green scrub and trees, even in the height of summer, was magnificent. She snuggled back into the seat as the sun shining through the window warmed her skin. She felt so calm and peaceful. Her head was filled with Dominic's scent. A fresh woodsy scent mixed with all male spice. The smell alone seemed to ease her mind and soul. Before she knew it, Dominic stopped the car.

"Hang tight a sec."

He prowled around the bonnet to her door. She kept her gaze on him the entire time. *Hmm, I could watch that man move all day and not get bored.* He opened her door, then held his hand out to help her from the SUV. She decided he was like a magnet. She could have easily stepped away from him but instead her body stepped in close to him—her brain didn't get any say in the matter.

He kept his hold on her hand, while the other went to her hip then swept up her spine to her neck, making her shiver at his touch. He gently tugged her ponytail until she tilted her head back. As his mouth descended toward hers, she slid her eyes shut to savor the sensations. He nibbled at the corner of her mouth before gently swiping his tongue along the seam of her lips. She gasped as she felt it all the way to her now curling toes. With her lips parted, he plunged into her mouth to take her over. She raised her free hand up to his hair, buried her fingers into his inky black soft hair to hold him to her. She felt that same spark that she had felt that first time he'd kissed her weeks ago.

She pulled back and gulped air in her lungs before uttering a "wow." She slowly opened her eyes to look up at him. He was watching her with passion soaked hooded eyes and then he slowly licked his lower lip like he was savoring the taste of her, not wanting to waste a single drop. Her gaze tracked the movement.

He leaned down, nibbled the edge of her mouth again while whispering to her, "You taste divine, my sweet Adele. I will never be able to get enough of you, but for now, I'd better stop. I have somewhere special I want to show you."

Pulling away from her slowly, Dominic headed to the back of the Rav. She chuckled when she noticed how stiffly he was walking now. Her own legs weren't feeling all that steady either.

He returned a few minutes later, walking normally, with his ruck-sac and her small backpack. He handed over her bag with a wink as he strapped his ruck-sac onto his back. Oh boy, even with a shirt on, the way his muscles flexed as he put that bag on just about had her drooling. He locked up the Rav then turned to her, reaching a hand toward her. Feeling brave, she didn't wait for him to move closer to her. She went to him, placing her palm against his and linking their fingers together. She risked a glance at his face. He was sporting a wide grin, looking very happy. She couldn't help but return the expression as he began leading her up the path through the scrub.

"We only have to walk for about five minutes to get where we're going then we can sit back in the shade and relax for a bit."

His deep smooth voice still affected her whole body the same way it had that first time. Adele felt light and content as they walked up the path holding hands. She wondered why she wasn't afraid; she should be running in the opposite direction. She did not want a man in her life, but Dominic obviously wasn't going to go away any time soon, and to be perfectly honest, even if only to herself, she didn't want him to go away. Dominic was divine. He was tall, had short ink-black hair, ice-blue eyes, and a body so muscular and defined she had trouble not drooling every time she saw him—and he wanted her, Little Miss Average. She shook her head at her thoughts, shifting her focus from inside herself to her surroundings, and taking a deep lungful of fresh mountain air.

She slowed and frowned when trees and rocks started to look familiar when she knew she'd definitely never been here before. The hairs on the back of her neck stood up as they came out into a clearing. She froze to the spot, unable to move as Dominic kept walking, unaware of her distress until her hand slipped from his. He spun around, looking worried.

"What's wrong, Adele? You've gone very pale."

She felt his warmth at her side a moment later but

she wasn't really tracking. He wrapped her hand around an open bottle of water and told her to drink. She did as she was told because her mind was reeling and she couldn't think of a reason not to. The only thing missing from the scene before her was her *chaton*. This was the field in her dreams, the field where she met her *chaton* and found comfort. She slowly turned a full circle before facing Dominic again. He had turned his back to her as he bent to spread out the picnic rug over the grass. When he stood, he faced her, still looking worried. He held his hand out toward her.

"Come here, Adele, I think you need to sit down before you pass out. I don't like how pale you've gotten."

She put her hand in his, taking comfort in the warmth that spread from his hand up her arm. He guided her to the rug and helped her sit down before he lowered himself behind her so that she was cradled between his large muscular thighs, his knees bent and at the same level with her shoulders. Without thought, she leaned her head against his one knee and closed her eyes while she took some deep breaths. All she could smell now was him; he surrounded her in all ways. Within seconds, she began to calm, but her world was still spinning. She opened her eyes and held her breath a moment when she felt him lean forward. What was he doing? When she felt his nose softly rub up her neck toward her ear and jaw, she leaned heavily against him. He nuzzled her just below her ear, and it felt familiar somehow, right. With a contented sigh, she reclosed her eyes and let go of all the remaining tension in her body and focused on enjoying Dominic's embrace. Ignoring for now the fact she'd imagined this place in her dreams. She felt so warm and safe surrounded by Dominic. There was also stirrings of stronger emotions in her heart, but she refused to look any closer at that. She wasn't ready to deal with those thoughts.

Dominic was regretting bringing her here. He'd guessed she would be surprised, but the way her face had drained of color the moment they'd stepped into the field, her body totally rigid and tense, was far beyond what he'd predicted.

Unsure how to handle her, he'd trusted his instincts that demanded he comfort and care for her. He'd curled himself around her as best he could as a man. When she'd leaned her head against his knee, exposing her long elegant neck, he simply couldn't resist. He'd run his nose gently up her neck while breathing deeply of her scent, taking it deep into his soul. When he'd started nuzzling her below her ear she finally let her tension go and he could breathe easily again.

He felt the stress pour out of her body and drain away. Now he sat with her all soft and relaxed in his embrace. His leopard wanted to purr in satisfaction, he had a job and a half to keep the noise inside. He was damn sure if she heard purring she would completely freak out and he didn't want to lose this moment that felt like pure heaven to him, so he stayed silent. He lost track of time as he sat there slowly, gently nuzzling his mate's neck, and delivering small kisses and licks to her soft sweet skin.

Her shoulders rose as she inhaled deeply before she moved to nuzzle her nose against the soft denim covering his knee. He grinned; she didn't know it, but she was covering herself with his scent, she was showing him her acceptance of him as hers. Dominic moved his mouth up to her ear.

"Please, Adele, don't keep pushing me away. I need you to let me in, please."

He could hear the desperation in his voice but there was nothing he could do. That's how he felt.

"I can't" —a sob escaped her— "can't keep pushing you away anymore. I'm not strong enough," she whispered so quietly that if he'd been wholly human he would have never heard her.

Dominic gently lifted and turned her around in his lap while putting his knees down, crossing his legs so she ended up straddling his waist with her bottom in his lap. He took her face between his palms. The tear tracks down her cheeks had his heart aching.

"My sweet Adele, you are the strongest woman I know."

Needing to connect with her more, he leaned in and gave her a quick kiss before he continued.

"Letting someone in, having someone to lean on, isn't a sign of weakness, Adele. We will both be so much stronger together."

Dominic lowered his lips to hers again, except this time there was nothing fast about his movements. He slowly, thoroughly devoured her mouth, making sure she felt him all the way to her soul, just like he felt her all the way to his. Everything else faded as heat and passion spread over him and into her. He felt her curl her arms tighter around his neck, holding him to her. As the tips of her nipples came into contact with his chest they both groaned. He had never felt like this in his whole life; he could smell her arousal, feel her burning up in his arms and she was taking him right along with her.

This day was turning out better than he could ever have imagined. Dominic's mind spun, the taste of his mate surrendering to him, the feel of her body willingly pressed up against his. He couldn't hold off any longer. He had to touch her—skin to skin. He pulled back slightly from her lips.

"I need to feel you, Adele. Will you let me touch you?"

She nodded her head slightly under his hands as she murmured, "Yes." He released the breath he was holding in a rush of relief. He moved to nuzzle her neck and placed reverent kisses along her collarbone up to below her ear. He hovered a moment just drinking in her scent. When she sighed, he pulled back a little. He wiped away the last of her tears with his thumbs before caressing her jaw, down her neck, and onto the collar of her shirt. She had on a thin cotton button-down shirt, perfect for hiking as it kept the sun off but wasn't thick enough to make someone hot. He loved that his mate was so practical.

He undid each button, brushing his fingers against the flesh he revealed as each one popped open. By the time he had all the buttons undone, both of them were breathing hard and he was aroused as all get out. He was as hard as steel. The heat radiating from her core that was resting over his erection was just about burning him through the denim of his jeans. He moved his palms up to her neck and slid them under the material, down over her shoulders, taking the shirt down as he went. It tumbled to pool at her elbows and he took a sharp breath in at his first glimpse of her.

"You are so beautiful."

His lips pulled up into a grin as her blush spread over her cheeks, then down her neck, and across her chest. She reacted so innocently to his compliments, like she truly didn't see herself as he did. Her white lacy bra was stunning against her pale skin. He could see a trace of the darker color of her nipples through the lace. Awareness of their connection flowed through him as he gently ran his fingers back up her arms then down her sides. He ran his fingertips over the underside of each breast, up the center, then traced the edge of her bra up to her shoulders. He hesitated after he slipped a finger beneath each strap. He would go no further than she was comfortable with, even if he was about to explode in his pants.

He tried to calm down his desire. The last thing he wanted was to push her too far and have her push him away again. He was well aware he could undo all his progress with Adele with one false move. He held his breath waiting to see if she would allow him to remove her bra and was so relieved as he watched her eyes dilate further.

"Dominic, please."

Her voice had turned husky with her lust and the sound had him shivering. He slowly let out his breath before he leaned forward and nibbled at her lips.

"How you honor me, my sweet Adele."

He slid the straps off her shoulders and let them fall down her arms. He gently gripped the front clasp and undid it before peeling the lace away from her flesh. He did it slowly so he could fully enjoy the revealing of her lush round breasts for the first time. Her nipples were rosy and tight. Standing up and begging to be worshipped by his hands and mouth. As her bra landed on the shirt pooled around her elbows, he palmed each breast and groaned in pleasure. The heat of her soft flesh seared him in the most delicious way.

"Oh, my sweet, sweet Adele, you are perfect."

Once again, she tensed up at him complimenting her. He wouldn't allow her to continue struggling with her self-doubts. She needed to know how perfect she was, so he continued to talk to her, to tell her just how perfect and beautiful her body was.

When a soft smile curved her lips and her muscles relaxed, he trailed off his words as he nibbled at the edge of her mouth. Then trailed kisses down her neck and over her collarbone. He briefly paused to nuzzle his face in her neck, absorbing her scent into his skin and soul. Then he moved slowly down, licking and nibbling his way over the outside of her right breast, around the underside. His stomach clenched when she gasped after he finally took her nipple into his mouth and swirled his tongue around it. She shuddered beneath him and her peak tightened further against his tongue. He could do nothing to stop the purr of satisfaction escaping his throat as he savored the taste and feel of his mate burning in his arms.

She went rigid for a moment before he managed to distract her by enclosing her other breast in his hand, while he continued to torment the one in his mouth. He felt her shudder and could smell how wet she was for him. Her hands moved tentatively over his shoulders and down onto his chest; he loved the feel of her hands on him. His muscles twitched and flexed beneath her hesitant touch. Her fingers got caught in the material of his shirt and she growled out in frustration.

"Skin...please, I want to feel your skin under my hands."

Dominic was more than happy to deliver on her request as he pulled his T-shirt over his head. Before he had his arms and head free, her sharp intake of breath had him grinning. A moan left him when her hot palms landed on his chest. His pectorals twitched as she smoothed her palms over them and when she scraped her nails lightly over his nipples, he shuddered on a groan. Bloody hell, she was going to have him embarrassing himself if she kept this up.

She continued her exploration down his torso, smoothing both her hands over his abdomen. His muscles tensed and rippled beneath her touch. He loved how her expression showed that she was totally enthralled by his body. Made all the time he spent keeping in shape worth it. Of course, he'd done it for his job, but now he was extra glad he'd stuck with it.

Her hands kept up their wandering as she trailed her gaze back up his body to his face. His lips quirked up in a lopsided grin as a very cute blush spread over her face and down her neck once more. He adored how easily she blushed around him.

In a rush, she snapped her hands away and he felt the absence immediately and missed the contact more than he'd thought was possible. He picked her hands up and lifted them to his mouth where he gently kissed each palm before holding them against his chest where he needed them.

"Don't be embarrassed, beautiful. I love the feel of your hands on me. Nothing has ever felt as good as you stroking my skin, please, don't stop what you were doing."

She tugged at her hands, trying to free them, but he refused to release her. Something else was going on here, other than a touch of embarrassment and shyness. He frowned down at her, trying to work out what it could be.

"You're laughing at me," she spoke in a hurt whisper.

His heart stuttered as a tear escaped and ran down her cheek when she closed her eyes.

"I've never been with a man, I don't know what I'm doing...and you...you are just so beautiful and I'm just so...average and you're saying things to me like that. *Merde,* I'm babbling."

Stunned mute, he didn't protest when she pulled her hands free. As he sat in shocked silence, she pulled her shirt back over her shoulders and lowered her face into her hands. Dominic couldn't believe how Adele saw herself. She was average? She was beautiful, stunning in every way. He wrapped his fingers around her hands, gently peeling them away from her face.

"Look at me, Adele...please."

He waited for her to turn her face up to his. Her eyes were rimmed red from her crying and it broke his heart to think he'd caused those tears.

"I was not laughing at you, beautiful. I would never laugh at you showing your passion. Watching your eyes light up, watching you look so happy, so enthralled, to be simply touching me, it makes me happy...more than happy; it makes me ecstatic."

He moved his hands to cup her face and he thumbed away the stray tears that remained on her cheeks. How could he get her to see what he saw?

"My love, there is *nothing* average about you."

Running his hands through her hair, he decided to tell her what he saw. Hoping she would see herself in the same light he did.

"Your hair is so soft, the waves glide through my fingers like silk. The color is totally unique, not quite black, not quite brown. When the sun shines off it, like now, it looks like you have a halo." He ran his thumbs under each eye. "Your eyes are like melted chocolate that I just want to dive into and drown in, and your lips" —he started nibbling at the side of her mouth— "just beg for my kisses. I can't resist."

He spent a couple of minutes kissing her with all the passion he felt for her, his mate. When she relaxed and her palms began to creep up his arms, exploring all the dips and rises of his muscles, he lowered his hands. Trailing them down her neck, and over her shoulders, pushing the shirt so it dropped back down her arms.

"Your skin is so soft, pure ivory silk. I can't stop touching you. I will never be able to stop touching you." His palms lowered to cup each of her breasts. "These are perfection. They are round, soft, with lovely rosy tips that stand up to attention waiting for me. They are just the right size to fill my hands—my very large hands." He nipped at her chin before he nuzzled up toward her ear. "And I just know, when you allow me the honor of exploring the rest of you, I will find utter perfection the whole way down to the tips of your dainty little toes."

Dominic lifted her easily, and moved her so she lay down on her back. Before she had a chance to protest, he lay beside her and began softly kissing his way down her neck, back to her irresistible breasts. He just couldn't get enough of her. He hadn't lied when he'd told her he would never get enough of her. She was his mate. Oh, how he wished he could claim her, complete the mating right this moment. But he couldn't, not until she knew all about him and accepted him. He would never start his forever with lies, even if they were only lies of omission.

He looked up at her passion-dazed face as he ran his tongue over her nipple and waited for her to look down at him. When she did, he finished his speech. "And the fact that I am the only man who knows your taste, the only one who has it on his tongue, the only man who has seen your perfection, brings me so much joy and makes me feel so honored, I simply don't have the words."

She opened her mouth to respond but before she could get a sound out he cut her off by sucking her nipple and as much of her breast as he could get into his mouth. He sucked until he felt the tip scrape along the back of the roof of his mouth. They both groaned together. Dominic settled himself between her legs and went to work worshipping his mate's body. He shivered when she began exploring his back and shoulders with her soft fingers. He couldn't hold back for much longer, the need to claim his mate was so strong. He moved back to her mouth and ravaged her for as long as he could stand the burn. When he pulled back, she was breathing as heavily as he was. She had a pink flush on her face and chest and looked good enough to eat. Right on cue, Adele's stomach let out a rumble. He chuckled as she gasped and flushed a deeper red.

"I think we need to get you fed, beautiful."

Adele sat up when he moved off her and reluctantly, he helped her get dressed. When he had all the buttons done up he looked up at her face. Her stare was glued to his chest, his pectorals twitched under the intensity of her gaze and her mouth gaped open ever so slightly. Dominic couldn't help the growl that escaped his throat. He watched her jaw click shut as her eyes flicked up to his face in shock. Damn, that growl hadn't sounded human.

"Sorry, beautiful. I didn't mean to scare you, but when you look at me like that, with heat in your eyes, it brings out my inner caveman."

Desperate to have her not analyze the noises he'd been making, he threw her his lopsided grin. He knew it would melt her toward him and sure enough, her lips quirked up in a small smile.

"So, caveman, what's for lunch?"

Kelly had been free for two nights and three days. She was tired after all the walking and so damn sore from her injuries. He'd worked her over well. Everywhere hurt. Her body was crying out for her to stop and rest but she couldn't give in, she had to continue on. There was no way she was going back to that hell, she'd rather die.

Her stomach growled and cramped bad enough it sent her to her knees. Damn, she was hungry. She breathed through the pain as best she could. When it finally eased off, she dragged herself up using a tree before she continued on. She'd been following a creek that had provided her with drinking water but food wasn't so easy to find. Her head was fuzzy and the desire to just lie down and sleep for a week was strong but thoughts of what he would do to her if he found her kept her going.

She came upon a lake and stopped to wash her face in the cool water and have another drink. She was going to have to find food soon or she wouldn't be able to keep going, the cramps were getting worse. What she needed to do was find a town, which meant she'd need to leave the creek and search for a road.

Gathering her remaining energy, she managed to get to her feet and up the embankment to find herself in an open field. As she walked, she glanced around and sucked in a breath when she caught a couple staring at her. Not looking where she was going, her foot hit something and she stumbled. When she landed heavily on her hands and knees panic rose up. Her breathing sped up, causing her ribs to hurt more.

She had to get away or they would take her back, but she couldn't get her body to respond. Nothing would move. She heard footsteps running toward her and just as their feet came into her field of vision, her eyesight began to dim and go black. She managed to groan out, "Please don't take me back to him." Before she lost the battle and the darkness took her into a blissful pain-free place.

Stunned, Adele could do nothing but watch as Dominic kneeled frozen in shock, looking down at the limp girl in his arms. She was having as much trouble as he was catching up with everything that had happened in the last five minutes. They had been happily finishing off their lunch, chatting away and having a great time then she'd heard something moving toward them from the lake.

Ever her protector, Dominic had stood and turned toward the noise so fast it startled her. Wondering what could be heading their way, she'd not expected it to be a bloodied tiny wisp of a girl. They had both frozen in shock for a moment. Adele slowly rose to her feet with a gasp of horror. She was just a child, couldn't have been much more than eleven or twelve years old and she had been badly beaten. She had an oversized blood stained T-shirt on with a jumper tied around her waist, some old track pants and ill-fitting shoes but the sight that held her transfixed was that every exposed piece of her skin was black, blue, green, or red.

Dominic snapped out of his shock and as he rushed to the girl, Adele followed him. Thankfully, he reached the girl just in time to sweep her up before she hit the ground when she passed out cold.

Needing the connection, to feel the calm he always brought her, she laid her hand on his shoulder. Slowly he stood up with the child in his arms. He was so gentle, so careful. His gaze locked with hers and she clearly saw the pain, sorrow, and horror in their depths. Adele was quite certain her eyes mirrored his emotions.

"She's so light, Adele, so small." He swallowed roughly. "What kind of bastard does this? To a child? Bloody hell, just look at her!"

Adele's heart was breaking simply looking at the poor little girl in Dominic's arms. As a tear escaped down her cheek, she forced her mind to focus and she switched into paramedic mode. She wiped the tear from her face and moved in close to the child. She gently pressed her fingers to the child's neck to check for a pulse, relief rushing over her as she counted the weak but steady beat beneath her digits.

"Bring her over to the rug, Dominic. I need to check her over before we take her in."

Adele walked behind Dominic as he headed over to their picnic rug and gently laid out the injured child, she was trying hard to remain focused on her and not how good Dominic looked with a child in his arms or how gently and carefully he cared for her. As he laid her out on the rug, she moaned and began to stir.

"She said something about a 'him' so I'm thinking it might be best if a man wasn't the first thing she sees when she comes around. The last thing we need is for her to freak out and injure herself further."

When she looked into his face, she winced at his pained expression.

"I know you would never hurt her, but she doesn't know that. I'll be as quick as I can here. We need to get her to the hospital as soon as possible."

She kept her voice low, not wanting to risk the girl overhearing.

"I'm going to need you to carry her to the car, so we need to tread carefully."

Dominic gave her a quick nod and went to stand off to the side, out of the child's line of sight. Her heart melted toward him even more; he was so compassionate and considerate of others.

She looked back down at the child, still a little in shock at the sight of such injuries on someone so small. Children were precious, a blessing, gifts that should be cherished and protected, not abused to within inches of their lives. The girl awoke, instinctively curling herself in a ball whispering "it hurts, please no more" over and over. Adele's maternal instincts took over, leaving her medical ones in the dust. She lay down beside the child, gently stroking her hair, coaxing her to uncurl from her ball. She murmured gently to her, nothing important, just soothing words in both English and French, trying to soothe her into relaxing a little. It soon began to work and she began to slowly uncurl. Adele looked up when Dominic sighed. It looked like her words were soothing him too; his eyes were closed and his face was slowly draining of its fury. When his lids rose again, he gave her a quick nod and then pulled out his phone as he stepped a little farther away from them.

Adele stayed on the ground wrapped around the child, stroking her messy black curls and whispering to her until she had completely uncurled from her ball. The girl raised her head slightly, big round grey eyes finding hers. Adele's breath froze in her lungs at the depth of the fear, pain, and sorrow held in those young grey depths.

"Can you tell me your name, *ma chère*? What do you want me to call you?"

She focused on keeping her voice low and smooth so she didn't startle the child.

"K-Kel-Kelly." She paused to take a shaky breath. "You're not hurting me? Please don't send me back to him," she pleaded.

The poor girl sounded confused at the concept that she wasn't being hurt. What the hell had she escaped from where being hurt was the norm?

"Oh, sweetheart, I promise I will never hurt you. My name is Adele and I'm a paramedic. All I will ever do is help you, *ma chère*."

As relief poured through her, Kelly started shaking. She was safe. This lady, Adele, would look after her.

She sensed in her soul that she was a protector. Her nightmare was over. Unable to stop, tears poured from her at the fact she was safe for the first time since...well, since ever.

"You promise you won't let him near me? Please, don't let him hurt me anymore."

She had to make sure Adele understood how important it was that he not get his hands on her again. Adele returned to stroking her hair, like her mother had done when she was a little girl.

"Shhh, *ma chère,* no one is going to hurt you. But we do need to move you. You're badly hurt and we need to get you to the hospital."

Panic flared bright within her.

"No, he'll find me there, he'll take me back. You can't take me to a hospital!"

A low growl startled Kelly and had her almost jumping out of her skin. Instinctively, she grabbed on to Adele as fear clouded her mind. Taking a steadying breath, she slowly turned her head toward where the sound had come and saw a massive man.

"Shhh, calm down. It's okay, Kelly. That's Dominic, he's a firefighter and a good man. He won't hurt you, he won't ever hurt you, Kelly, I swear it. He's just a little angry, but not at you, *ma chère.* He's very cross at the one who has hurt you so much, isn't that right, Dominic?"

"That's right, Kelly." The man put his hand over his heart. "I swear to you that I will never hurt you. I will never allow anyone else to hurt you again. Will you let us take you to the hospital? Adele will stay with you. I promise she won't leave you. And I promise I'll stand guard, I'll wait right outside your room and make sure no one who shouldn't gets in there. Does that sound good, Kelly? Will you let us help you and keep you safe?"

Dominic's voice was so calm and soothing that Kelly knew that he too was a protector like Adele. Kelly instinctively knew Dominic was a completely different kind of man to her father and him. His ice-blue eyes flared with anger but like Adele said, it wasn't aimed at her. She could see the pain and sorrow for her in his gaze too, and it reassured her that this gentle giant would never hurt her. Adele's voice brought her back from the daze she was in.

"Kelly, will you let Dominic carry you to our car? Or would you like to try and walk?"

She would have loved to be able to walk her way down the path but she knew that wasn't an option anymore. She'd pushed her body beyond what it could handle already.

"I don't think my legs work anymore."

Never taking his gaze from hers, Dominic slowly crouched by her side on the ground and on the count of three lifted her, then she was being cradled against a solid warm wall of muscle wrapped in the picnic blanket. He was so gentle with her, no one had ever held her so tenderly. She wondered if this was what fathers were meant to be like, warm and protective. She was grateful for his gentleness, as every touch, every move hurt so much. All the stress and her pain caught up with her. She didn't try to fight it this time. Soaking in the tenderness of Dominic's hold, she laid her head against his hard chest and allowed the darkness to carry her away again.

Chapter Eight

Cole dragged himself out from under the covers, sat on the edge of his mattress, and rubbed his hands over his face. Stretching his neck until he heard a crack, he glanced at his bedside table to check out the time. Bloody hell, he'd slept for five hours. He hadn't realized how tired he'd been.

He grunted as he rose to his feet. Better go check his slave. He doubted she'd be able to move on her own for a couple of days after the workout he put her through, but he'd feel better with her chained. Those delicious thoughts gave him the motivation he needed to get his body and feet moving.

He was in a fantastic mood, humming even, until he reached the stairway to the basement. The door was open; he always kept the thing shut. It was neater that way. He could see fresh blood smeared on the steps, hand, knee, and toe prints as if someone had half crawled, half dragged themselves up the stairs. His eyes followed the smears across the carpet to the front door where he noticed his shoes were gone. Damn it all to hell. He beat feet down the stairs to double-check, cursing when he got to the basement and confirmed it was indeed empty.

Bloody hell, he shouldn't have given in to his worn-out muscles. He should have made sure she was chained-up and secured before he went to lie down. It's what he'd always done in the past. Why hadn't he this time?

A sense of urgency fueling him, he ran back up the stairs, taking them two at a time. He wasted no time getting dressed, he simply threw on whatever he reached first. She couldn't have gone far, he'd worked her over for a solid six hours. Damn it, the girl shouldn't even be conscious yet, let alone running around town. He'd probably find her passed out in his driveway or just down the road. He grabbed his keys and headed to the garage.

An hour later, he pulled back into his driveway furious. He hadn't been able to find a trace of her. His mind spinning from his rapid firing thoughts, he was in a near panic.

How the hell could she have gotten away from him?

She was his, damn it. He *owned* her.

She would be back.

He would get her back.

He had to get her back.

Once his mind slowed down enough that he was back under a moderate level of control, he headed into the house to pack a bag. He'd go on a little road trip to find his slave, shouldn't be hard. How far could she have gone? She hadn't left his house in, what, five years now? Yeah, he'd find her tomorrow or maybe the next day...and when he did get her back, she was going to be permanently chained. He'd buy a longer chain that would reach down to the basement. He would never let her go. She was his alone and her punishment for this little adventure was going to be brutal and one she would never, ever forget. He'd make sure of it.

Dominic strode through the hospital hallways with purpose. Kelly had been here for two days. Due to her injuries they were keeping her heavily sedated so her body could focus on healing. When they'd first arrived with her, Dominic had rallied the cats and organized them to take shifts to keep her guarded around the clock. Dominic had promised that little girl he would keep her protected, and he never broke a promise. Aside from that, it's what his kind did. Snow leopard shifters had essentially been made to be guardians. They'd been created to protect snow leopards from extinction by a couple of Tibetan monks long ago, so the need to guard and protect was soul deep in their entire breed. Nothing spoke to that need like a seriously abused innocent little girl, or a big-hearted woman looking after that child. Adele had spent the last two days with Kelly, only leaving her side to attend to other emergencies. She hadn't been out of the hospital. Hadn't slept in a bed. Hadn't eaten a proper meal. Tonight, that would change. Dominic was taking care of his mate whether she wanted him to or not. She was looking paler each day and would get sick soon if she didn't start looking after herself and that was simply unacceptable to Dominic.

Kit was on *guard-cat* duty. She sat outside Kelly's door in the hospital hallway with her long legs stretched out, crossed at the ankles. Her cherry red Doc Martins reflected the fluorescent lights. She had her arms crossed over her chest. Her tight black muscle shirt and dark denim jeans made her look every bit as dangerous as she was. She sat still as ice but her eyes watched everything that happened around her. Dominic knew she wouldn't miss a thing and if someone tried to get to Kelly, they would get a rough welcome. Dominic almost hoped someone would come and try to take Kelly, then they could deal with the bastard and move forward, breathing easier. That, plus watching Kit fight was amazing. That woman had moves for sure. As she saw him approach, she unfolded herself from the chair, stood up, and stretched, looking every bit the feline she was.

"That coffee for me, boss?" she asked, then grinned.

"Hey, Kit. Yep, it's all yours. Thought you could use a jolt of real stuff over the crappy hospital grade."

He handed over the takeout cup to Kit. Kit lifted the lid, took a deep inhale, and sighed.

"Now that's what I'm talking 'bout, real coffee."

After she took a sip and groaned in bliss, Dominic got serious.

"You seen Adele? She still in with Kelly?"

Kit nodded as she swallowed her next mouthful of

coffee.

"Yep, she's still in there with Kelly. You planning on removing her?"

"That was the plan. That woman has a heart the size of a mountain but she's going to run herself into the ground if she doesn't start eating or sleeping properly soon."

"I hear you there. Clint's starting to worry about her health too." She fished a key out of her pocket and handed it to Dominic. "Why don't you take her back to my place? There's plenty of food there and you'll have more privacy than at yours."

"Thanks, Kit, you're a gem. You know if I took her back to mine, Mum would have her fed and rested, all right, but I wouldn't get a damn look in at getting any alone time with her."

He smirked as he thought about how much his mum would love to pamper her future daughter-in-law given half the chance.

Kit chuckled.

"Yeah, your mum is a doll, but she wouldn't help your chances of alone time with Adele one bit."

Leaving Kit to enjoy her little slice of coffee heaven, Dominic quietly opened the door into Kelly's room. He stopped in the doorway to take in the scene before him. Kelly lay unconscious in the bed, her pale skin just about a perfect match for the white sheets except for the bruising that colored about ninety percent of her exposed arms, neck, and face. Her jet-black curly hair was a mess around her petite face and stood out against all the white. Even though she clearly looked unwell, she was looking a boatload better than when they found her. Her face looked relaxed and peaceful now. Like she knew she was now safe and could focus on healing. And she'd been cleaned up. No more blood and dirt covering her.

He moved his gaze over to Adele, drinking her in. She sat in a chair next to the bed, holding Kelly's hand loosely with her head resting on the bed next to it. She was sound asleep. Her hair was a mess; he assumed it had originally started out in a braid but now more of it was loose than in the hair tie. He didn't like that her cheeks looked a little sunken in or the grey smudges under her eyes. Slowly, he walked up to her, crouched down by her side before he gently ran the back of his knuckles back and forth across her cheek.

"Adele? C'mon, wake up, beautiful. It's time to go."

Adele blinked and slowly raised her head. Dominic could tell she wasn't fully awake; she looked so sweet and sexy all sleep rumpled. He palmed her chin and she tilted her head into it, nuzzling his palm as she murmured, "My *chaton*," before kissing his palm, then settling her head back down on the bed and reclosing her eyes. Dominic couldn't help but grin, he'd been spending as much time as he could with her in her dreams, hoping that by hanging out with his leopard she would sleep better, be calmer, more relaxed during the day. She obviously really liked his visits if she was dreaming of him even now when he wasn't creating the dream. That was a good sign and meant she had accepted him—as a leopard. He gently shook her shoulder.

"C'mon, sleepyhead, you need to wake up so I can take you home."

Adele woke slowly from her dream. She'd been cuddled up with her *chaton*. She had spent so much time with him over the last two days. It seemed like whenever she closed her eyes he was there waiting to comfort her.

Someone gently shook her shoulder...yes, that's what had woken her, someone telling her something about home. She rolled her head to the side and opened an eye. Dominic. Of course, it was Dominic. Who else would it be? He bent down, kissed her lightly on the cheek, and nuzzled her with his nose. Hmmm, that felt so good...and familiar somehow, but she was too tired to focus on why.

She sat up slowly, stretched, and looked down at Kelly. Her skin was finally gaining a pink hue rather than a ghostly white one. Slowly but surely her body was healing from her massive injuries. Yesterday, Adele had spoken with Kelly's assigned Child Protection Service Officer, Deirdre. Turned out, Kelly wasn't in the system. It was like she didn't exist, which meant she had nowhere to go.

Adele felt extremely protective over Kelly from the second she'd seen her, so it had been only logical to offer to be her guardian on a permanent basis. Deirdre had told her that if she could get her own place and prove that she could take care of a child, then they would allow her temporary custody of Kelly once she was released from hospital. A lot would have to be done before permanent custody could be awarded to anyone. The first priority was to get her healthy. The feel of strong arms lifting her out of her seat jarred her from her runaway thoughts.

"Dominic, what are you doing? Put me down. Right now."

She growled at him, with no real heat. She rather liked being in his arms, but she couldn't leave Kelly; she had to stay until she was well. She'd promised.

"Adele, I'm taking you home where I am going to feed you, and then I'm going to tuck you into bed and watch over you to make sure you get a full night's sleep," he said in a firm voice.

"But I can't leave, what if she wakes up? What if someone comes for her?"

Panic rose inside her, and she started trembling in Dominic's firm embrace.

"I promised her."

"Adele. Look at me. I get that you promised Kelly. I understand that you want to take care of her. But you can't do that if *you* get sick. You're burning yourself out, beautiful. You will be in no condition to look after her when she wakes up if you keep this up. Kit is on guard duty. She's sitting right outside the door. How about we leave the door open? That way if Kelly so much as rolls over, Kit will be in here with her, okay? You know Kit. You know that no one will get to Kelly while she's here watching."

Deep down, Adele knew Dominic was right, but she still struggled to leave her. Her mind was so muddled she couldn't keep her thoughts straight. Her spinning thoughts wore her out but she could see by the look in Dominic's eyes she was never going to win this one. She silently accepted defeat and snuggled against his warm muscular chest where she allowed herself to drift off to sleep as he carried her off.

Dominic looked down at the sleeping woman in his arms. She was so strong, yet so fragile. He carried her from the room, stopping briefly to let Kit know to keep the door open and to make sure Kelly was not left alone in the unlikely event she woke up. Then he took his precious bundle out to his car. He gently placed her in the front seat and strapped her in, tilting the seat back so she would be comfortable. In no time, he had it started and they headed out of the carpark. It only took five minutes to get from the hospital to Kit and Adele's place. She hadn't stirred once since he left the hospital; his poor mate was absolutely knackered and definitely needed some TLC.

He parked in the drive and went to open up the house

first before coming back to carry Adele inside. The feel of her in his arms was amazing, but she needed to get a good night's sleep, so he took her into her room and laid her on the bed. Wanting her to be comfortable, he removed her shoes and socks.

He glanced up at her then. She was so beautiful, with her dark hair against the pale pillow. She looked peaceful in sleep and he would love nothing more than to lay down beside her. He sighed and rubbed his aching chest, he didn't doubt that if she woke to him holding her it would scare her.

Since she'd been at the hospital for so long, she'd changed from her clothes into hospital scrubs. Not wanting to disturb her sleep, he carefully pulled the pants down over her slim waist and the gentle swell of her hips and thighs, over her perfect knees and slender calves, and off over her pretty dainty feet. Then he slowly removed her top up over her rib cage, over her chest, and gently pulled her arms through and lifted it off over her head. He was sure Adele would not like it if she woke naked, so he decided to leave her in her plain cotton knickers and sports bra. He smiled. His mate was so practical.

He made quick work of tucking her quilt around her body, then moved to her hair. Removing the band, he finger- combed it and smoothed the stray hairs from her face. Finally, he gave her a kiss on the forehead, whispered, "Good night, my love," and left her to sleep.

Dominic watched as Adele shimmered into the

dream, sitting on the picnic rug. She began to look around her, seeming to examine the landscape in fine detail. His lips curled into a wide grin. She was trying to work out if it was the same as the real one.

He let her go for a minute and when she closed her eyes, rubbed her fingers over her temples, he padded over to her, purring so she knew he was approaching— and because he was happy to be near her again. He lightly brushed his face against the back of her neck and she tilted her head to the side, giving him access. He was more than happy to take the invitation and nuzzled his nose into her neck, licking where her neck and shoulder joined. His rough feline tongue picked up so much more of her taste than his human one. He couldn't wait until she knew about him so he could taste her fully in the real world, not a muted dream. He felt her body slacken, felt her stress drain away. As usual, once she relaxed, she began to verbalize her thoughts for him. He never would have thought it possible to learn so much about someone without him uttering a word to them.

"I have so much that I need to do, chaton. *Kelly needs a home, she needs to be loved and taken care of."*

He lifted his head slightly as she twisted around and hugged him close. She buried her nose in the fur on his neck. Oh yeah, he loved how it felt to have her in his fur, feel her breath on his skin.

"I want to be the one who looks after her, but I need a place of my own. Deirdre, the Child Protection Officer, said I need to be 'stable' which means being in

my own place where Kelly can have her own room and space. I'm sure Kit will help me sort it all out. But if she's helping me do that, she can't watch over Kelly. Who else can I trust with her?"

Who can she trust? Really? What was he? Invisible! He gently pulled back from her, waited for her to look into his eyes. Then he lowered his gaze to the rug, before looking back at her face. He repeated the process a couple of times until he saw her eyes brighten with understanding. Finally!

"Dominic? You want me to ask Dominic for help?"

He nuzzled her cheek with a purr to let her know he was all for that plan. She released a low sigh.

"I know he would help me, but it means letting him in. Trusting him. What if he hurts me? What if I let him close and he leaves?"

Her pain-filled whisper made his heart ache for her.

"Everyone my mother loved abandoned her, then she abandoned me. Left me alone. Oh, chaton, *I don't want to be alone anymore."*

Her tears seeped through his fur onto his skin as she tightly wrapped her arms around his neck and clung to him as she sobbed. The ragged sound tore him up; he would never leave her. How on earth was he going to prove to her that he would never hurt her? He gently caressed her neck and shoulder with his fur and whiskers while he pondered the problem.

Dominic awoke to discover he'd wrapped Adele up in his arms as they'd slept. He'd stripped down to his boxer-briefs and had lain down next to her before he pulled her into a dream. Her pain and sorrow was so strong he'd obviously reacted to it in the real world too. Instinctively, without conscious thought, he'd drawn her close to him, wrapping her up in his arms to comfort her.

How he wished she would open up to him in reality like she did in their dreams so he could help her. He couldn't believe how hard it was to not give himself away when talking with her during the day. He'd planned on telling her everything at the lake, but she'd had enough trouble coping with the fact the field was real, he'd thought she would have totally flipped out if she found out the snow leopard was real too. Then Kelly stumbled in and he hadn't been able to get much time with her since, not that he minded given the circumstances. The way Adele cared for and protected Kelly spoke volumes about her heart and soul.

Adele rolling into him pulled him from his thoughts. He looked down at her as she blinked up at him. A frown creased her brow; she wasn't expecting to wake to him in her bed. He smiled gently at her as he traced his finger up the line of her nose, over her eyebrow, then down her cheek bone to her lower lip, which he proceeded to caress with his thumb.

He tried hard not to chuckle, as she opened and closed her mouth a few times before she finally mustered some words.

"What are... Why are..."

She wasn't really awake yet. Since he didn't have an easy answer for her, he cut her off by covering her mouth with his, devouring her mouth with his lips and tongue. By the time he pulled back, they were both breathing heavily. His body was on fire for her and his erection was so hard it ached. Her arousal scented the air and he was soaring high with pleasure. He stroked her face and hair while he trailed light kisses over her jawline up to her ear.

"Dominic. Please..." She breathed out on a shudder he felt through his whole body.

"Please what, beautiful? Tell me what you need."

Dominic gently bit the lower edge of her ear between his teeth, feeling the wave of heat come out of her body as he did. He wanted to hear that she wanted this, wanted him.

"I-I don't know what I need, Dominic. But please do something."

She spoke between short breaths; he could see her eyes were glazed over with desire. She looked stunningly sexy. But as much as he wanted to lay here and drink in her beauty, he was also burning up and wanted another taste of his beautiful mate.

"My sweet Adele. Will you trust me to look after you?" he whispered, before kissing his way from her ear, down her neck, and over her shoulder. He nudged her until she rolled onto her back, then he moved to cover her. He was careful to use his arms to hold his weight off her. She closed her eyes and took a deep breath. When she opened them they looked somber, her desire shelved while more serious thoughts dominated her mind. His stomach cramped with concern; was she going to say no? If she did, he would respect her choice and leave. It would be the hardest thing he'd ever done, but he would. For her. Locking her gaze into his, she quietly spoke the sweetest words he'd ever heard.

"Yes. I'll trust you."

Dominic looked down in wonder and awe at his mate lying beneath him. She'd just said yes, for real. Not just in his head this time, but out loud. He couldn't stop the huge grin that quickly spread over his face.

"Thank you, my sweet Adele. I promise I'll take good care of you. I'll never leave you alone. I promise."

Her brow creased in confusion. Damn, he shouldn't know about her fear of being left alone. Before she could ask him anything, he lowered himself and took possession of her mouth until they were both breathless. His head reeled with his mate's scent surrounding him. Finally, his mate was in his arms where she belonged. He showered her in light kisses and licks, working his way down her body.

As he reached her breasts, she ran her hands in his hair and held him to her. He brushed the tip of his nose over her tight nipple through the smooth material of her sports bra. His mouth went dry when she moaned and arched up into him. Making the most of her torso being lifted off the mattress, he shifted his weight so he could run his hands up her delicate rib cage, slowly taking her bra off, revealing one glorious inch of flesh after another.

The second her lush breasts sprung free from the confines of her bra, he couldn't resist. He released the bra so it sat bunched up under her arms and palmed each breast. He groaned at how good they felt in his hands. Licking his lips, he bent down to suckle her beautiful rosy nipples one after the other. He ran his thumb back and forth over the one not being ravaged by his lips and tongue. His heart soared as he heard her moan out his name in pleasure. She started to wriggle and move beneath him. He lifted his head to look at her face.

The sight before him held him totally transfixed. As soon as he'd lifted himself from her, she had arched farther toward him before she'd grabbed the bottom of her bra and lifted it over her head, her gorgeous breasts thrust out toward him. She looked like a goddess with her back arched, her arms stretched above her head, and her hooded eyes burning him with their passion. Without breaking eye contact, he lowered his head to her again. He palmed each breast, pushed them together so her nipples touched, then he filled his mouth with both her hard rosy nipples and sucked in hard short bursts. Her whole body shuddered as she gasped. Hmm, she liked that. He did it again a few times before he couldn't stand the burn any longer.

Her scent was driving him insane. He could smell her arousal, and he would put money on the fact that her knickers were soaked at this point and he really, really wanted a taste of his mate's nectar that smelled so damn good. He released her breasts after delivering one last lick to each and slid his hands down her rib cage. He could feel her bones beneath her skin more easily than he had at the lake. He frowned, had she eaten at all since then? He needed to look after his mate. She needed to be healthy with some meat on her bones.

When he hooked his thumbs around the sides of her knickers and pulled them down, all thoughts of feeding his sweet mate disappeared, replaced solely with thoughts of feeding himself—on her.

As he peeled the material down her calves, she tensed up. He smiled at her as he tossed them aside; she was so exquisitely innocent. Every muscle in her body was tense and she'd squeezed her eyes shut. He could just about hear the cogs turning in her mind. Using only the tips of his fingers, he began running small circles over her ankles, keeping his movements slow, reverent.

"Let go, Adele, you're thinking too hard, just let go and feel."

His fingers slowly traveled up her calves.

"You are so beautiful, and you feel so good under my hands. And your smell" —he breathed in deeply, shuddering as his head went a little light from taking in her natural scent mixed with that of her arousal— "you are driving me insane with it. You are my heaven, my sweet Adele, I need you."

He started massaging the soles of her feet, nibbling the tender skin at the arch. His heart lightened with joy hearing her sigh of pleasure as her body relaxed. She blew out a breath and frowning, locked her gaze onto his.

"I've never...you know...been with a man before. I've never felt like this before either, and to be honest, it's kinda scaring the hell out of me."

She rushed out her confession then quickly turned her head away and closed her eyes, hiding them from him, like she was expecting rejection. His heart broke a little as a tear slid down her cheek. Her eyes flew open when he gently wiped it away with his thumb. She turned back to look at him. Her eyes showed all her emotions clearly. The fear, the insecurity, the anticipation. He would never reject her, never cause her pain. Why couldn't she believe him?

"My sweet Adele, don't be afraid of me. I will never hurt you. I'd already guessed I am the only man you've allowed to touch you. You can't understand how happy that makes me. We're going to take this real slow and if I do anything you don't want me to, just say the word and I'll stop. I promise."

A flash of relief passed over her expression. He nipped the arch of her foot before he spoke again.

"Oh, and, Adele? I've never been with a woman before you either."

He chuckled softly at the look on Adele's face. Clearly she hadn't thought he would be a virgin.

"Don't look so shocked, beautiful. I've simply never felt the desire to touch a woman before I met you. But since meeting you, touching you is all I can think about."

He moved up and began stroking her from shoulder to hip with a feather-light touch. Before long, he felt her relax back into the mattress.

"That's it, my sweet Adele, just relax and feel."

He continued his seduction with kisses and whispered words as he worshipped her body from head to toe. He stayed away from the sweet spot between her thighs on his way down to her feet. If he started off by touching her where he wanted to be the most, he'd never finish his journey to her toes and he wanted to know each and every inch of his mate's precious body. He kissed the tips of her toes before working his way up the inside of her leg. He grinned when he reached the back of her knee and she twitched and giggled.

He adored the sound of her giggling. Hmm, he could just imagine how much fun it would be to tickle her into oblivion, but that would have to wait until another time. He slowed the pace down as he kissed his way up her inner thigh. He loved she was so caught up in her pleasure she hadn't tensed up.

He trailed his fingers in small random patterns over her inner thighs, slowly going higher and higher. As he ran a single finger down the crease at the top of both her thighs, she jerked slightly and giggled again. He grinned; she was damn ticklish. He made a mental note of each one of her spots so he could revisit them later—again and again.

He ran his fingers toward her belly button, gently swiping over where he so desperately wanted his mouth on the way up. She tensed a little as he passed over her dark curls.

"Oh, my sweet Adele, you are exquisite and so beautiful."

Dominic felt a great sense of pride as he looked up at his mate's face. Her body was limp, boneless under his touch. He waited for her passion-soaked gaze to find his before he lowered his head to place a sweet kiss just above her curls, then running his tongue down over her slick folds. He hummed in pleasure at the taste of his mate's cream. Like her scent, it was deliciously sweet with a hint of vanilla, tantalizing his taste buds and flowing down his throat. He couldn't stop himself. He covered her core with his mouth and delved his tongue as deep as he could, lapping up all the nectar he could get her to give him. She arched, pushing herself closer to him, pushing him deeper. He continued to torment her sensitive flesh, lost to the passion and pleasure of his mate. He hummed as he stroked her, sending her higher.

It didn't take long before he felt her walls begin to tighten around his tongue. She groaned and he looked up at her as she thrashed her head back and forth. Her brow creased and he realized she mustn't have ever brought herself to climax before. That this whole experience was totally new and foreign to her. She confirmed his thoughts.

"Dominic, what's happening? It hurts. I think."

She groaned and writhed. Dominic lifted his mouth from her core, replacing it quickly with his fingers. Her silky heat felt so good on his skin.

"You're about to climax, beautiful. Just let go, don't fight it, just flow with the sensations. Nothing to be afraid of, love. Come for me, Adele, let me taste you. Gift me your first orgasm."

His words combined with his fingers twirling and going in and out of her seemed to be working in sending her higher. Her walls grabbed at his fingers but she still hadn't been able to trip over and take the plunge. He lowered his mouth back to her, keeping his fingers where they were, and then he flicked his tongue over her clit. She bowed off the bed, trembled all over, then spilled more of her cream for him. He sighed with pleasure as he swallowed every last drop. Oh, how he wanted to purr...it was extremely difficult to hold himself in check.

He growled out his pleasure as she grabbed fistsful of his hair. He continued to lap up her release, like a kitten would a bowl of milk. He kept his fingers inside her, helping her ride out the waves of sensations that crashed through her body. As he felt her tremors lessen and her body go limp, he reverently kissed his way up her body until he was face to face with her.

"Thank you, Adele. That was the most precious gift I

have ever received. I will treasure it always."

He lowered his mouth to hers and gave her a hot scorching kiss, pouring all his love for her into it. He released her mouth and rolled to the side, turning her around so he spooned up against her back. He wrapped one arm protectively around her waist, burying the other in her hair and sighed in satisfaction when she went limp and her breathing evened out.

Chapter Nine

Kelly awoke slowly to the sound of machines beeping close by. What was making that noise? He didn't have anything that sounded like that. Without opening her eyes, she took a deep breath and winced as her ribs protested the movement, but what made her mind come to a halt and her heart skip a beat was that her neck felt bare. She swallowed to confirm her throat was unrestricted by the collar.

She sat bolt upright, opening her eyes and pressed her hands to her throat. Her head spun at the sudden movement and spots swam before her eyes, obstructing her vision. Her hands were touching bare flesh. The collar was gone...but how? As her vision cleared, she saw she was in a white room, on a hard white bed with rails on either side so she couldn't escape. She dropped her hands from her neck, looked down at them. There was a tube going into the back of one of her hands that was attached to a bag full of clear liquid hung on a pole next to the bed. She wasn't sure what it was but it didn't hurt so she left it alone. Her gaze wandered up both her arms. There were a few bandages and her skin was covered in bruises that were mostly faded out to greens and yellows. Only a couple were still grey, black, or blue. She looked down her front. She was wearing a stiff white shirt type thing.

Where the hell was she?

How did she have clothes again?

She looked up in confusion and trailed her gaze around the room beyond the bed. She stopped still when her eyes landed on a woman sitting there looking straight at her. She panicked and tried to push herself away from the woman, but she couldn't move. She was attached to the beeping machine and to the bag of stuff. The rails on the bed wouldn't allow her to break free. She whimpered as she thrashed to get free. Pain ripped through her with each jerky movement, but she couldn't focus to stop. Her body and mind had left her behind.

"Shhh, Kelly. You are safe. You're in a hospital. No one here will hurt you, *ma chère*. You are safe."

The woman kept repeating herself as she slowly moved closer to Kelly. Focusing on the woman's calm movements gave Kelly the chance to control her body's frantic movements. Did she know her?

"My name is Adele. My friend, Dominic, and I found you wandering by the lake. Do you remember?"

"I don't know...what happened to me?"

Her last memory was of him coming home early and dragging her down those stairs. She rubbed her temples, trying to get her brain to focus, to remember what happened.

"We don't know what happened to you, *ma chère*.

You were very badly injured when we found you so we brought you here to the hospital. You told us you were worried someone would come and take you back, so we've kept someone outside your room guarding you. I have been here watching you as much as I can. You haven't been alone the whole time you've been here. No one will hurt you ever again, Kelly."

Adele's voice was calm, soothing, and helped to anchor her. Suddenly pain pounded the inside of her skull and she closed her eyes tightly, clenching her teeth against the agony. As memories flooded back to her, she pressed her palms to her eyes...oh crap, the things he'd done to her, threatened to do to her. She remembered everything now, getting away, being found. She dropped her hands, desperately holding on to Adele's worried gaze.

"He was going to rape me. He told me that tomorrow he would finish my training. That I would be fully his forever after that. I-I got out. I ran away."

Confused, Kelly frowned as tears flowed from Adele's eyes. This woman who had only just met her seemed so upset by her pain. No one had ever offered any sympathy toward her, not even her own mother. Adele reached her hand slowly toward Kelly's. When their hands were nearly touching, Kelly leaned forward to grab hold of Adele's tightly. Her touch was warm, gentle, safe.

Adele moved closer to the bed. Kelly kept her gaze on her while she lowered the side rail and slowly lay down next to her. She allowed her body to be pulled into Adele's embrace. The comfort she offered was too much and tears began to fall as she fell apart in the safety of Adele's arms.

"He won't get near you again, Kelly. I promise I'll do everything I can to protect you."

When her tears finally began to lessen, a sudden heavy wariness washed over her. Adele's soothing hand began stroking her curls.

"You were so brave, *ma chère*, running away. You saved yourself. You were so strong, sweetheart. Now, you have help. We will all help you get better and even stronger."

Kelly couldn't remember ever being cuddled so lovingly. It was a strange sensation but one she decided she liked. So much better than being hit or whipped. She snuggled into Adele and breathed in her smell. She smelled like vanilla and sunshine—and safety.

"How long has it been?" she asked on a yawn.

"You've been here eight days, *ma chère*. You were very badly injured so we kept you asleep so your body could heal without causing you any more pain. You're going to be sore for quite a while. You have a number of cracked ribs which take time to heal."

Adele's voice was so gentle and soothing. Kelly wished she could stay forever in Adele's embrace feeling safe and secure, but she knew better than most that life wasn't that easy. She took as deep a breath as she could before bravely asking her next question.

"What is going to happen to me when I have to leave? I have nowhere to go. I have no one."

She buried her face into Adele's shoulder as a feeling of hopelessness enveloped her and she started crying again. How did she think running away would help? She would have been better off if he had simply killed her like he had her mother. While she cried, she felt Adele rest her cheek on top of her head and begin to hum to her. When her tears slowed, Adele spoke.

"It's okay, Kelly. Don't you worry about a thing. When you leave here, if you want, you can come live with me. I've been talking with the Child Protection Agency and since they can't find any of your biological family, you will need to go into Foster Care. I've been going through all their tests so I can take you in. I promised to keep you safe, Kelly. I meant it. You will never be alone again, *ma chère*."

Adele's words made Kelly so happy she started crying all over again. Maybe, just maybe her life would be better now. She cried until the exhaustion overtook her and she fell asleep snuggled in Adele's warm arms.

Conner put his phone off speaker and held it up to his ear.

"You still there, Dom? Did you get all of that?"

"Yeah, I'm here, bro. That poor kid. I can feel Adele's pain from here, man."

Conner could clearly hear the pain in his brother's voice. The mating bond must be a strong one, if it allowed mates to feel each other's emotions like that. Conner had been paying close attention to his brother and Adele, trying to learn all he could about the whole mating thing. He was hoping he'd start having dreams soon. Surely his mate would be turning twenty-one soon. He was getting close to his twenty-fourth birthday now. He didn't like the idea of a huge age gap, but more importantly, he was impatient to meet his mate and start courting her. His brother's voice pulled him from his thoughts.

"How's Adele looking? Do I need to come over there?"

Conner was the current guard-cat on duty. He'd rung his brother as soon as he heard Kelly wake up. He'd put his brother on speakerphone so he could hear the conversation between the girls without Conner needing to relay it all later. He hated relaying conversations. Speakerphone was so much easier. Added bonus, he couldn't get in trouble for getting things wrong.

He silently poked his head through the doorway to see what was happening before he pulled back out of view. He didn't want to disturb either of the girls.

"Adele is on the bed with Kelly, looks like the poor kid has fallen back asleep. Adele's stroking her hair and humming to her. She could probably use someone to talk to, and you know I suck at this stuff, so you probably should high-tail it over here."

Dom chuckled at him, his brother knew him better than anyone, knew how awkward he was around emotional people, especially women.

"You'd be fine, Conner, but I'll head over. I have to finish up here first. See you soon."

"Cool, see you then."

He ended the call, rested his head back against the wall and let thoughts of finding his own mate fill his mind as he kept a close eye on the hallway around him.

Dominic had been in the office with his dad drawing up the rosters for the next month when he'd received Conner's call. As he hung up, he felt his father's gaze on him. He slipped his phone onto the desk and scrubbed at his face with both hands. What should he do now? Had he and Adele cemented their relationship enough for this test? He really wasn't sure. He hated feeling like this. He was the cool, calm one, the one who planned everything out. Suddenly, he felt out of control, nothing was planned and the few things that were, weren't panning out. The fact his mind, body, and soul were all constantly burning to claim his mate did not help matters in the least.

"Stop thinking so hard, son. I can hear your cogs turning from over here."

Dominic dropped his hands to his knees and looked up at his dad with a frown.

"Kelly. She woke up. She's awake."

Dominic felt like a tool for not being able to construct a better sentence for his dad but his brain was so busy with everything, it wasn't in the mood for wasting time on grammar.

"Ahh, so the young lass is awake and I'm guessing the lovely Adele was there for the occasion? And your little brother was playing spy for you?"

His dad had an eyebrow raised and was sporting a slight smirk.

"Hardly spying, Dad. Conner's on guard duty and you know as well as I do he hates having to remember stuff so he can relay it. He chucked me on speakerphone so I could hear everything that was said first-hand."

Dominic couldn't stop the shudder that ran through him at the memory of what Kelly had told Adele.

"Care to share with your old man what was said? Don't think I didn't see you shudder just now, son."

Dominic took a couple of minutes to fill his dad in on the details.

"Well, looks like your mate is going to be mighty busy real soon. Why don't you see if Adele will come over to the house for dinner tonight? Your mother has something she wants to discuss with her."

Dominic raised an eyebrow at his father. What was his mother up to this time?

"What's Mum planning? Should I be worried? Or scared?"

Jake barked out a laugh.

"Neither. This time. It's nothing to worry about or be scared of. She's been thinking about some things young Kelly is going to need. You know how since she stepped back from full-time teaching last year she's been looking for something to fill her time? Well, she's thinking about tutoring. She was hoping Adele would let her help get Kelly up to speed and into school, which, I suspect might take some doing. Doesn't sound like she's been out in the world much, if you know what I mean."

Dominic couldn't help but chuckle.

"Trust Mum. Neither Adele nor I had even thought about that side of looking after Kelly. I'll do my best to get her away from the hospital for dinner. With Kelly awake, it's probably going to be harder than ever to tear her away."

"I'm sure you'll find a way, son. Now, I heard you say you'd be heading over there. You better get a move on. I'll finish up the roster and get it out to everyone."

Dominic sighed with relief that he could go straight away to Adele. His dad was a lifesaver. He paused on his way out the door.

"Thanks, Dad, you're the best."

"Just you remember that when my birthday rolls around," he responded with a wink.

On his way to Kelly's hospital room, Dominic stopped by Clint's office.

"Hey, Doc, got a minute?" he called out as he knocked on the doorframe of his office.

"Sure, Dominic, what can I do for you?"

Clint's voice sounded tired. Poor bugger, being head of the hospital meant he was under some serious pressure.

"Heard Kelly woke up earlier, wondering if you could give me an idea of how long she'll be in here? Adele wants to take her in when she leaves, a time frame for how long we have to get organized would be great, Doc."

Dominic watched in amusement as Clint flew out of his chair.

"She's woken up? When?" He snatched the pager from his belt and cursed. "Damn it, dead battery again! I swear the current box must be made up entirely of duds. Follow me, Dominic."

Dominic understood Clint's frustration. Mobile phones were starting to take over but pagers were still vital to all emergency services. For a doctor, missing a page could be the difference between life and death. He followed behind Clint as he strode out of his office toward Kelly's room. They briefly stopped at the nurses station so Clint could hand over his pager with instructions to ditch the box of batteries. As they approached Kelly's room, Conner got up from his chair and stretched.

"Hey, Dom, Doc. Was about to come looking for you. Adele was wondering why you didn't answer her page."

"Hey, Conner, the joys of technology, my man. Damn thing was dead. Is she still awake?"

"Not sure. Last check she was curled up with Adele sleeping. Poor kid."

Dominic watched as Conner shook his head. Yeah, his brother was as pissed as he was about the abuse Kelly had suffered.

He and Clint entered the room and sure enough, Kelly was sleeping and Adele was still on the bed with her. The sight before him was instantly imprinted on his soul. Adele would make an awesome mother. He fell a little more in love with her as he stood there watching. She had Kelly protectively embraced in her arms with her cheek resting on top of Kelly's curls, and her eyes were closed as she quietly hummed.

Adele raised her head from Kelly to look at them as they approached the bed. He loved how she could sense his approach; he sure as hell sensed whenever she was anywhere near him. He remained standing behind Clint. He didn't want to get in the way of any poking or prodding he might need to do.

"Pager dead again, Clint?" she asked with a slight hint of a smirk. His mate was a cheeky one when she wanted to be.

"Yeah, damn batteries. I asked Lyn to throw out the whole box. Dominic tells me Kelly woke up. What happened?"

Dominic drunk the sight of his mate as she relayed to Clint how distraught Kelly had been upon waking and what she had recounted upon her memory returning.

"Poor little mite, how on earth did she manage to get away from the monster?" Clint shook his head, his disgust easy to read in his tone and posture.

"I guess the threat of rape was motivator enough to give her strength to take a few risks."

He noticed how Adele tightened her hold as they spoke. So protective. So perfect.

"I'm glad it did and I'm glad we found her. Now she has us to keep her protected," Dominic added in a firm voice. He needed Adele to realize that Kelly wasn't the only one who was never going to be alone again.

Clint cleared his throat, looking sadly down at Kelly.

"Well, don't suppose you could try to wake her for me, Adele? I'd like to check her over and then I can give you an idea of when she might be able to leave the hospital."

Chapter Ten

"A week. I have seven days to get everything organized or Kelly goes into the system."

Adele's panic rose as she paced around her office. Clint had checked Kelly over, then she'd curled up and was asleep within minutes. Poor kid was so wore-out. Thankfully all her injuries were healing up well and she would make a full recovery—physically anyway. Dominic snagged her hand as she rushed past and pulled her against his muscular chest.

"It will be fine, Adele. Take a deep breath and calm your mind down a notch. Everyone will help, you'll see."

He took her face between his palms and kissed her. Oh yeah, her mind slowed down a notch or two now. Stuff a deep breath, Dominic's kisses worked much better. Adele's thoughts scattered under the onslaught. Just like every other time he'd kissed her, his mouth was lethal to her concentration. She wrapped her arms around his neck, deepening the kiss. Dominic pulled back slightly from her lips. She grinned at how heavily he was breathing.

"Come to dinner with me. At my house. Tonight."

"I don't know if I have time. I have so much to do now."

"This will help. I promise. My parents want to get to know you, and my mum, she's got some ideas on how to help Kelly with her education. I bet Deirdre will be impressed if you have a plan all worked out on that front."

Adele had rested her head over his heart as he spoke. Tilting her head up, she put her nose against his neck to inhale and surround herself with his scent. Another night in his arms would be nice. Really nice actually.

After a moment of shoring up her courage, she kissed Dominic's neck, nibbled her way up to his ear where she whispered, "Okay, I'll come over for dinner, on one condition."

Dominic groaned deep in his throat as she nibbled his jaw.

"And what would that condition be, beautiful?"

His voice was hoarse and sounded strained.

"You come pick me up...then take me home after, and" —she paused a moment to nibble his jaw some more— "stay with me the night."

Dominic's hands, which had dropped to her waist, tightened their hold as he took a sharp breath.

"Are you sure, Adele? You need to be certain, one hundred percent sure."

She trailed her hand over his pectoral muscles, marveling at the way they clenched beneath her palm.

He was so sweet, worrying about her decision.

"I'm done running, Dominic. I am most certainly one hundred percent sure."

Dominic wrapped her up in his embrace, lifting her off the floor as he stood straight with his face buried in her neck.

"Oh God, Adele, I love you and tonight will be so special and so perfect. I'll never leave you. I promise."

Adele's heart sang at Dominic's desperately whispered words.

"This is so crazy. We've only know each other for such a short time, but yeah, Dominic, I love you too."

As the last syllable left her mouth, Dominic spun her around before putting her down and kissing her senseless again.

Adele ran her fingers through her hair as Dominic pulled up to his house. She got out and took in the surroundings. The house was set back from the road, far enough that the scrub hid the house from the view of passersby. There were a couple of paddocks on either side of the house, where what looked like Alpacas were quietly grazing. The house itself was massive, but it wasn't ritzy. Adele thought it looked homey and warm. She looked over the two-story brick house; it had been rendered white and it looked almost like an overgrown cottage, especially with its two beautiful bay windows on either side of the front door. There was a series of four attic windows poking through the stone grey

Colorbond roof. She grinned. She'd always loved the idea of attic rooms. This place was like her fantasy home come to life. She couldn't wait to see inside.

Adele was pulled from her trance when Dominic came up behind her and wrapped his arms around her waist and pulled her body flush against his. He lowered his head into her hair and she heard him inhale deeply before his body shuddered slightly.

"Oh, Dominic, your parents' house is gorgeous!"

She felt Dominic raise his head. Obviously, he didn't actually look at the house he lived in. She couldn't help but giggle, such a typical male.

"Don't tell me you've never *seen* the house you live in before?"

Dominic chuckled in return.

"It's home. I've never really seen it as anything other than that. I guess it's a good-looking place. I know Mum and Dad do a fair amount of work to keep it at its best. Let's head inside. I can give you a tour if you like?"

He chuckled again and she decided she loved the sound, especially when he was holding her and she could feel it vibrate through her body.

"I guess I should say, if Mum leaves you alone for long enough, I can take you for a tour."

She attempted to respond but before her lips parted, she felt his head lower to the tender skin between her neck and shoulder where he laid a gentle kiss that set her on fire from the top of her head to the tips of her toes. As she stood trying to calm herself, he released his hold on her and stepped back. As if sensing she was extremely aroused, he gave her a moment in the cool night air to regain her composure before he slid his hand over hers and led her down the path to the front door. As he reached his hand for the door handle, it swung open to reveal a rather excited woman who Adele assumed was Dominic's mother. Her heart melted when Dominic leaned in to kiss his mother on the cheek. He was so sweet. She imagined a lot of men would be too embarrassed to kiss their mother in front of their girlfriend—or in front of anyone for that matter.

"Evening, Mum." He gently pulled Adele so she stood in front of him.

"Mum, I'd like to introduce you to my special lady, Adele."

Startling her slightly, his mum rushed forward and grabbed her hands in hers.

"It is so lovely to finally meet you, Adele."

Adele frowned slightly, *finally* meet her? She glanced at Dominic. She'd only known him a short time, a matter of weeks. Dominic gave her a quick shrug and a wink, like he knew what she was thinking but didn't think she should worry about it. She turned her attention back to his mother.

"The pleasure is all mine, Mrs White. Dominic speaks very fondly of you."

Adele caught the look that passed over Dominic's face. It was one of barely contained laughter. She gave him a raised eyebrow glare. He stopped nearly laughing, gave her a slight nod and a lopsided grin. Oh, she couldn't resist that grin. And damn, but the man knew it and used it against her relentlessly. Adele felt so nervous. She'd never had a boyfriend before so didn't have a clue how to act around his parents. The way his mother was blushing and fussing at her, she was pretty sure she was stuffing it up royally. At least Dominic seemed to be enjoying the show.

"Oh, none of that Mrs White stuff, love, you'll make me feel like I'm back in the school yard! Just call me Sophie. Now, dinner's almost ready. Why don't you two go in with Jake, he's in the dining room."

Sophie released her hands, gave them a pat, then left them alone in the foyer. Before they could move from the foyer, Adele grabbed Dominic's arm.

"Please, won't you tell me what had you so amused?"

She cocked an eyebrow and feigned a hurt attitude.

"You were so preciously nervous, beautiful. And you had Mum fussing and blushing like a teenager. If our roles were reversed, you'd have a hard time not laughing too." He leaned in and gave her a quick kiss. "C'mon, let's go find Dad."

Adele couldn't help but grin as they entered the dining room. There was Jake, six foot four, wide muscular shoulders, powerful arms, and he was gently laying out placemats and cutlery. Even from the back, his big body looked out of place doing something so mundane. Adele raised her hand to cover her mouth as her body shuddered in a near silent giggle. Dominic's hand tightened on hers before releasing her with another lopsided grin and a wink. He stepped over to his dad with a shoulder nudge hello and grabbed the cutlery from his hands.

"You know you never get it right, Dad. Mum will hang you out to dry if you muck it up when we have a guest."

From the humor in Dominic's voice, Adele guessed he was just stirring up his dad.

"Can't help that I use my right hand for my fork. You know, everyone else could just get used to it instead of giving me grief every chance you lot get... Oh, hey, Adele."

He came over to her, giving her a quick kiss on the cheek.

"Lovely seeing you again."

He promptly went back to the placemats to finish setting them out.

"Well, I guess since my table setting abilities are no longer required, I'll go organize the drinks, shall I? What's your poison, Adele?"

"Oh, I'll just have some of whatever you are all having. Thanks, Jake."

Adele's eyes followed Jake as he disappeared out the room toward the kitchen, before she focused on Dominic being all domestic with the cutlery. A fully house-trained man; she wished her mother could see this. Fleur Petit would never believe it without seeing it. She shut her eyes, sucked in a breath, and winced at the sudden onslaught of pain the random thought of her mother brought on. She opened her eyes to find Dominic right in front of her looking very worried. He caught her hands in his.

"What's wrong? Are you okay? You look like you're in pain."

She looked into his eyes, allowing their cool blue ice to soothe her. The feel of his thumbs rubbing back and forth over her wrists calmed her further.

"I'm fine, *mon amour.* I just had a thought that jarred a memory. I wasn't expecting it, that's all."

She smiled as best she could, vainly trying to reassure him she was okay. "Fake it till you make it" was her motto just at the moment.

Adele could see understanding in his gaze, how on earth this man could read her so well was beyond her, but somehow he knew. He knew her heart still wept for her lost mother. He tilted her head up and lowered his mouth to hers, giving her a passion-filled kiss that made sure her mind had no room for any thoughts other than of him and his taste. She was totally melting into him when she heard a chuckle. Glancing around Dominic's arm, she saw his parents placing dinner on the table with large grins in place at their show of affection. She blushed as she buried her face against Dominic's chest that was vibrating with his laughter.

Dominic glanced over at Adele as he plugged his seat belt in. She looked so adorable and sweet. Her eyes were half shut, and she had just a hint of a smile on her face with her hand resting on her tummy, just like he did after he ate a satisfying meal. His mother's roast lamb could do that to a person. Dominic grinned as he remembered her hoeing into dessert. Fresh fruit salad with cream—he chuckled to himself—cream with fresh fruit salad would be a better description of her dessert. His mate apparently really liked her cream.

"What are you chuckling about this time, *mon cher*?" Adele's sweet voice sounded content. He really liked that he was at least partly responsible for that contentedness.

"Just thinking about your love of cream, beautiful."

She arched her brow at him before giggling.

"I'm a girl of simple tastes, Dominic. I love my fruit salad, especially when it's fresh, and especially when it comes with cream."

Dominic chuckled as he started the car and headed down the drive. After he drove out on the road, he got up to fifth gear as quickly as possible so he could lay his hand on her thigh. It felt nice, like he was claiming possession of her.

"So, what do you think of Mum's ideas for Kelly?"

He didn't want her—or him—getting too nervous about the night ahead.

"I think it all sounds great. I hadn't even thought about school yet; getting my own house has been all

I've been focused on. But she's right, Kelly is going to need some serious tutoring and help. Not only with the academic stuff but I don't think she's ever socialized much with anyone, let alone other teenagers. It's going to be one hell of a journey for all of us."

Adele's voice sounded worried, but Dominic wasn't. He knew his mate was strong, definitely strong enough for this challenge. Plus she had plenty of help available.

"Yeah, there is a lot to do. But you're not alone, Adele. You have me. You have this whole town to support you with this. You know that, right? This community is great when it comes to helping out when someone needs it most; you'll see for yourself soon enough."

"Hmm, I'm learning that already. It's been hard to adjust to. Sunshine, where I lived near Melbourne, wasn't like this. Everyone pretty much kept to themselves. I've been on my own for so long, it's taking some time to adjust to having all these people that want to be in my life and learning to open up to them. Trust is hard for me."

"I know, beautiful. But you won't ever be alone again. I promise you, I will never leave you alone."

He felt her gaze on him as he drove. He couldn't wait for her to believe him, in him. He didn't know how to get her to take his word as truth so he decided he'd just keep telling her. Eventually, she'd see by his actions that he meant his words. She was staring hard at him and thinking equally as hard. He could just about hear her brain ticking over.

"Don't think so hard, beautiful. Just accept it and relax."

"I keep expecting to wake up and this to all be a dream. You're too perfect, I just—I don't feel like I deserve you."

Her tone reflected how confused she felt, and Dominic's heart stuttered for a moment.

"I'm real, Adele. I love you and I'm one hundred percent committed to you, forever. I will keep telling you until you believe me."

"I want to believe you. I really do."

Dominic brought her hand to his lips and kissed her palm before laying it against his cheek to nuzzle into it.

"You'll see, beautiful. I'll prove it to you with actions and words. Whatever it takes." He could hear the steel in his voice, but he couldn't help it. He was dead serious about Adele, and he needed her to understand he was in this forever.

Adele's gaze didn't shift from him, but after a few minutes he felt a shift in her focus. The air in the car was suddenly thick with her scent. His little mate was aroused. Staring at him in the light from the passing street lights, Adele had gotten herself worked up. He could relate. He was already hard as steel at the thought of what would happen tonight, and her eyes on him were making him even hotter. At this rate, he'd be embarrassing himself by coming before the party began.

Finally, he saw the drive to her place up ahead. He

slowed the car, turned into the drive, and pulled up in front of the garage. He cut the engine then looked over at Adele and groaned. Her eyes were hooded in the darkness of the car, and he could hear her rapid breathing. The smell of her arousal increased as he watched her. She was as turned on as him. He ran a hand over the side of her face, holding her steady while he leaned over for a kiss. As soon as his lips touched hers, she parted them for him, inviting him in. He took the invitation without a moment's hesitation, deepening the kiss, consuming her mouth until they were both breathless. He slowly pulled back and released her face.

"I think we best move this inside, love."

Adele could barely function enough to get out of the car after the powerful kiss Dominic had laid on her. He'd completely possessed her, dominated her. And she'd loved it. She managed to grab hold of her handbag but the door handle was a different matter entirely; her fingers simply refused to function properly. Within moments, Dominic was there, opening the way for her. As she went to slide out, Dominic stepped up to her so she slid down his body until her feet hit the ground. Her head, which had just started to clear, went reeling again as she found herself completely surrounded by his strength and heat. Despite his strength, he cradled her against his hard body gently. Which turned out to be handy, because if he hadn't been holding her when he kissed her again, she would have ended up on the ground when her knees buckled. She moaned into him through the kiss. She was so turned on and they hadn't even made it inside the house yet! She nipped his bottom lip, which earned her a growl. Low and sexy, deep in his throat. She pulled back as much as she could in his tight embrace.

"We really need to get inside, *mon amour.* The neighbors don't need us to provide their entertainment for the evening."

Adele shivered when Dominic took a fast step back from her. She instantly felt cold, empty. It was crazy; he was standing right in front of her. She looked up to see him gaze around the street, like he was checking to see if they had in fact given any neighbors a show. She idly wondered what he'd do if they had. Then he gazed down into her face and she melted against the car as his heat stole her mind.

"Keys, beautiful."

On autopilot, her hand reached into her handbag and grabbed out her house keys. She was so far under his spell she didn't realize she had dropped them into his waiting palm until she heard him chuckle quietly. Obviously realizing she was using the car to keep her upright, he bent forward and pressed his shoulder against her tummy. She let out a small squeak of surprise when she ended up over his shoulder in a fireman's hold.

"What on earth are you doing, Dominic? I can walk, you know."

Embarrassment heated her cheeks and dulled her arousal.

"I'm carrying you inside, beautiful, because I'm not so sure about your ability to walk, and I can't wait much longer to have you. This way is quicker."

Okay. So he may have a point about the walking thing. She couldn't quite believe it, but now that the initial shock had worn off, she kind of liked this whole caveman thing he had going on. With one palm firmly holding her thigh, Dominic opened the door with his other hand. He lowered her feet to the floor and then turned to close and lock the door. Before he could turn back around, she came up behind him, molding her curves to his back. She needed to be connected to him.

A zing of satisfaction raced through her when she heard him groan. She began to lay gentle light kisses over his upper back. She didn't know what she was doing, but it felt so good to be touching him. Honestly, she was feeling more than a little frisky now that she knew where things were going. She wanted Dominic like she'd never wanted anyone before. She couldn't stop thinking about him. Day and night, thoughts of this man consumed her mind and body. She wasn't worried about not knowing what to do next; she was pretty sure Dominic was too dominant a male to allow her to take the lead, especially this first time.

Sure enough, moments later, she found herself with her back up against the front door. Dominic ground his hips into hers, his thick erection rubbing against her lower belly. With a will of their own, her legs parted to make more room for him. As his mouth nipped and nibbled its way over her neck and up her jaw to her ear, he ran his hands down her sides, over her hips, and down her thighs. He cupped her bottom and lifted her up.

"Wrap your legs around me, beautiful."

His voice was so hoarse, and she loved he was as turned on as her. His hands remained on her as she quickly wrapped her arms around his neck and her legs around his waist. She couldn't stop the gasp as her sensitive flesh landed on the hard ridge of the erection through his jeans. The thin cotton of her cargos and thin satin-and-lace of her G-string provided little barrier from the roughness of the denim against her.

Dominic lifted her away from the door and hissed in her ear as he inadvertently rubbed against her. Shivering, she nuzzled her face into his neck, breathing his scent deep into her. She loved that he was on edge. She could feel how taut all his muscles were around her. Feeling light and carefree, she laughed when he ran to her room. She kept up her attack on his skin with kisses and nips to his neck and shoulders. He stopped short at the end of her bed, releasing her so she could slide down.

As soon as her feet landed, she remembered the candles she'd planned on lighting. She began backing away from him.

"Where do you think you're going, beautiful?"

He growled playfully at her.

"I won't be but a minute, just wanted to light some candles so we can turn the light off."

She gave him a quick wink as she headed for her bedside cupboard. She lit the candles quickly, then headed over to turn off the light. She chewed her lower lip as he looked around her room but relaxed when she noticed the huge grin her was sporting. She was glad he liked what she'd done to her room. She'd gone to a lot of effort for tonight. Her room was spotless, the sheets clean and fresh, made up with hospital precision—some training just stuck, she couldn't help it. She did notice his eyebrow rose slightly when he glanced at the bed. She couldn't wait for him to see the other surprises she had for him.

She briefly thought about what she had spent her afternoon doing. She'd gone shopping and splashed out on some sexy lingerie. She squirmed as she thought about it and felt the G-string pull tight against her skin. Yeah, she was rocking a lovely little baby-blue satin-and-lace ensemble beneath her cream cargo pants and baby-pink fitted shirt tonight. She'd also stopped in at the salon. She'd gotten her usual eyebrow and leg wax done before working up the nerve to be big and brave and have other places waxed. Man, had that stung like a bitch. She smiled to herself as she wondered what Dominic's reaction would be.

She was still hovering by the door, lost in her thoughts and feeling nervous, when Dominic turned slowly toward her with his eyes full of passion and hunger. He tilted his head and crooked a finger, indicating he wanted her to come to him.

"Come to me, my love."

His voice was all deep and smooth and sent shivers of delight and desire over her whole body, pooling in her lower belly. Adele was rapidly losing control. Dominic had her so worked up she couldn't think straight. Tentatively, she walked over to stand in front of him. Damn, he smelled so good. Her eyelids drooped when she took a deep breath. He chuckled.

"Like what you smell, my love?"

Was he kidding? She was completely addicted to what she smelled.

"Hmmm, I do. You smell like the forest, fresh but spicy. I love it."

She nuzzled her face into his neck when he lowered his head into hers and inhaled deeply against her throat.

"Your scent is simply intoxicating to me, my love. Its natural woman and vanilla and just now, it's laced with your delicious arousal."

Dominic's words had her head spinning, again. She barely noticed his hands trail down her sides and under the bottom edge of her shirt. He grabbed the bottom and lifted it over her head. She smiled when he sucked in a breath and whispered, "Nice, love, very nice," as he traced the edge of the lace and satin bra with his fingertip. He lowered his head to hers to devour her mouth once more as he unbuttoned and unzipped her cargos. He pulled back slightly as her pants dropped to the floor to pool around her feet.

"Hmm, aren't you full of surprises tonight, my sweet Adele."

His voice was heavy with his arousal, which only added to hers.

"I wanted it to be special," she confessed quietly as she looked at the floor.

She was a little worried about his reaction now that it had come time for her to reveal herself. She felt Dominic's hand slide up her neck and tilt her head up until she was looking at his face.

"I love you, Adele. Tonight *will* be special and I love that you went to all this effort. It shows me that you love me too."

He kissed her before she could respond. She reached for the bottom of his shirt and began lifting it up his torso, running her hands over his ribbed stomach as she went higher. He pulled back from her mouth and took his shirt off. She licked her lips as she took in his chest and arms. He was massive and so muscular. She ran her palms up his tight abs and over his pecs, which clenched beneath her touch, over his broad shoulders then down his thick arms. She gripped his left bicep, tilting it toward her. He had a tattoo down the outside of the upper half of his left arm. She'd seen glimpses of it before but never had a chance to have a good look before now. She ran her fingertips over the detailed black design of what appeared to be an almost oriental-looking umbrella with a lotus flower at the base and a ribbon coming down from the bottom of the umbrella.

"It's a Tibetan Umbrella. It symbolizes protection."

His tone was proud; this tattoo was special to him. Not just some ink he'd gotten on a whim. She grinned widely. Protection. How appropriate.

"It's beautiful."

She released his arm and continued her exploration of his exposed skin. It didn't take long for him to lose patience. He bent down, placed his hands around her waist, lifted her up, and gently tossed her on the bed. Where she couldn't help but giggle as she bounced once. He was so strong and she loved when he lifted her. It made her feel petite and precious. He unlaced each of her shoes and took them, her socks, and her bunched up cargos off. Leaving her feeling very sexy in her bra and G-string.

He quickly toed off his own shoes, removed his socks, then went for his fly. She could feel him watching her but couldn't draw her eyes from what his hands were doing to check. He lowered his fly, revealing black boxer-briefs. He took off his jeans. As he stood back up and hooked his thumbs into the front of his briefs, she felt her breathing speed up and was certain her G-string was soaked; she was that turned on. He was killing her with his slow striptease. She wanted to tell him to hurry up but her mouth was too dry for her to speak. He took a deep breath and lowered his boxer-briefs, releasing his hard throbbing erection to the cool air in the room, and her hot stare.

Adele sucked in a breath. Her butterflies were going berserk at the sight Dominic presented before her. He stood tall and confident, with his erection long and thick and pointing straight at her as if directing which way he needed to move. She took in his whole body from feet to head and she settled on his beautiful face. She could see the hint of vulnerability in his eyes. He was worried about her opinion of him.

"You are amazing, *mon amour*. So beautiful. So strong. But you're too far away. I can't touch you, or be touched by you."

He kneeled on the edge of the bed and began slowly crawling toward her with his head dropped down. He looked almost feline in his smooth movements. An image of her *chaton* sprung to mind as she watched him approach her. He licked, kissed, and nipped her skin from her toes up, until he got between her legs. There, he held his nose against the satin and pressed in, inhaling deeply as he nuzzled his nose against her clit. With no hair there, the sensation had her gripping the mattress.

He rose slightly, took the edge of her G-string in between his teeth, and lowered the garment down her legs. Watching him remove her clothing with his teeth alone had a gush of cream leaving her, coating the tops of her thighs as she rubbed them together. She arched up under the intense emotions flowing through her. He quickly returned to her after tossing her G-string away somewhere.

"Hmmm, more surprises, my love."

Dominic couldn't believe what he had in front of him. Adele had waxed every hair on her body from her ankles to her hips; her flesh was bare to him. He ran his knuckles over her mons, the skin so smooth and soft he shuddered. Using his thumbs, he parted her lower lips. He could see she was glistening and the tops of her thighs were slick too. She was into this as he was. Trembling, he couldn't stand it any longer. He wanted to explore her more but the scent of her cream was just too intoxicating to ignore. Holding her open, he leaned forward, flattened his tongue, and licked her back to front before sucking down on her. As soon as his mouth closed over her, she came, filling his mouth with her sweet cream. He groaned as her taste exploded across his taste buds and flowed down his throat. *Nirvana*. She tasted so good. He kept at her until she had come twice more before he moved up her body. Her hips cradled his body, his hard length pressed against her folds where her heat and moisture scolded him. He kissed her with all the love he felt for her as her hands came up to hold his face to hers and she began rocking her hips ever so slightly beneath him. Suddenly she jerked away from his lips; he opened his eyes and cocked an eyebrow at her sudden movement.

"Protection, we need protection." she rasped out.

He rolled off her and watched as she reached over to

the top drawer of her bedside cupboard and pulled out a box of condoms. He chuckled.

"You really did think of everything, didn't you, love?"

She passed the box over with a sly smile.

"I bought them, but I've got no idea how to use them. I do believe that's your department."

He took the box from her while shaking his head. He loved her sense of humor. He leaned in and kissed her briefly before setting about opening the box. He had one out and ready to put on when he got distracted by watching Adele reach behind her to unclip her bra. Watching her lush breasts spring from their confinement had his erection bobbing and his blood on fire. She noticed he'd stopped and smiled slyly.

"I'm not distracting you, am I, *mon amour*?"

"In the best possible way, love. You are so beautiful."

He finished putting the condom on and lowered himself back over Adele. He wanted to take his time and savor this first time with his mate, but he was so worked up it might be a short trip through the park. He silently vowed he would make it up to her later. He kissed her lips and trailed his mouth down to her breasts where he worshipped them until she was writhing beneath him and he could smell the fresh cream she was pushing out for him.

He pulled back to look down at her passion-soaked face. She truly looked like a goddess. He lined his erection up with her entrance and began gently pushing forward. Her heat burned the tip as he pushed into her tight channel. *Total nirvana*. He felt like he was coming home; he was right where he would always belong. He watched as she arched her back under him as he continued to push into her slowly. She grabbed at him. Grabbed fistfuls of his hair and dragged him down to her mouth. He went to her willingly. He consumed her mouth as he slid his way farther into her tight wet heat. He felt the slight resistance of her virginity and winced as he broke through it. He hated hurting her in any way. He swallowed her cry and held still while her body adjusted to having him fully inside hers. He needed a moment too, to absorb how wondrous it felt being inside his mate for the first time and knowing that he was the first and the only man that would ever be inside this divine woman lying beneath him. She'd moved her hands to grab at his shoulders as he'd entered her fully, and her nails were sunk into his skin. The little bites of pain had him flying higher.

After a minute, Adele loosened her grip on his shoulders and started tentatively rocking her hips against him.

"Are you okay, Adele? I hate that I hurt you."

Her eyes were still closed and her forehead creased. He was worried she was still in pain.

"It only hurt for a little bit, *mon amour*. Now I just feel...full; you take up so much room inside me. I need, I need you to move, Dominic. I need you moving inside me."

She started rocking harder against him and his control snapped. He placed his left hand possessively around the front of her neck, gently holding her down. He kissed her again as he took over control, thrusting into her over and over. Each thrust jacked him higher, burning brighter. Her body clenched around his as her orgasm steamrolled through her body. He couldn't fight it any longer, not with her walls caressing him like they were. He slammed into her one final time, tilted his head back, and roared as he found his release.

Dominic had never felt so complete than he did with Adele asleep beneath him. She'd passed out from the pleasure. He grinned like a fool as he slowly eased himself from her body. He pulled off the condom, grabbed a tissue, and tossed it in the bin by her bed. He then snuggled Adele into his side as he spooned up behind her. He held his right hand out and examined his claws. They still hadn't receded back into his hand. Once she knew about him being a shifter, that she was his mate, he would claim her completely and mark her. He was so glad he'd talked to his father about all this. If he hadn't, he wouldn't have known to be careful to keep his right hand away from her skin. At this point his mark would scare the life out of her. He was sure any girl would panic if they woke up after a night of sex to discover what looked like four wide scratches revealing snow leopard spots beneath tattooed onto their skin. He sure as hell would in the same position. So he lay there, listening to his mate's breathing even out, her heart rate settle, and watched as his claws receded and his nails reappeared as human. Soon he'd confess everything and claim her.

Chapter Eleven

Cole slammed his way through the front door of his motel room and headed to the bathroom to have a shower and clean the dirt off. He felt a little better than earlier, thanks to finding that stray dog to torture, but it wasn't his slave. It had been weak and died on him. He then had to bury the damn thing. Which was why he'd had to settle on a stray and not a woman. He was too far from the coast to toss the body. Attracting the attention of the authorities would not help him find his slave.

Damn it, he needed her back.

He needed to feel his hands on her skin.

See her skin marked up by his touch.

Hear her screams.

He'd spent the last two weeks searching and still no sign of her. He'd spent the first week scouring Strahan, but the only trace he'd been able to find were some bloody handprints on a Salvo's clothing bin near his house. Now he was in Queenstown and he'd been methodically searching the town for any sign of her but to no avail. Bloody hell, he wished he'd bothered to find out what her name was. He'd not cared what her—or her mother's—name had been while they were under his control. It hadn't been important. They were both simply his slaves, possessions, that didn't need a name. But now that he couldn't find her, he really wished he'd gotten one from either of them to make it easier to trace her.

After he finished cleaning himself up, he sat down at the table in his room with a map of the Cradle Mountains and the surrounding region. Which way had she gone? There were only two main roads out of Strahan: one that headed east to Queenstown and another that headed north to Zeehan. There was a main road that ran from Queenstown to Rosebery that cut across close to Zeehan. Probably best to take that road; given that she'd had two weeks, he doubted she would be on the road between Strahan and Zeehan. If she was, it would be because she'd died from her injuries.

Shit.

She better not be dead.

He started rubbing the center of his chest at the ache that formed at the thought of his slave dead. He needed her. She was his and she didn't have permission to die on him. He squeezed his eyes shut against the pain that suddenly shot through his skull. Damn it, he needed to calm down or he'd be useless. Without his slave to workout on, he was having trouble staying focused on anything. He needed to workout to stay balanced, to feel like he fit in his skin. His dad had shown him how to stay in control of himself, and he had taught his son well before he died in a car wreck when Cole had been sixteen. For the last ten years, Cole had been perfecting what his dad had taught him. If only his dad was still here, he'd know how to find his slave and then he would have helped Cole discipline her for leaving. That would have been some beautiful father-son bonding time right there. Damn, but he did really miss his old man.

Cole sighed as he started packing away his things neatly in his suitcase. He would leave first thing in the morning and head to Zeehan. It would probably take at least a few days to search the town for signs of her. He would have to be careful though, there were people in Zeehan who didn't like him and would cause him a great deal of trouble if they found out he was around. So he would have to be quiet and quick about it before heading up to Rosebery.

Adele looked up from her bowl of cereal to watch Dominic move around the kitchen. He'd only put on his jeans when they'd finally got out of bed, so his upper body was on full display, and she was making the most of it. As her gaze roamed over his exposed skin, her belly clenched and an ache settled in lower. As if he could sense her eyes on him, Dominic glanced over his shoulder at her with a lopsided grin and winked at her before he closed the fridge and came over to her at the table with his breakfast.

"Keep looking at me like that, beautiful, and we won't be leaving the house at all today."

He leaned over to gently kiss her before sitting down.

"Hmmm, well, as nice as not leaving the house sounds, I've got too much to get done."

That and Kit would be home soon from her night shift of guarding Kelly. As much as Kit might approve of her and Dominic finally getting together, Adele was fairly certain the woman didn't want to witness it first-hand.

"So, what's on the agenda for this bright and beautiful Saturday morning?"

Adele couldn't help but preen as she heard how happy Dominic sounded to be spending the day with her.

"House hunting. There're a few that look good."

She grabbed the pile of printouts she'd compiled over that week and handed them to Dominic to look at.

"The one on the top is my favorite."

Dominic cocked his eyebrow at her.

"The house is painted purple."

She barely contained her laugh. She'd known he would say something about the color. She couldn't hold back her grin as she spoke.

"I know, right? I love it, and it will make giving directions easy."

Dominic looked at the page again and winced.

"I guess that's one way of looking at it."

She reached over and patted his arm, poor Dominic. He looked like she'd just shot his dog or something.

"The more important things are that it has three

bedrooms, a bathroom that actually has a bath, a nice big wood heater, a large kitchen with a brand new oven and cooktop, and a huge fenced back yard. Lots of room for Kelly to have all the things she needs."

She watched as he read the description below the picture and his frown slowly eased away.

"It's not too far from the hospital either, which is good. I reckon Kelly would be able to walk to school from there too if she wanted to. When is it available?"

"It's vacant at the moment. The previous tenants moved out last week. Perfect timing, and it's only $130 a week so I'll be able to afford to buy some furniture to put in the house too. I guess we need to start looking for all that stuff."

She frowned as she grabbed her pen and jotted down a few notes about furniture she'd need to buy on a piece of scrap paper. How on earth was she going to get all this done in a week?

"How about we take a tape measure with us and measure up the house, then we can go do a round of the second-hand shops and see what's available that will fit?"

She smiled as she looked into Dominic's eyes. He thought of everything, especially the little things she always forgot. She would have to go to the furniture shop before realizing she didn't know how big the rooms were.

"Sounds great."

Dominic stood in the driveway next to Adele and the Real Estate Agent, Marlee Van Dyke. He was holding Adele's hand and felt her excitement vibrating through her. He looked up at the house. It really was purple. The photos hadn't been exaggerated as he'd hoped. Some moron had actually clad the house in light purple iron paneling. From the outside, the house didn't look anything special—aside from the purple factor—just your average ironclad home with a fenced back yard and carport. He could tell Adele loved it already so it looked like he was going to have to get used to a purple house, not that he expected to be moving in with her next week. It was too soon for that but at some point they would live together—apparently in this bloody purple monstrosity.

Sighing, Dominic allowed Adele to drag him up the drive behind her. She was quietly laughing at him.

"Something you find amusing, beautiful?"

He was pretty sure it was his reaction that had her amused, but he couldn't resist the chance to tease her a little.

"Don't you like purple, Dominic?"

Her voice was laced with false innocence.

"I like purple just fine. Just not on a house. Especially when it's the only color."

That earned him another chuckle. Marlee opened up the front door and ushered them inside then led them around the house on a quick tour. Dominic was having serious trouble not wincing as each room revealed more purple horror. Even the metal edging around the shower door was bloody purple!

However, Adele was right about the kitchen; it was nice and big and the stove was brand new. Focus on the positives, that's what he needed to be doing. The bedrooms had built-in robes so that was money saved. With his tape measure in hand, he headed off to start taking measurements of the rooms while Adele and Marlee finished going through the house. He needed to distract himself from focusing on the purple everywhere. He made sure to measure the windows too. The deep purple curtains were going. There wasn't going to be a discussion on that one. There was a limit of how much he could endure and the curtains pushed way beyond it. He finished up and found the ladies chatting in the lounge room by the front door.

"There you are! I was starting to wonder if you got lost. I can move in as soon as I want. I was thinking Wednesday. That will give me a few days before Kelly gets released to get everything set up. Do you think you and Kit could get the day off to give me a hand?"

Adele's voice was so excited Dominic couldn't help but smile at her.

"Sure, beautiful. You'll have all the help you'll need. I promise."

He flashed her a wink.

Adele smiled as she stood in the driveway of her new home: No 14 Wattle Avenue. She was fingering the front door key in her hand as she looked up at the house. It was a pretty thing, ironclad and painted purple. She knew a lot of people who wouldn't be caught dead in a purple house, but she loved the color. It wasn't anything special, just your average three-bedroom house with a fenced back yard and carport. But it had been available for her to move in straight away and the rent was in her price range—and most importantly, it had everything the Child Protection Service had demanded she needed.

Kelly. The poor little girl would remain in the hospital until Friday. Tears welled in her eyes at the thought of how badly she'd been beaten. Adele brushed them away from her cheeks. Kelly's pain was over now, and she would never be hurt like that again. Adele would make sure of it.

As Adele unlocked the front door, she heard footsteps coming up behind her. Before she had time to turn around to see who it was, she was lifted in the air with ease. She squealed in surprise until Dominic silenced her with a hot kiss. It had only been four days since Dominic had made love to her for the first time and rocked her world. Her cheeks heated in memory, but damn, the man was sexy.

"Dominic, what on earth do you think you are doing?"

Her voice was all husky at the heat Dominic brought out in her by simply holding her.

"Why, my love, I'm carrying you over the threshold. You don't move into a new house every day and you have to make sure you do it *just* right."

He sounded all serious but the glint in his eyes gave him away. Adele couldn't help but laugh. She wrapped her arms around his neck and kissed him on his cheek.

"Well then, *mon amour*, we'd best get inside before the others arrive and beat us over the threshold."

Adele beamed as Dominic carried her through the doorway. He was so sweet. He had a huge grin on his face, like carrying her was the best thing he'd ever done. She wasn't sure how she managed to catch this tender, sweet, strong man, but she was certain she'd never, ever want to let him go.

As soon as they were inside, he bent down and nuzzled into her neck. She heard him inhale against her skin. He always inhaled against her skin like that; it tickled, made her giddy, and gave her butterflies every time.

"Welcome home, Adele."

Then he proceeded to devour her mouth with his. When the need for air forced them apart, they were both breathing heavily.

"Hmmm, as much as I'd love to continue, we need to check through the house quickly before the others get here. I want to make sure it's all clean and ready."

Dominic had her so turned on, Adele was struggling to speak normally.

"I don't want to put you down just yet, beautiful. How about I carry you around on a tour?"

His voice was husky, as if he was as turned on as her.

Before she could muster a response, he started for the kitchen. He strode up to the bench and sat her down, planting himself between her legs and she kept her arms wrapped around his neck.

"Hmmm, I think we need to christen all the rooms with a kiss at least. Got the front room covered, now for the kitchen."

He leaned in to kiss her and she tilted her face to him, silently encouraging him to take what he wanted from her. She was melting into his kiss when she felt him tense. She was about to ask what was wrong when she heard car doors. She raised an eyebrow as he placed her back on the ground. Just what was he up to? He had that lopsided grin that he knew melted her. It also normally meant he was about to, or had recently, done something he wasn't sure she'd be okay with.

Adele was grateful that Dominic let her walk out the front on her own feet. As much as she loved being wrapped up in his arms, she'd like to keep those moments private. Dominic had mentioned he'd recruited a couple of the guys from the station to help her move. Naturally, that was what she expected to find, just a couple of the guys. She took one step out her front door and froze with her hand still on the handle. Two small moving trucks were being backed down her drive while a group of men walked up her drive from the car parked out on the street.

"Dominic, I thought you said a *couple* of guys would be helping us? And there is no way in hell all the things

I bought from the second-hand shop would need two trucks to move! What on earth have you done?"

She turned to find Dominic looking a little sheepish. "Surprise."

He quickly came up to her and wrapped her up in a hug.

"I did only mention it to a couple of the guys, but word spreads fast around here. You know that. When people found out you were doing all this so you could take Kelly in, they started donating things. You've pretty much got everything you could ever want or need now."

Adele felt her eyes prick with tears and she blinked fast to try to stop them but it was no use, they began to fall. Dominic wiped them away and gave her a quick kiss.

"Don't cry, baby. Think of it like a 'welcome to the family.' You're part of Rosebery now."

Dominic's words just made her tears flow faster and she clung on to him. She curled into his chest as he scooped her up and walked back into the house. He took her straight out the back and sat down on the wooden bench with her on his lap.

She felt like a fool, falling apart because people were being nice to her, but she just couldn't get her head around all these people here to help her. She felt Dominic's hands rubbing over her back, arms, and legs while his cheek rested on the top of her head. His touch helped soothe her and bring her back down. After ten minutes or so she'd calmed right down.

He ran his hands through her hair, dragging the bits that had stuck to her tears on her face and tucking them behind her ears. He gave her a soft kiss on her forehead that was so tender it broke through her walls and she began to speak.

"I'm so sorry. I didn't mean to fall apart like that."

She took a few deep breaths, inhaling Dominic's masculine scent, allowing it to further soothe her.

"No one has ever been so nice. I'm not used to people doing things for me, helping me. I'm not sure how to handle it all."

Adele looked up at him, using her eyes to plead with him to understand what she meant. He lowered his head and gave her a chaste kiss on the mouth.

"My dear sweet Adele, everyone you meet loves you. Everyone who has met Kelly loves her. You are about to find out exactly what being a part of the emergency services family is all about, because everyone wants to help you and Kelly settle in here and make a life for yourselves."

He helped her to her feet and taking her hand in his, led her back into the house.

"Now, you better start telling everyone where you want all your new furniture and stuff or you'll spend the next couple of weeks searching every time you want something."

The rest of the day flew past as Adele instructed everyone on where to put all the furniture and other stuff. She'd only been able to afford the basics for the house and had assumed the place would look rather barren for some time until she could afford everything she'd wanted. Now she found she had every piece of furniture and appliance she could have ever possibly wanted.

She went to check on her bedroom. Dominic hadn't let her in there yet and her curiosity was rapidly winning out over his instructions not to sneak a peek. Just before she reached the door, she heard a whole heap of beeps coming from all over the house. Suddenly there were men flying out from everywhere to leave the house. She plastered herself against the wall so she wouldn't get trampled. They must all be on call. Dominic came through the bedroom door and stepping in front of her, he wrapped her up in his arms. She sighed; this was her favorite place to be in the whole world.

"Sorry, beautiful. We just lost all of our helpers."

"That's okay, I wouldn't mind some quiet time. Do you need to go too?"

"Nope, you'll have to continue to put up with me. I'm off rotation today."

He began nuzzling her cheek in a most feline manner.

"Are you going to let me see my room yet? The suspense is killing me," she pleaded, before Dominic's ministrations caused her brain to completely cease to function.

"Hmmm, can't have you dying, now can we? So I guess I'll just have to let you in."

He was chuckling as he pulled back and gave her a wink.

"I need you to close your eyes for the grand unveiling."

Adele closed her eyes and wondered what the hell he had done to her room that warranted all this. Dominic held her hands, guiding her through the doorway before moving to stand behind her. Wrapping his arms around her waist, he rested his chin on her shoulder and whispered in her ear, "Open your eyes, my love."

Adele opened her eyes and took a sharp breath in.

"Oh wow!"

She was facing her new bed. Well, "bed" was an understatement. It was huge and beautiful. She had always wanted a four-poster bed; they looked so romantic in movies and magazines. The frame consisted of bold straight solid Tasmanian Oak pieces with six sheer white curtains hanging down and tied off to each post, on both sides and the end. The bed had been made up with lots of pillows and a big fluffy quilt with a beautiful white lacy cover on it. But the thing that caught and held her attention most of all was hanging above the bed against the back wall, centered between the posts. The most amazing framed photograph she had ever seen hung there. It was of a snow leopard stalking toward the camera in a field of wild grass. The funny thing was, the picture looked exactly like the snow leopard from her dreams. How bizarre.

Dominic kissing and nibbling his way up her neck pulled her back from her thoughts, and she quickly glanced around the room at the rest of the furniture. It was all solid Tasmanian Oak and stunning. She had never owned a single piece of brand new furniture before in her life and now she had a whole bedroom suite that looked like it was all brand new.

"So, do you like your new room, beautiful?" Dominic asked as he nibbled on the edge of her ear.

"Oh, Dominic, I love it. It's all gorgeous."

A sob broke out of her throat and she turned around and wrapped her arms around his neck and cried into his chest.

"Adele? Are you okay? I wanted to make you happy, not sad. If you don't like it, we can return it and you can pick whatever you like."

She could tell by the tone of his voice she had scared and worried him with her reaction.

"The room is perfect, *mon amour*. It's just, I've never owned anything new before. No one, aside from my mother, has ever given me anything. And I've always dreamed of having a four-poster bed to sleep in...it's just all so much to take in. It's been one hell of a day on my emotions."

Adele let herself go in Dominic's tight embrace. She nuzzled her nose into his neck as she began regaining her composure. He swept his arm behind her knees, swiftly picking her up before he sat on the bed with her on his lap.

"Why a snow leopard? How did you know I liked them?"

She twirled her fingers in the short hair on the back of his head. He shifted a little, like the question unnerved him.

"I don't know. I just saw it there and it made me think of you, so I took a gamble and bought it for you. Also, Kit said you'd love it when she saw it."

His tone was a little strained, like maybe that wasn't the whole truth. She was simply too overwhelmed by her day to try to work out what he might be hiding.

"Well, I do love it. It looks so at home here in my bedroom...much like you do."

She gave him what she hoped was a seductive smile.

"I do believe this room needs to be christened, maybe with a little more than a kiss?"

Dominic chuckled.

"Why, my sweet Adele, I do believe you're right. We best correct that."

Her heart sang when he covered her mouth with his and lowered her to the bed.

Chapter Twelve

Cole's mood was rapidly getting darker. He'd spent five days searching Zeehan, finding not even a trace of her anywhere. He raised his hand to his swollen jaw. To top off the brilliant time he was having, yesterday his "friends" had found him and decided to spell out the benefits of him leaving town. Bastards. Damn, he needed to vent. Maybe he'd have to look for another stray dog or something tonight. Where the hell was his slave?

He chucked his bag in the tray and shut the lid, hopped in, and took off toward Rosebery. He hoped he found her soon. Animals just weren't the same and he was starting to really lose it.

It didn't take long to get to Rosebery, and Cole couldn't believe his eyes as he drove down the main drag through the town. After weeks of looking, there she was. Relief poured through him as he watched her walking across the street in front of him. Thankfully, there were two cars between him and her so she didn't notice him.

She was with a woman, holding her hand and staying very close to her side. Damn it. He couldn't just take her if she was being watched over. He was going to have to plan this out. He forced himself to turn onto the next street away from her and headed out of town. He needed to sit and think about how he was going to work this.

He found a deserted car park facing over the river, swung his ute in, and killed the engine. He sunk back into his seat with a smile on his face. She was alive. And soon, very soon he would have her back where she belonged. He just needed a plan on how to get her. The way she was cuddled into that woman wasn't good. He doubted he would be able to catch her alone. He would have to take both of them. Maybe if he used his old Ruger pistol, the one he'd bought off that rough-as-guts captain a couple of years back. Yeah, he would grab the slave, hold the pistol to her, and make the woman come too. Cracking his knuckles, he grinned. That'll definitely work.

As he was about to start his car to head back into town, he noticed movement off the side of the carpark. A bitch and her pups were sniffing around the edge of the gravel. He smirked as an idea came to mind. Hmm, looked like he'd get his workout tonight after all. Then he'd leave them for his slave to find in the morning. Make her suffer a little of what he'd been suffering since she left him, and give her a hint at what she could expect to happen to her when he got her back.

Kelly braved leaving the house on her own for the first time. She'd walked out the front door, across the road, through a vacant block of scrub, and had ended up here, sitting on a large flat stone that jutted out over the river. The sun had heated the stone a little and it felt warm against her bottom. She guessed by late afternoon the stone would become too hot to sit on. She looked out over the river, watching the water flow and the odd fish that swam close to the surface. She loved watching water; it was so peaceful and calming. The sound of water had always helped soothe her nerves, not that her nerves needed soothing so much anymore. That thought took her back, reminding her this last week of peace was an anomaly in her world. Pain and suffering were much more familiar to her. She lightly fingered a fading bruise on her knee as her mind revisited her dark place and the man who had made it hell.

Something dripping on her knee brought her back to reality and the peaceful river before her. She was now sitting with her head resting on her knees, her arms wrapped around her legs, and she was crying. She brushed her tears away and focused on the water. Two weeks, three days. That's how long she'd been free from hell. Her nightmares were finally getting better. She idly played with the key that hung around her neck on a blue hospital lanyard. She had a feeling living with Adele was what was making them better. Thinking about Adele made her smile. Adele had been so good to her. She'd panicked when Dr Maynard told her she could leave the hospital. She didn't know if Adele had meant what she said about taking her in. After Adele told her she would, she had spent less and less time with her at the hospital. Now she knew why; she'd been getting everything ready for her on the outside. When the doctor had walked in with her discharge papers, Adele and Dominic had been one step behind him with big grins, ready to take her to her new home.

Her biggest shock was when they got her home. She liked that word: Home. She'd never really had one before, but as soon as she saw the purple house, she knew it was home for her. Everything in the house was neat and clean and girly. Most importantly, there were no bolts or chains. Not even a basement.

She'd dropped down on her bed when Adele had shown her around her room. She had a beautiful white iron framed bed with a pretty pink and purple cover and sheets and a big window that let the bright sunshine in. The wall of built-in cupboards filled with clothes and toiletries had left her in awe. She had never owned so many clothes in her life. She couldn't stop the cringe at the memory of him ripping her clothes from her when he had first taken her as his slave. She hadn't owned any clothes at all since.

An animal's soft whimper interrupted Kelly's thoughts. She stood up rubbing her arms, trying to shake free from the hold her past had on her. She walked up the bank a little and followed the noise. When she got to the top, she saw a garbage bag resting next to a large tree trunk. She was pretty sure that hadn't been there when she'd come over earlier, but whatever.

She kept looking around for an animal until she heard the plastic bag move. Kelly ran over to the bag and ripped it open using her nails. She fell back on her butt in shock. Inside the bag there was a dog and four puppies. The adult dog was obviously dead as were two of the puppies. The two live puppies didn't look well; they were all very skinny and they had all been harshly beaten. Kelly froze as she focused on the injuries and really saw them. They looked familiar. Oh crap. He'd found her. She was sure of it. She took off the fleecy jacket she wore and bundled up the two live puppies before she ran as fast as she could back to the house and back to the safety of Adele.

Adele was drinking her coffee and watching out the front window in the direction Kelly had gone walking. Nerves knotted her stomach. It was her first time out alone and Adele wanted to make sure she was okay. She'd given Kelly a house key on a hospital lanyard so Kelly would know she could come and go whenever she wanted, and if she got lost, anyone who saw the hospital name on the lanyard would take her there if Kelly couldn't remember their address. Not that Adele intended to let her out of her sight long enough for her to get lost. She lowered her mug as she noticed a shiny black ute drive past slowly. Strange. When it kept going, she dismissed it as simply someone looking for a specific house number on Wattle Avenue somewhere.

She took another sip of coffee and looked back

toward the river. If Kelly didn't come back soon she was going to have to go find her. Sophie was joining them for a meeting at the school about getting Kelly settled in socially and for some basic testing to work out how much help she was going to need. Adele had a feeling it was going to be a lot, the poor little thing could barely read or write.

Adele just about dropped her mug when she saw Kelly running toward the house. She was sprinting as fast as she could, and holding her jacket bundled in her arms. As she got closer, Adele saw blood on the jacket and on her shirt and her heart went into overdrive. What the hell had happened? She shoved her mug on the table sloshing coffee everywhere on her way out the front door.

"Kelly, *ma chère,* what happened? Are you hurt?"

Adele wrapped her arms around Kelly when she skidded to a stop in front of her. When Adele felt something move against her, she pulled back from the sobbing child and looked down. There were two little white puppies poking their noses out of the jumper.

"He did this. He's found me. Oh, Adele. He's found me!"

Kelly was in a panic. Adele could see it in her eyes that her mind was lost to the emotions and memories that were swirling in her mind.

"Come inside, *ma chère.*"

Glancing up and down the street, she couldn't see anyone, but instinct led her to usher Kelly inside and double-check the door was locked behind them. She grabbed her phone from her pocket and rang Dominic. He answered her on the second ring. She quickly told him what had happened and he was on his way before she ended the call.

While she waited for Dominic to come over, she grabbed some dark towels, a bucket of warm water, and a sponge before heading back to Kelly and the puppies.

"How about we try to clean them up a bit? Then we can take them to the vet once Dominic gets here, okay?"

She spoke calmly; Kelly was still shaking in panic and needed a distraction. Adele didn't want to risk going to the vet without Dominic just in case the bastard that had hurt Kelly and these puppies was lurking around waiting for them.

Dominic was struggling to not shift as he sat in the waiting room at the veterinary clinic. His body was vibrating with rage. Kelly's abuser had tortured a female dog and her four pups then left them out for Kelly to find. It was beyond cruel. It also meant the bastard knew where Kelly was living, and that presented a risk to his mate as well as Kelly. When they finished here, he was going to organize the cats to continue their protection detail. Unfortunately, there were too many other people in the waiting room for him to make the calls. He couldn't risk someone overhearing him. He needed to arrange to have at least one shifter on guard duty each day then he would start spending the nights at their house to make sure they were safe.

He looked up when he heard a door open and saw a frowning Adele usher Kelly out of the examination room where they'd been with the two live pups and the vet, Natalie. Kelly clung to Adele as they made their way over to him. She was hanging on so tightly Adele was having trouble walking.

"How are the pups?"

He kept his voice low and ran a hand gently over Kelly's curls, which had her clutching tighter to Adele.

"Natalie said one isn't looking good but the other has a good chance of surviving. They've got him drinking some formula so that's a good sign. His front right paw has to be set, which they are doing now. He'll have to stay here for a while but maybe when he's better we might be able to keep him. I'm going to ask the agent about it once we know if he's going to survive."

Adele had been rubbing circles on Kelly's back the whole time she talked and the poor kid was starting to relax and loosen her grip. Although, she clearly wasn't listening or paying attention to what was going on around her. Poor little thing must be in shock.

"C'mon, let's get you girls home."

The drive back was a quiet one as all three of them were lost in their thoughts. Dominic pulled into the driveway and headed up the front door with them. Once inside, Adele suggested Kelly might like to go have a shower and she headed off to her room.

"What are we going to do, Dominic?"

"I need to call the others. I'm going to set up a roster of guards for you and Kelly, just like we did at the hospital. Then I'm going to call the detective who saw us about Kelly. Let him know what's happened. We'll go from there. We will catch this guy, Adele."

He pulled her against him and held her tightly. He was terrified of what this bastard was going to do next. Clearly, he was as mad as a cut snake.

"I can't hear water running in the pipes. I better go check on Kelly. I don't like how she's been acting."

"Yeah, can't say I'm happy about her losing her spark either. She was doing so well. I'll step out to make the calls. Last thing Kelly needs is to overhear me talking about it all."

Adele tilted her head back and he leaned down to gently kiss her.

"I'll wait for you here. I noticed how she flinched earlier and I don't want to upset her more," he whispered against her lips before he straightened.

"You know it's not you that scared her, right? She's reverted back to what she knows, and that's to fear men."

"I know, beautiful. I'm not offended, only pissed off that she's suffering again."

His heart ached for that little girl and he hoped they could catch this bastard soon so they could get back to helping her heal physically and mentally.

Taking a deep breath, he headed to the carport as Adele headed back to Kelly's room. He didn't want to be too far away from them while this guy was out there. But there was no point in being in Kelly's face. That would only scare her more.

Chapter Thirteen

Cole had followed his slave and the woman yesterday until they headed back to their house. A disgusting purple monstrosity that only a girl would ever live in. He'd gone home to retrieve his gun and got his workout in while he was there. He'd driven past this morning just in time to see his slave walking across a vacant block opposite the house.

He'd left the bag of dogs out for her to find. He'd then gone and stashed his ute at a public car park up the end of the next street before walking back. He returned in time to see her running across the street and the woman came out to meet her. He'd stayed back, hidden amongst some bushes until another car pulled up. A man got out, went inside for a short time before all three headed out again. Once the car was out of sight, he went around to the vacant block behind the place and pried a panel of the fence free. After slipping through, he leaned the panel back in place so anyone passing by wouldn't notice it was not fixed. He'd gone through the house before settling in the kitchen. He was certain they would be gone for a while with those dogs so he made himself a coffee and a sandwich before sitting down.

He'd just finished washing up and putting away his dishes—damn OCD could be a pain in the ass, especially when he didn't get regular workouts—when he'd heard a car pull up the drive. He'd quickly made his way down the hall to his slave's room where he then stood against the wall by the door and waited. He winced when he heard three car doors slam before the front door opened. The deep sound of a male's voice had him silently cursing.

The man that had come to pick them up had come in with them. That bloke was one big bastard, no way Cole could take him on and the two girls. He was trying to form a new plan when his slave came through the door. Alone.

Her head bent down, she was not paying attention. Good. His trick with the dogs had worked in throwing her off kilter. He snapped forward, quickly wrapping a hand over her mouth and an arm around her waist.

He lent forward to whisper in her ear, "Hello, slave. I've told you how pointless it is to hide from me. Did you forget?"

As soon as he'd started speaking, she'd gone batshit crazy fighting against him. She'd gained some strength over the last weeks. He grinned; she was going to be so much more fun to play with now. Despite her efforts, he kept her in a firm grip. There was no way he would make it out until at least that man left, so he just held her tight against his body while he breathed her scent in and listened for the front door.

He could hear snippets of the conversation through the wall and had heard the man say he'd make phone calls from outside while the woman came back here. Once he heard the front door close, he smiled. This was going to be fun. Now, he just needed to get the two girls quietly out the back door with him before that big bloke finished the phone calls, and he'd be home free with his prizes.

"I'm going to release your mouth now, slave. You scream and I'll shoot you, then I'll take the woman you seem to like so much as my slave. Understand? Nod if you do." He growled out his words right into her ear.

He loved how she stiffened at his threat. He waited for her to nod, which she did right as he heard footsteps come down the hallway toward them. He released her mouth and grabbed his pistol out of the back of his pants. He held it against the side of her temple and waited for the door in front of him to open.

The door swung open slowly as he heard the woman begin to speak.

"Kelly, are you okay in here?"

Well, there you go. Her name is Kelly. Not that it mattered now. She would never escape him again. Or need her name.

"Oh, Kelly's just fine. For now," he said in a low voice.

She cursed and froze to the spot when she spotted his pistol against his slave's head.

"We're going to take a little drive, the three of us. Me

and Kelly here have some catching up to do. Don't we, slave?"

He moved his arm from her waist and took hold of a fistful of her hair. He looked the woman over from head to toe. She was a pretty thing, built how he liked a woman to be.

"And I think I might just save you for later. Now, here's what's going to happen. We're going to move real slow and easy down the hall and out the back door. We're going to go through the back fence, then we're going for a car ride. You're driving. Me and my slave here will sit in the back. If you so much as twitch in the wrong direction, she gets a bullet. Do we understand each other?"

He watched as the woman slowly nodded before she turned to go back out the hallway to follow his instructions. Such a good girl, maybe he should keep her too. He did like obedient slaves. He followed along behind with his slave firmly in his grasp.

Adele had been stunned when she'd walked into Kelly's room and found her being held at gunpoint. Now she was driving a stolen car with the bastard and Kelly sitting in the back seat. Her mind was moving from stunned to flat out pissed. How dare this bastard break into their home and lie in wait for them! She took a deep breath; she needed to calm down and think of something. He was obviously taking them somewhere and no doubt it would be secluded. Kelly hadn't spoken much about where he'd held her, just that it was in Strahan and that he'd killed her mother, before nearly doing the same to her. Adele vowed to herself that she would not allow that to happen. She'd promised Kelly she would be safe. This bastard was making her break her promise. That just wasn't going to fly with her, not at all.

She needed to let Dominic know what was going on. No doubt he'd found them missing by now and was looking for them already. He was so calm and capable. She was certain he'd be able to help them get out of this.

As quietly as she could, she slipped her phone out of her pocket. Careful not to move her head, she put the phone on silent. Sweat began to bead on her forehead, she was so worried he would catch her reaching out. If he took her phone, she had no way of contacting anyone. She said a quick prayer of thanks she had put Dominic's number into her speed dial. In quick succession, she dialed, muted the call, and put it on speaker. She slipped it into the front pocket of her hoodie and hoped the thin fleecy material wouldn't muffle their voices too much and that Dominic would work out what was going on.

She nervously checked the mirror to see if he had caught her. Phew, he was still focused on Kelly, talking in low tones to her. Kelly began sobbing at whatever it was he said and he looked up and caught her eye in the mirror. She shot daggers at him with her gaze, and the bastard had the nerve to laugh at her for it.

"Where to now?"

She had to get him talking, had to somehow let Dominic know where they were heading. He sat forward and she could feel his warm breath on her ear; she couldn't fully suppress the shudder of repulsion that ran though her. He chuckled at her again, a horrible evil sound.

"Just keep heading south, toward Strahan. When we get closer I'll give you more directions."

He sat back and began murmuring to Kelly again. She was kind of glad she couldn't make out what he was saying, but her heart was breaking for Kelly as she heard her continued sobs.

After about forty-five minutes of driving, he sat forward again and directed her to pull into the driveway of a nothing-special brick house on the outskirts of town. As she killed the engine, she glanced at the gumleaf key-chain. Joys of living in small town Tasmania; a lot of people left their keys in their cars. The owner of this one left it in the damn ignition so it hadn't been real hard for them to steal it.

Taking in a deep breath, she looked around the area. If she'd been on her own, she could probably make a run for the trees behind the house. She glanced back to Kelly in the mirror. She didn't want to leave her behind, but if he got both of them inside, she wouldn't be any help to her. If she could get away, she could come back and save Kelly.

"Now, this is what is going to happen. You are going to slowly get out of the car. Then you are going to open my door. Then we're all going to go inside that house. Don't even think of running. I will shoot you. Now move it."

Adele's emotions were going nuts inside her head. She was angry, scared, nervous, and hopeful that Dominic would get here in time to save them. She inched out of the car slowly and reached back to open the rear door as he'd requested. She caught Kelly's eyes—she was pleading her to run. It was written clear as day in her big grey eyes, along with a heavy dose of fear and sorrow.

She opened the door, keeping her hand on the handle. He began to inch his way out, with one hand still gripping the gun aimed at her and the other dragging Kelly by her hair after him. It was a slow process. When he started to lift himself out, his gun arm dropped down and his head was in the perfect position. Before she could fully think it through, she shoved the door hard and fast with both hands before she spun around and ran like hell toward the trees behind the house. She could hear him curse a blue streak behind her as she put distance between them.

She didn't know how far she would get before he caught her so she took out her phone while she ran. She needed to check if Dominic was listening. She unmuted the call and took it off speaker.

"Please, please be there, Dominic."

"Adele? Can you hear me? I'm right here, beautiful."
Damn, his deep voice had never sounded so good.

"Dominic, help. He's got us—"

A loud bang cut her off and she felt pain flare
through her hip. She stumbled but regrouped quickly
and made it to the tree line. She paused behind a thick
tree trunk to look at her side and put the phone back to
her ear.

"...answer me damn it! Adele? What the hell is going
on?" Dominic's voice was frantic now.

"I'm okay. He shot me. The bastard shot me! It's just
a graze, over my right hip. I'm okay."

She ignored the pain and started walking through the
trees to get farther from the house. No matter what, she
had to stay focused; she had to get back and save Kelly.

"Do you know where you are? Where's Kelly?"

"He's brought us to the outskirts of Strahan. The
street name was Mountain View Lane. It's a small dirt
road. Third house on the right. He was waiting in her
room, Dominic. He made me drive. I got away. But he's
still got her. I can't hear him coming for me. I think he's
taken her inside the house. I have to go back. I promised
I'd keep her safe, Dominic. I have to go get her out."

"I know you promised, love. You're doing real well,
ringing me like you did was brilliant. But you can't go
back in there. It won't help her, he'll just get you too.
We are already on the road coming to get you both.
Please just stay hidden and wait for us to help you get
her out. Can you do that for me, Adele?"

She knew he was right. Her mind was a mess of thoughts that just wouldn't be logical.

"Please hurry, Dominic. I'll try to wait."

"How about you tell me what he looks like? Anything distinctive?"

She pictured him in her mind and gave Dominic the best description she could.

"Umm, he's a little taller than me, so about five foot five. He has really short hair, like he cuts it himself with clippers, but I could still tell it was ginger. His eyes, they're brown and you can see the evil in them, Dominic. He radiates it."

She couldn't stop the shudder that ran through her as she remembered his dead evil eyes.

"Bloody hell, that sounds like one of the blokes that got fired from the docks after the fire a few weeks back. What was his name?" Adele could hear voices in the background as Dominic was obviously in a car with the others. "Cole Jones. That's the bastard's name, and he's got a place on the outskirts of Strahan. Damn, with what Alex told us, we should have put this together sooner, the timing all makes—"

"Umph."

Adele cursed as pain radiated up her leg from her now injured ankle as she landed on all fours and dropped her phone. She snatched it up and looked down to see what she had tripped over as she spoke.

"Sorry, Dominic, I tripped...over a bloody wire!"

She looked around in a panic, expecting a gunshot or an arrow or something to come flying at her. Yes, she watched way too much TV.

"You tripped on a what? Are you okay? What happened?" Dominic fired questions at her over the phone.

"Yeah, a trip wire, but nothing happened. I'm fine, my ankle's not real pleased with me though."

She reached down to rub at her ankle before getting back on her feet and limping on.

"If nothing happened, the bastard must have it linked to sensors. Keep your eyes open, love, he'll probably be coming for you now he knows where you are. Put your phone back how you had it before and try to stay as quiet. We're coming as fast as we can but are still about twenty minutes away. But we *are* coming for you Adele, for you and Kelly. Just hang on. I love you, beautiful."

The sincerity in his voice had her eyes blurring with tears. Oh, how she loved that man. She hoped like hell she would get through this so she could show him. It seemed so cruel she finally found some happiness and was going to lose it before it really even began.

"Please hurry, Dominic, I can hear him coming. Oh shit. I love you too, so much."

Adele quickly sorted her phone out and put it back in her pocket. Just as she started moving forward again, she felt his hot heavy hand on her shoulder. As she spun with the force of him jerking her arm, she remembered what Kit had begun showing her.

Kit had told her that medics could find themselves in the thick of things, and she should know at least a few moves so she could help herself if the need arose. She sent up a quick thanks for Kit's foresight as she raised her fist so she could use the momentum of her spinning to crack him a beauty in the jaw. As soon as she made contact, her hand felt like it was on fire. Damn, that hurt! Kit failed to mention how much it hurt to punch someone in the face.

He released her to grab his jaw and curse. She didn't waste time; she took off. She weaved between trees as best she could, making sure to watch the ground this time. She didn't need any more tripping interrupting her escape. She did her best to move silently but her aching ankle and hip slowed her down and made moving difficult. She must have been running for a good ten minutes before he caught her again. This time he grabbed her ponytail and pulled her into his body hard and fast. She stomped her foot, aiming for his, but missed. Damn it. That always worked in the movies!

She raised her elbow forward and swung it back into his ribs. Yes! Contact! He released the hand in her hair and lowered his arm to protect his now—hopefully—sore ribs. His other arm was around her waist. She started to turn to get out of his hold.

"Bloody hell, bitch, you'll pay for all that."

She'd just moved from beyond his arm's reach when she felt pain radiate through her skull as her head snapped back. The bastard had backhanded her! She hadn't even seen his hand before the pain kicked in, knocking her to the ground. She panted through the throbbing in her face. With her ever increasing count of hurting body parts, she had no chance of further fighting him off.

After a minute, he dragged her back to the house. Her head spinning from the blow, and her hand, ankle, and hip throbbing she couldn't do anything other than stumble along behind him.

He dragged her through the house and down a flight of stairs. As they went through the door leading down she said, "Basement," as clearly as she could, hoping like hell Dominic could still hear her and he wasn't far away. She had a sinking feeling she wasn't destined to be coming back up these stairs alive.

"Shut up, bitch. Fuck, I think you stuffed my jaw again. It'd only just stopped hurting. Damn it." Good. She hoped it was hurting like a bitch. Her hand certainly was.

"Only fair since you shot me." She bit out before she really thought about how dumb it was to backchat a psycho.

He tightened his grip on her arm, digging his fingers painfully into her flesh as he dragged her down the rest of the stairs. Yeah, that was definitely going to leave a mark.

As he threw her forward into a room, she froze as her brain momentarily shut down. Kelly was bound with her hands above her head hanging from a hook that was embedded high on a wall. Her head hung down but the tears dropping to the floor were easy to see. The most disturbing thing was all the red around her. The walls and floor were heavily stained with old blood. Adele's vision blurred as she thought about how much of that red was Kelly's.

She snapped to attention as she realized that Cole had turned his back on her to grab some rope from a nearby table. He really wasn't the brightest bulb in the box. She steadied herself and landed a solid kick to the side of his knee. When she heard the satisfying crack, she spun and ran for the door and stairs. She was about half a dozen steps up when he grabbed her ankle and pulled. All the air in her lungs was forced out of her as she landed with a thud on the stairs. Thankfully, she'd gotten her hands up so they took most of the impact rather than her face. Still, the pain that shot up her arms from the impact had her brain short-circuiting. She vaguely felt him drag her back down the steps. Once he had her on the floor of the basement hall, he delivered another wicked backhand that really messed with her brain function.

"Try anything else and I *will* start putting bullet holes in you, bitch," he sputtered.

He bound her hands together and dragged her back into the room. He lifted her up and hung her bound hands from a hook in the ceiling, not far from Kelly.

As Adele teetered between being unconscious and conscious, she focused on Cole as he laid out various weapons. Bloody hell, was that a metal rod? A whip? She had seen Kelly's injuries, but she hadn't really thought about what would have been used to cause them. The reality of what he was going to do soon helped her get her brain firing up again. He laid out a couple of knives next, checked his gun, and tucked it into the back of his jeans.

"Now, slave. Like I told you in the car, you did not have permission to leave me, yet you did. You. Are. Mine. Forever. Now, before we start on your punishment, there's one thing I need to do."

He reached over the table and Adele heard the rattling of a chain. He turned around to reveal a bloodstained thick brown leather collar complete with padlock and chain attached. She followed the chain and it appeared to go out the doorway and up the stairs. As he started toward Kelly with the collar, Kelly's sobbing grew louder and she pulled at her hands but there was no way for her to escape. She'd not been tied up with rope like Adele, but was bound in locked leather cuffs. He snapped the collar around her neck and locked the padlock.

"There. Now that's never coming off again. Not even down here. You will never escape me ever again, slave."

As he went back to the table, he pulled his shirt over his head. He carefully selected a knife from the table before he headed back toward Kelly. Adele struggled to get free to help her. She screamed as loud as she could for him to get away from her. Tears burned her eyes as she pulled on the ropes bounding her hands. She didn't care about the pain that ripped down her arms with renewed fire or that her fingers had gone numb. She was not going to let him hurt her! She'd promised, dammit! She looked at Kelly as he approached her with the knife. The look on her face broke her heart. There were no more tears streaming down her face and her eyes were glazed over like she'd left herself. Or like this was an everyday occurrence and nothing to get worked up over. Just something that she needed to block out to survive. Her rage took over as she thought about the abuse Kelly must have suffered to be reacting so calmly to this situation. She pulled harder on her hands and finally felt the ropes loosen.

"Hmm, keep screaming, bitch. It makes a lovely soundtrack and soon we'll be adding to them, won't we, slave?"

Kelly's monotone response of "Yes, sir" made Adele's vision turn red.

Where the hell was Dominic and the boys?

Dominic was literally vibrating. Being stuck sitting in a car—in human form—having to listen to his mate being beaten was not something he was dealing with very well. They pulled into the drive behind an old Hyundai Excel. Jake turned the engine off then faced his son.

"Dominic. Look at me. And listen up. You need to find your calm, son. You go running in there with no plan, you'll all get shot."

"I know, Dad. You heard what he's done to her. You hearing her screams? I can't sit here...I have to get in there."

He jumped from the car and bolted toward the house.

"Dominic, hold up! We go in together, just like always."

Conner's voice managed to break through the anger haze filling his mind and he stopped a moment to let his brother catch up. When Conner got to him, he grabbed his head between his hands and rested his forehead against his.

"Deep breath, Dom. We will get them out. Together."

Conner released him as Kit came running up behind them.

"I'll get the door, boys, no need kicking it in and announcing our arrival, now is there?"

Within seconds, Kit had the door unlocked and all three silently entered the house. Dominic felt his heart stop and his knees began to buckle as they entered the house and Adele's rage-filled screams rung out from a doorway leading down some stairs. Silently, Conner caught him and stood him back up, before he nudged him with his shoulder and they headed toward the stairs together. Kit had moved off to search the house. She mouthed the word "empty" as they all reached the stairwell.

With his heart beating double time, Dominic led the way, with Conner and Kit right behind him. Within seconds, they were at the bottom of the stairs in a dark hallway. Dominic pressed up against the wall next to the door for a moment and listened to the movements inside the room to get a position on where everyone was. Using hand signals, he let Conner and Kit know where they were. He pointed at Kit and mouthed "Adele & Kelly." He looked to Conner and nodded. No words were needed; they would take out the bastard then help Kit get the girls out. Dominic held three fingers up, counting down.

Three.

Two.

One.

He made a fist then spun and bolted into the room. He roared as he changed into his leopard. The sight of Cole taking a knife to Kelly's shirt was more than he could stand. Add to that the sight of his blood-covered barely conscious mate and there was no chance of him holding back. At the sound of his roar, Cole spun around.

"What the fuck?"

He was quick to pull out his pistol but not quick enough. Dominic had leapt into the air, aiming his sharp teeth for the bastard's throat by the time he got his shot off. Dominic felt pain and fire rip through his hind leg, but it didn't distract him from his goal. He landed with his front paws on Cole's shoulders, knocking him to the ground. He didn't waste a moment, sinking his teeth into the soft flesh of his throat and ripping it out with a triumphant growl. Once he heard Cole's heart cease beating, he looked up around the room. He winced as he caught the horrified look on Adele's face. Then he locked his gaze onto hers and he couldn't fight the blackness that took over his vision.

Seconds after Adele had wondered where Dominic was, he appeared in the doorway like an avenging angel. Her heart lurched at the sight of him barreling into the room. Her body slumped when Conner and Kit followed him in. Rescue had arrived in the form of three very fierce-looking firefighters. The relief of imminent rescue evaporated as quickly as it had begun when she heard a deafening roar vibrate the entire room, rattling the tools on the table. She glanced around to see what had made the noise and saw what appeared to be a bubble of blue electric energy surrounding Dominic. Moments later, Dominic was gone and a snow leopard appeared. Whoa, hang on a minute. Holding her breath, she carefully catalogued the large cat's spots and features against her memory. Bloody hell, it was her *chaton* standing where Dominic had been just moments ago. Sucking in air to her burning lungs didn't help her spinning mind and she began to see spots as she attempted to process what she was happening.

Dominic was a snow leopard.

Her snow leopard.

Her *chaton* that had been visiting her dreams for the last nearly five years.

But hang on, shape-shifters were just legend, weren't they?

Maybe she was unconscious and dreaming that her *chaton* was here charging in to save the day. Yeah, that had to be it. She could so see herself having this dream. Suddenly feeling calmer that this must all be her imagination, she raised her gaze and jerked back in shock. Kit was right in front of her. Her face was a mask of seriousness, fury, and purpose. Adele stared at her friend, noticing the glint of pain in her eyes. The muscles of her neck and shoulders looked hard and strained as she was obviously clenching them. She took a knife from the holster on her belt and reached up to cut the ropes around her hands, freeing them from the ceiling hook. Fresh pain fired through her hands and fingers. She gasped out in pain as Kit carefully lowered her arms. As soon as they were all the way down and her blood flowed back to her previously numb fingers, agony began to overwhelm her. It was more than she could stand and she crumpled to the floor as her limbs refused to function anymore. Kit was there the whole way, wrapping her in her warm embrace, anchoring her in the mist of the chaos that had taken over her mind.

"Shh, Adele. You're safe now. I've got you."

Adele started to think that maybe this wasn't a dream after all. Surely, she wouldn't dream up this amount of pain.

A loud crack of a gun going off cleared her head of fog and brought her eyes up to look over Kit's shoulder.

Her *chaton* latched on to Cole's throat and tore it free with a growl. Its animistic brutality was so far outside her realm of normal that her mind couldn't register it.

Then all she saw was red.

His hind leg and a rapidly growing pool around his rear paw.

So red.

Too much red.

He was losing a serious amount of blood. Her eyes flicked up as she felt his gaze on her. They held contact briefly before he collapsed and lay in a heap of black-and-white fur, out cold on the cold concrete floor. Then as if they were linked, she felt her eyelids droop, the light dim, and she joined him in the darkness that pulled at her.

Jake paced the front yard. Even with him blocking, he could feel the pain, sorrow, and fury flow from the open front door of the house, but he didn't know who was putting out what. The waves of emotion crashed against him, making it hard for him to breathe. This is why he got sick at jobs that involved injuries. He was strongly empathetic and the intense emotions of the gravely injured made him physically ill. When he knew that not only were his two sons in the mix, but two women and a child that he held very dear too, it was even harder to bare.

Especially when he knew Adele had to be injured. His lips quirked a little as he thought about the fight they'd heard between Adele and Cole. She'd knocked him a few beauties by the sound of it. Good on her. He hoped they'd hurt like hell; it was the least he deserved.

How could any man raise a hand against a female— adult or child? That bastard needed to be taken out. Jake might look human most of the time but his heart was that of an animal and at the moment the animal inside him was begging to be the one to deliver the justice of taking the bastard out.

His radio squawked, grabbing his attention. He snatched it off his belt.

"Rosebery P1 here. Please repeat."

Conner's voice came over the line sounding serious and strained.

"Rosebery P2. Come in, Rosebery P1."

"I'm here, Conner. Was that a gun going off earlier? What the hell is going on down there?"

He didn't have the patience to worry about radio protocol, nor could he keep his emotions from his voice. He noticed as he spoke, the others had gathered around him to listen in. All the cats that were on duty were here. The others were on their way. Including Clint and Sophie in the ambulance. If a shifter got injured, Clint was the only one who knew enough about them to be able to help.

He'd also rung Alex on his private mobile in the car. Detective Alex Ross often rung Jake for his opinion on cases, and for assistance in finding people that were proving hard to catch. Over the last few years, they'd had a couple conversations about a serial rapist and murderer in the Strahan area. As future Alpha, Jake had told Dominic about the case. His son may have seen something he didn't that would be helpful. When Adele had explained what her attacker had looked like, and Dominic had remembered the link to the docks, Jake had rung Alex. They'd previously discussed the profiler's report that stated he worked near or on the water. Naturally, Alex had wanted them to back off and let him bring the police in, but Jake had told him straight out that was not going to happen. The police would take longer than they would to arrive at the scene, and with Dominic's mate being held, there was no way he'd sit back and allow someone else to take over. Even the police.

Thankfully Alex knew about their kind and had reluctantly agreed to stay on the sidelines. He was however waiting at the station for their call to come take Cole in. Jake didn't think that would be happening. No way would Dominic leave that bastard alive if he'd seriously injured Adele or Kelly. He could tell that already Dominic had bonded with the young girl. She was as much his as a biological daughter would be. But he hadn't said that to Alex. He knew the man wouldn't be able to sit by if he'd known Dominic was likely to commit murder—no matter how justified.

Breaking his thoughts, Conner's voice rang out loud and clear.

"We need medics, Dad. Two, one."

242

Long ago, they'd created a code for radio chat. Conner's "two, one" meant two humans, one shifter. They had to be careful over the airwaves to not give themselves away.

"Who?" Jake heard the fury in his own voice as he growled into the radio, and he didn't care. He was furious.

"Dominic. Gun wound, right leg. He's out cold from blood loss. I'm tying it up now to try to stop the flow."

"And the girls?"

He was almost afraid of the answer, but he had to ask. Something bad had to have gone down for Dominic to have shifted and lose focus enough to get shot.

"Adele is banged up pretty bad, Dad. She passed out soon after Dominic did. Kelly seems to be physically okay, but her eyes are glazed over and she's not responding to anything. She didn't even flinch when the gun went off. Kit's just unlocking her collar and cuffs now and she's not even twitching."

Conner's voice was filled with pain and anguish, which cut Jake straight through the heart. Then his actual words registered.

"Kit's unlocking her what? Where is the bastard?" He all but growled into the radio. He'd collared her? Like she was a damn pet?

"D T."

D: Dead, T: Throat.

Good, Dominic had ripped his throat out and killed him. Alex was going to hate him when it came time to explain to the medical examiner about cause of death, but it was an appropriate reward for the bastard.

"A fitting end. Ambulances are on their way. ETA five minutes." He looked around him, pegging Jordan and Joel with a hard stare. "The twins are coming down to get Dominic out of there. You and Kit bring the girls up. Over and out."

He put the radio back on his belt as the twins jogged through the door to go get their Leap brother.

"Right. We need the stretchers and all our first aid gear. And blankets, we're going to need blankets, " Jake's voice was strong as he fell into captain mode.

He headed to the back of the work SUV that he came in with Dominic, Conner, and Kit to grab out the first aid stuff and blankets. Just as he and the others laid down all their supplies, he heard movement from inside. He looked up in time to see the twins carry Dominic outside. His son's one hundred and twenty kilo leopard form hung loosely in their grip, his tongue lolling out the side of his mouth. The thing that had Jake dropping to his knees was the sight of the blood-soaked shirt tied firmly around his son's hind leg. Blood slowly dripped from the bottom of his paw as the twins lay him down on a blanket that Nick had set out. Nick already had the first aid kit open and was grabbing out gauze and bandages to apply pressure to the wound as they heard the ambulance siren get closer.

He felt a firm grip under his elbow and Xander spoke softly in his ear as he helped him to his feet.

"All hands on deck, boss. You're needed. Push it aside to deal with later, just push it aside. I know you can do that, for them, you can do it."

Jake turned to look at Xander.

"When this is over, I need you to bring a team back and burn this place down. We need to cover up the way that bastard died. Then I'll call Alex in."

"Was already planning on it, boss," Xander replied calmly.

A noise from the house brought Jake's gaze back in that direction and he froze anew as he watched Conner come into view with Adele cradled against his bare chest. Oh hell no. He took in her injuries as he looked her over from head to toe. Her face was swollen, a bruise already forming on her cheek. Her bottom lip was split and a dribble of blood had dried down her chin. Her arms were by far the worst; the rope burns around her wrists had cut through her skin and blood was seeping down her arms and he could see it slowly dripping from her elbow and streaking down Conner's pants. One hand looked red and swollen too. There was a large slice through her shirt and pants over her hip; he could see the weeping wound beneath. She had short ankle socks on with her sneakers so he could also see the bright red line where the trip wire had cut into her ankle, along with the swelling around where she'd probably sprained it.

Jake took a couple of deep breaths and did his best to push past all the pain and emotions that were currently bombarding him—his own and the ones from everyone else here. He built a wall in his mind and shoved it all behind it, refusing to allow any of it to affect him today. As Conner laid her out on another blanket, Jake opened his first aid kit to grab out what he needed. He gently took one of Adele's arms and laid it out flat so he could begin cleaning and bandaging her wounds. All the while praying hard that his son's mate would survive her injuries.

He glanced up as Kit walked through the door carrying Kelly. Damn, Conner was right. The poor girl wasn't with them anymore. He concentrated briefly on her emotions but couldn't get a read at all—and didn't that just say it all? It was going to be a long road back for that young girl. As he turned his attention back to Adele's injured wrist, he heard the ambulance pull up and footsteps racing across the gravel toward them.

Chapter Fourteen

Adele resurfaced to reality in a rush. One minute she was floating peacefully in the pitch-black cocoon, which held her safely and free from pain, the next she was blinded by the bright sunshine and her body felt like it was on fire. The level of pain rolling through her body overwhelmed her and held her paralyzed as she attempted to push past it, to breathe through it. She decided that unconsciousness definitely had its benefits. She squeezed her eyes closed and took some deep breaths. Starting at her feet she began to take a mental catalogue of her injuries; as she did, her mind flashed back to how she earned each wound.

Her right ankle ached and a strip across the front stung: thank you, trip wire.

Her legs felt okay, no pain, just a bit achy.

She could feel a low burn radiating from her left hip: thank you, gunshot. She hoped the burning sensation was it healing and not an infection taking root; that was all she needed.

Her abdomen and chest felt fine.

Her shoulders were stiff and achy, must be from all the thrashing about she did trying to get to Kelly.

She tried to move her fingers and couldn't. Both arms hurt something fierce. Pain was pulsing from both wrists up her arms: thank you, slamming into the stairs.

Her right hand throbbed in time with her heartbeat: punching him in the face. She smiled a little at that memory; damn, it had felt good to get a shot in.

As she smiled, she felt pain over her cheek and it felt swollen: thank you, backhand number one.

Her split lip was also hurting: thank you, backhand number two.

Her head was pounding and her brain felt a little foggy. It probably didn't really appreciate being rattled around so much.

She reopened her eyes and squinted through the bright sunlight down at her body that simply refused to follow any command she tried to give it. Her eyes zoned in on her arms and stayed there. Her right was encased in a hot-pink fiber-glass cast from just below her fingertips to halfway up her forearm, the left had a splint and bandages from her elbow all the way down. No bloody wonder she couldn't get them to move and they hurt so much. She idly wondered how many bones she'd actually broken...

A noise to her left shifted her attention in that direction. Kit was sitting there watching her carefully, almost clinically, like she wasn't sure if she'd be welcomed or kicked out. Adele tried to talk but her mouth was so dry, nothing came out. Kit was on it in a heartbeat, jumping up and bringing a cup with a straw in it to her mouth.

"Small sips, doll, that's it."

Her friend's soft voice was soothing and helped her focus.

"How long?" she whispered hoarsely.

She wanted to say so much more but couldn't get her dry throat to cooperate. Hopefully Kit would work out what she meant.

"Today's your fifth day in the hospital. Do you remember what happened? How you got here?"

Whoa, she'd been out for nearly five whole days? Damn. Did she remember? She didn't think she would ever forget anything about that day, however there were parts that were a bit hazy.

"I remember. Kelly? She okay?"

Her voice still hoarse, she pleaded with her eyes, hoping Kit would continue to understand what she needed.

"Kelly's still here too. She's not good, Adele. She's gone deep into shock. It's like she's disconnected her mind. They have her on a drip to keep her fluids up and they've been using massage to help with the circulation in her muscles. I think Clint is hoping that you can reach her. If you can't, it's not looking good for her. She'll have to be institutionalized. Poor baby. We're all hoping like hell she snaps out of it. Sophie's been spending as much time with her as she can. She does seem to relax a little when Sophie's there."

Adele briefly flashed back to the basement, to the

moment Cole had snapped shut the lock on Kelly's collar. It had been that moment her eyes had glazed over, her tears had stopped falling, her spirit broken and stomped into the ground. That poor girl.

As her mind ran over what happened next that day, she suddenly understood Kit's timid approach to her when she first awoke. She cocked an eyebrow as she stared hard into Kit's face. The water had helped her throat and now she could say all she wanted to and she wanted some damn answers.

"You knew, didn't you? You weren't shocked when Dominic turned into a-a leopard," she finished in a rush.

She was still having trouble processing what she'd seen in that basement.

"Umm, yeah, Adele, I knew. I know you have lots of questions, and I'll answer everything I can. Just, please, don't write him off because he didn't tell you. You need to know that he wanted to, he'd planned to tell you on your picnic but then Kelly stumbled in and he just couldn't find the right time after that."

"How do you know?"

Adele had a really good feeling she knew what the answer was going to be, but she needed to hear it for it to be real.

"I'm pretty sure you've already worked that one out, Adele. I'm a shifter like Dominic."

"Just how many of you are there?"

Adele felt like nothing in her life was quite as it seemed on the surface. She wondered what other legends were true. Maybe there were vampires working the mine and faeries running the school.

"There are thousands of us around the world. Here in Rosebery, it's pretty much the entire fire crew plus a few others and their families, of course."

Adele stayed silent as she digested what Kit had told her so far, until a scary thought had her pegging Kit with a hard stare again.

"How are you created? Dominic wasn't going to-to turn me somehow, was he?"

She could hear the edge of hysteria in her own voice but didn't care. She needed to know this. She watched Kit's eyes as they briefly widened in surprise.

"Calm down. It's nothing like that, Adele. You have to be born with the right DNA to be able to shift; it's passed through genetics. I'll leave the story of our original creation for Dominic to tell you some other time."

Speaking of Dominic, why wasn't he here? How badly had he been hurt rescuing them?

"Where is Dominic, Kit? He wasn't badly hurt, was he? Why isn't he here?"

She was getting worked up again, and her head was pounding. She took a deep breath or two, trying to calm down before her head exploded.

"Dominic's not far, and he was hurt but he's going to be just fine. It's going to take more than a bullet to stop him. He's off getting his stitches out and should be back any minute now. You should know, he hasn't left you since they took care of his wound. He's going to be pissed you woke up without him here. Clint had to just about drag his tail out of here so he could take the stitches out."

Just as Kit finished speaking, Adele felt a tingle trip up her spine and she looked up at the empty doorway in time to see Dominic's large muscular frame fill the space. The sight of his beautiful face with his ink-black hair all messy and the thick stubble growth over his jaw was enough to make her heart swell and ache. She might not understand how he could be a shifter, might be pissed that he hadn't told her about it all earlier, but her heart, it simply didn't care. She loved him.

Dominic slowly crept into the room, with a slight limp. He probably should have a crutch until his wound healed. No doubt he was too macho to accept it. Just like Kit, the look on his face said he wasn't sure what his welcome would be from her. Her mouth opened and the words poured out before she could even think to stop them.

"It's been you all these years, hasn't it? You are my *chaton*."

She held his gaze as she waited for his response. He raised his hand to rub the back of his neck.

"Yeah, it's been me." He winced, as if he knew she was going to be pissed.

"How? Why? I dreamt of you for four years before I ever met you!"

Her voice rose as her mind tried to wrap around

everything that was being loaded on it—and it all made the pounding pick up intensity again.

Dominic started to creep closer to her bedside, like he wasn't sure how close she'd allow him. She watched him as he slowly, smoothly, grabbed a chair and sat down next to the bed near her head. She watched as he raised his hand to her face, then hesitated a moment, hovering his hand over her uninjured cheek. Not quite touching but close enough she could feel his heat. She couldn't resist the need for contact and turned her head into his palm and his comforting heat. As she did, she heard him release his breath and sigh as he caressed her cheek. His touch soothed and anchored her. As her breathing evened out and the pounding in her head eased off, he began to talk to her in his deep smooth voice that she loved so much.

"I first dreamt of you on your twenty-first birthday. Then, when your mum got sick, your pain reached out to me. I tried to come to you as man in your dreams, but you wouldn't see me, so I went as a leopard. Your pain was mine, love, I had to try and help you. I didn't know where you were so I had to go into your dreams to help you."

He stopped, taking a deep breath as he lowered his gaze to her hand.

"But why? Why did you dream of me in the first place? And why couldn't I keep away from you after we did meet?"

This whole thing was confusing her, none of it made

sense.

"The simple answer is because we're mates. We were made for each other, destined to be together."

His voice was quiet, like he knew she'd struggle with the information. And she was most definitely struggling. He continued on before she had a chance to respond.

"When a male shifter's mate turns twenty-one, he begins to dream of her. Seeing glimpses of her face and hair; as time goes on, he will see more of her. Eventually, if he still hasn't met her, he will see places and things she holds dear, which will enable him to go in search of her. But I've heard that takes many years before it will happen."

"Predestined mate, huh? So tell me, Dominic. Do you really even like me? Or is it just this mating thing that is forcing your hand and making you seek me out?"

Adele was starting to get angry. She did not like the idea that he would be with her, just putting up with her, because he thought he had to. She wanted a man who loved her for her, who *wanted* to be with her.

"I mustn't have explained it right. Please don't be angry, beautiful. Let me try again. Being destined mates means that we are, quite literally, made for each other. Our personalities are designed to complement each other, our bodies to fit together. We are perfect for each other in every way *because* we are mates."

Dominic shuffled his chair closer and leaned in to kiss her lightly on the tip of her nose before laying his head down next to hers so their foreheads touched.

"Adele, I. Love. You. How could I not? You are beautiful both inside and out. You have a heart as big as a mountain. You show compassion and empathy to everyone you meet and you protect your own more fiercely and completely than anyone I've ever known. Just look at your current injuries. You could have just kept running away and saved yourself or you could have let him take Kelly in the first place. But you didn't. You went too, you stayed close when you got away. You fought hard, damn hard to get to her and save her. A child who was a stranger to you mere months ago. I admire and respect you so much, Adele."

He took a deep breath before he stroked her cheek, stared into her eyes, and continued.

"Don't you understand? You complete me, Adele. When I'm with you, I feel whole. When I found out that bastard had you, that I might not make it to you in time, my heart stopped and my soul cried out in agony. You are as vital to me as air, my sweet Adele. Marry me, and I promise I'll spend the rest of my life showing you just how much I love you."

It took a full minute for Adele to comprehend what Dominic was saying. No one had ever said things like that to her before and she was having trouble working out what to do...then his final sentence sunk in. He wanted to marry her?

"Did you just ask me...to marry you, Dominic?"

"Yes, Adele, I did. Will you? Will you say yes? Be my mate, my wife?"

She stared into Dominic's eyes as she thought about his proposal. There was a small part of her still unsure about the whole shifter aspect but deep down she knew what her answer was. She loved him with all her heart and he completed her just like she did him.

"I love you, Dominic. When I was being dragged down those stairs, when I thought I wasn't ever going to come back up, it was you that filled my thoughts. The idea that I would never see you or be held by you again made my heart bleed for the loss. Then when you came charging through that door to rescue us, I knew for certain that you would be the only man I would ever love. So, yes, I will marry you, Dominic."

He gave her the biggest smile she'd ever seen and with tears in his eyes, he leaned forward and kissed her gently so as to not hurt her split lip. He was such a kind man.

Dominic knew he was grinning like a fool as he and Kit walked into the jewelry shop, but he didn't care what anyone thought. Adele had said yes. He was going to marry his mate. Kit's laughter snapped him out of his trance.

"Sorry, what was that?" He focused on the smiling sales assistant in front of him.

"Can I help you, sir?" the young lady asked, apparently for the second time.

"Ah, yeah, you can. I need an engagement ring."

"Do you have any ideas about what you're looking

for?"

In answer, he just looked blankly at the assistant. This was why he'd brought Kit—he had no idea. The assistant obviously picked up that he didn't have a clue and started with simpler questions.

"We can start with what color gold you would like. Do you like yellow or white?" Well, that one was easy.

"White, definitely white."

He glanced at Kit and saw her nod in agreement.

"And the stone? Maybe a traditional solitaire diamond?"

Okay, this is where it was going to get messy. He was sure.

"I'd definitely like a diamond to be the main stone, but I'm not so sure about the solitaire part."

Diamonds were forever and so was this marriage, so there definitely had to be a diamond in the mix. He didn't need to see Kit's nod of approval to know he was right this time.

"One last thing, what price range are you looking at?"

Oh man, he had no idea. He looked to Kit for help and was grateful when she stepped up and saved the day

"He's looking for the perfect ring, the price is not the main priority."

She gave him a quick wink.

"Okay, then. I'll just go and get a selection out for you to look over. I'll be back shortly."

He watched her walk away and start gathering rings

on a viewing tray. A few minutes later, she returned with about a dozen rings. There was every color stone imaginable and he didn't know where to start until he saw the perfect ring amongst the others. He reached forward and picked up the white and black ring.

"Ah, a fine choice, sir. The ring you have is fourteen-carat white gold. As you can see, it has a main round cut diamond surrounded by a circle of genuine natural black onyx and on either side are smaller round cut diamonds with a black onyx tear shaped surround. Then smaller diamonds are inlaid in the band. This ring also comes with a matching wedding band that nestles beautifully in against it."

Dominic only half heard the grand description and sales pitch...he was quite certain this sales lady could sell ice to Eskimos if she had a mind to. He held it out for Kit to see up close.

"You're right, Dominic. That's it for sure. Adele's going to love it."

Twenty minutes later Dominic and Kit were back in his car, heading away from the shopping center.

"Where are we going, Dominic? Hospital's the other way, in case you forgot."

Damn, Kit could be a smartass when she wanted to be.

"I haven't forgotten, Kit. We're picking up a present for Kelly."

He'd spoken with Natalie earlier and she'd told him that the surviving puppy was doing well and could be adopted at any time. If anything was going to get Kelly to snap out of it, that little puppy would. As he pulled into the veterinary clinic's car park, Kit let out a curse.

"You are kidding? Why the hell did you bring me along for this? You know I don't do dogs. I'm strictly a cat person—in more ways than one."

"Give it a rest, you baby. We have to get Kelly to snap out of her trance. I'm hoping having the little puppy to look after will give her something to focus on other than all the shit that's running around her head. We have to at least give it a try. And it's not like I'm going to make you nurse him on your lap or anything. He'll sit in the back, in his seat belt. You won't even have to pat him if you don't want to."

They got out and headed up to the entry, Dominic chuckling as Kit grumbled under her breath the whole way about the lengths she went to for friendship.

Adele counted the holes in the ceiling panels as she waited for Dominic to come visit. He'd said he had a couple of errands he needed to attend to that couldn't wait. Then he was going to help Adele into a wheelchair and they were going to see Kelly. Adele had been awake for two days now, so that meant she hadn't seen Kelly for seven days. She was desperate to get to her, and nervous about whether she could get her to open up.

As she thought about Dominic, she felt a little giddy. She was going to marry him, be his wife. A pang of sadness gripped her as she thought about how much she'd have liked to have her *maman* see her get married. She closed her eyes as a tear slipped down her cheek. She still grieved for her mother like she had only died yesterday, not over four years ago. She felt the familiar tingle up her spine that told her Dominic was near. Before she could wipe the tear away and compose herself, he was at her bedside.

"Adele, what's wrong? Are you in pain?"

His voice was filled with concern for her. Oh, she so loved this man. She shook her head a little before opening her eyes to look into his ice-blue irises.

"I'm fine, Dominic. I was just thinking how *Maman* won't see me get married."

Dominic swiped his thumb under her eye, wiping away another tear.

"But she will be watching, beautiful. She will always be with you, in your heart and in your soul. She always will."

Adele hated that she still couldn't really move her arms, because she desperately wanted to wrap them around his neck and hold him to her. She settled for nuzzling her face into his palm and leaving little kisses in her wake. Dominic wrapped his arms around her the best he could and simply held her, comforting her...until she heard a strange sniffling noise. She lifted her head out of Dominic's neck and blushed as she realized they weren't alone. Dominic chuckled as he obviously saw her blush.

"Don't be embarrassed, beautiful. It's only Kit. Why

don't you see what she's got," he whispered right in her ear.

Adele lifted her head away from Dominic and glanced toward the door and saw the last thing she'd ever expected to see. Kit stood there cuddling a little Dalmatian puppy.

"I'm not sure what is more shocking. Kit actually cuddling a puppy or the puppy itself," she said then chuckled.

Kit had always proclaimed to not have time for any canine. Dominic barked out a laugh.

"Yeah, you should have heard her grumbling the whole way into the vet's, then as soon as the little guy came out and went straight up to her, sniffed her shoes and whined to be picked up, she was done for. She wouldn't even let me put him in his seat belt. She insisted on nursing him on the way over. I wanted you to give him to Kelly, but I'm not sure Kit will give him up now."

Kit paused in her patting long enough to flip them off.

"What can I say? He's cute and soft. And Kelly won't be able to look after him until she leaves the hospital; he can stay with me until she does. Can't you, little fella?"

She finished off in the squeaky high voice people used for pets and babies. It was so out of place coming out of Kit, Adele couldn't help but laugh again.

Ten minutes later, Adele was in her wheelchair with

Dominic pushing her down the hall to Kelly's room. Kit was walking beside them, making a fuss over the puppy the whole way. As they entered the room, Adele's heart ached. Kelly was just staring at nothing. Not blinking, not moving, barely even breathing. She looked so pale and rather frail. Even her curls were looking flat. Dominic wheeled her up to the side of the bed as Kit hung back in the hallway for a few minutes.

"Hey, Kelly, I'm so sorry I couldn't come see you sooner, but they wouldn't let me. I was too sick still."

She watched Kelly's chest rise and fall a bit deeper than before.

"Please, *ma chère*, look at me. Come back to us. You're free now. He's gone. Dead. He can never hurt you again."

She only just saw the twitch of her fingers. She turned to Dominic as an idea formed.

"We need to show her she's free. She went into shock when he put the collar on her, so maybe if you place her hands on her neck, so she can feel for herself that her neck is bare and free it might help."

Adele watched Kelly closely as Dominic very gently picked her hands up in his and placed them, palm down, over her neck. Kelly's eyes closed and her hands moved all over her neck in slow jerky movements. Oh, thank heavens it was working. She was coming back to them.

"You are free, Kelly, and we are all here for you. Please look at me, *ma chère*."

Relief filled her when Kelly slowly turned her head

and her dull grey eyes flicked over Adele's body, taking in her cast and bandages before they settled on hers.

"He hurt you. It's my fault."

Tears began to run down her face as she reclosed her eyes. Adele looked up to Dominic in desperation.

"Please, Dominic, lift me onto the bed with her, she needs me."

Dominic nodded his head once then gently lifted and placed her on the bed so she lay next to Kelly in a way that wouldn't cause her arms further pain. Kelly slowly curled against Adele like a little kitten and cried into her embrace. She used all her strength to drag her left arm over so it rested on Kelly's side—as close to a hug as she could manage. She lowered her head so her cheek rested on her hair.

"Kelly, what happened was no one's fault but Cole's. He chose to do all he did. No one forced his hand. Please don't blame yourself, none of this was your fault, *ma chère*."

She started to hum just like she had that first time until Kelly calmed.

"We brought you a present, Kelly. Would you like to see it?" Adele asked in a soft voice.

Kelly moved her head back a little to look over her side toward the door. She didn't pull away from Adele's body so she couldn't see her expression but she heard the hitch in her breathing.

"Hey, kiddo, look who wanted to come say hi. This is the little puppy you rescued; he's all healed up now.

Would you like a cuddle?"

Kit brought him over and Kelly shuffled a little away from Adele as Kit lay the puppy down between them. The puppy went straight for Kelly, licking her neck and face.

Kelly laughed.

Adele cried.

She was back and was going to be just fine. Relief poured through Adele as she watched the light come back into Kelly's beautiful grey eyes and a smile appear on her face. Dominic came up behind her and lay his hand on her upper arm and he bent down to kiss her head. Kit stood close on the other side. All three watched with tears in their eyes as Kelly joyously played with the little puppy.

"I think you should name him, Kelly," Dominic said in a soft low tone. Kelly looked up in confusion.

"But he's not mine."

Her gaze flicked from Dominic to Adele.

"If you want him, he's yours, *ma chère*. Kit is going to look after him until we're both out of here, then he'll be coming home with us." Kelly cuddled the puppy in close and closed her eyes as she nuzzled him.

"Thank you, so much."

She moved the puppy away a little and stared into his face.

"Hmm, a name...I remember once I saw this show on TV about Indian culture and stuff. It said 'Raksha' meant protection and the moon. I think I want to call him 'Raksha.'"

"That sounds beautiful, Kelly. Raksha, our little protector."

Adele rubbed his ear as Dominic and Kit told Kelly she'd chosen the name well.

Chapter Fifteen

It was ten to six, Tuesday morning, and Jake, fresh from the shower, sat down in front of his computer and fired the thing up. He sipped his coffee while he waited for it to boot up. He shook his head; people kept claiming technology was saving people time. The amount of time he spent waiting for technology to do what it was meant to, he had serious doubts that he actually "saved" any. Once it was up and running, he activated his webcam and loaded up Skype, ready for the monthly Alpha meeting.

Choden Sangye was already on and waiting. Choden was the very first snow leopard shifter created. Unlike the others after him, he was immortal. For a two hundred and sixty-eight-year-old, he was surprisingly attuned to the modern world and all its technology. He was up bright and early, his clock would currently read one forty-five a.m.

Over the next ten minutes, all the others joined them. Dishi Wee, Tristian Laprise, Maddix Torres, Obi Traore, Fernando Molina, and Joe Fairley was the last to join them, as per usual.

With everyone now online, Choden started things off

with a welcome in Tibetan. They then went through the usual stuff: deaths, births, and matings in each of the Leaps. They moved on to the Lost Ones lists they each had been compiling. They compared and updated their lists and discussed what each Leap was doing in order to seek out their Lost Ones. Once that discussion was done, they tackled general business.

"Jake, tell me, how is your eldest, Dominic, recovering?"

The fact Choden knew something had happened didn't surprise Jake. Choden seemed to have some super powers, one of which enabled him to somehow know what was going on within all the Leaps around the globe.

"Dominic and his future-mate are both healing from their ordeal. The child, Kelly, has also thankfully snapped out of her shock and is recovering. The doctor is confident that all three will make a full recovery."

He then spent a few minutes answering questions about what had happened before Obi spoke up.

"So, your son has found his mate. This is good. The next generation's Alpha is now secure for your Leap, Jake. You must be pleased."

"That's the thing I don't get, Obi. I always assumed Dominic would be next Alpha, but his mate is wholly human. So now I must start observing the other young males in our Leap for signs of the next Alpha. I'm not sure how I'm going to get everything I need to done, or tell Dominic that he is not going to be Alpha when I've been grooming him for it for so long."

Choden cut into the conversation.

"Jake, my brother, I have two pieces of wisdom from Buddha for you. Firstly, 'There is nothing more dreadful than the habit of doubt. Doubt separates people. It is a poison that disintegrates friendships and breaks up pleasant relations. It is a thorn that irritates and hurts; it is a sword that kills.' And secondly, 'Do not dwell in the past, do not dream of the future, concentrate the mind on the present moment.'"

While Jake was still trying to process what Choden had meant with his "pieces of wisdom," the meeting adjourned and everyone signed off. Choden knew something; he knew what was going to happen but obviously wasn't going to share it yet. He had a nasty habit of being fond of free will and wouldn't tell anyone anything unless he deemed it necessary in order to maintain balance. Jake jotted down the quotes while they were still fresh in his mind. He would have to think over them later. For now, he needed to get down to the station. He was back being captain while Dominic's injury healed and while Adele and Kelly needed him. He drank the last mouthful of his cold coffee, winced, and left his office.

He stopped on his way down the hall when he caught sight of a movement in the spare room. He stepped into the room and was stunned. Someone had set off a pink bomb in there.

"Honey, what are you doing?" he asked Sophie as his

eyes attempted to adjust to all the pink in the room.

"I'm making up a room for Kelly. She'll need somewhere to stay until Adele gets released, and I thought we could keep it set up so she can stay here whenever Dominic and Adele want some private time. She's never had much of anything, so I wanted to make it special."

He walked up behind his wife and wrapped her in his arms. He nuzzled her neck, breathing in her scent. Even after over thirty years of marriage, her sweet scent was still his favorite smell.

"How about you add some white? I think you've gotten just slightly carried away with the pink. She is nearly a teenager, honey. I'm not sure she's going to be quite so into pink as this room needs her to be."

He spoke softly with an edge of humor. He didn't want to hurt his wife's feelings, but he didn't want to hurt Kelly's eyes either. He waited as Sophie scanned the room, then let out a sigh.

"I guess you have a point. Only having had boys in the house, I got excited at being able to do a girl's room. But now that I've stood back and looked at it, it is a bit much, isn't it?"

"I'm excited too, honey. We're getting a daughter and a granddaughter all at once. And making a room for Kelly to have as her own is a wonderful idea."

He turned her around, held her face in both his hands, and proceeded to kiss the daylights out of his beautiful mate and wife.

Excitement had Adele restless. After two long weeks in the hospital, she was more than ready to leave, and Clint had finally said she could. She was sitting up in her bed waiting for Dominic to come and take her home. Sophie and Kelly had already been in to visit. Kelly was released a few days ago and was staying with Jake and Sophie. Apparently, Sophie had done up one of the spare rooms for her and Kelly was ecstatic about having a whole room that was hers alone at their house. She was going to stay there for a few more days while Adele got settled back in at home. She suspected Dominic may have requested to have a few days of just the two of them. A wide smile pulled at her lips as she thought about being able to spend whole days and nights alone with Dominic.

As if he'd heard her thoughts, she felt the familiar tingle that meant he was near. Moments later, he appeared in the doorway. She sat mesmerized by his powerful stride as he came over to her. He had completely healed from the bullet wound and wasn't even limping anymore. He had told her shifters healed at a faster rate than humans. He bent down over her, stroked her face, and gave her a breath-stealing kiss.

"Good morning, love. You ready to run away with me?"

He kissed her again before she could respond. A cough from the doorway broke them apart. She looked up blushing at Clint who had caught them.

"Got all your paperwork here, Adele. I just need to check your left wrist. I think we should be able to take the splint off. You'll still have to wear a soft brace for a while but it will be easier to get dressed and move around than with the splint."

After a thorough examination, Adele now had a soft bandage brace on her left wrist, which meant she now had use of that hand.

"You'll need to be careful with that right wrist and hand. You might want to have it in a sling for a while so you don't accidentally bump it. You have two fractured knuckles and a few broken bones. It's going to take time to heal."

"It's okay, Doc, I'll make sure she doesn't do anything too strenuous."

Dominic gave her his cheeky lopsided grin and a wink, which sent the butterflies dancing in her belly, like it did every time.

"Well, okay, then. I'll just get Dominic to sign your release, Adele. I think it'll be a while before your right hand is up to writing. I dare say you'll get pretty good at writing left-handed."

Dominic felt a wave of relief as he helped Adele out of his car and into the lounge room. His mate was healing and out of the hospital. His leopard felt much better knowing she would be in his arms where he could protect her personally. He settled her on the couch before he went out to collect her bags and lock up the car. While he was in her room putting her bags down, he got the ring out of his pocket and held it enclosed in his hand as he went back out to Adele. He'd been so relieved when Clint had taken the splint off her left hand. She could wear his ring now. He came through the door to see Adele staring up at him with absolute adoration shining from her eyes.

"Is it because you're a shifter or because we're mates that whenever you're close I feel a tingle up my spine?" she asked.

He grinned like a fool at her question. He went over and knelt in front of her before he answered her.

"It's because we're mates, love. I feel it too."

He leaned in and gave her a slow gentle kiss.

"I know you already said yes, but I didn't do it properly before."

He rearranged himself to kneel on one knee before he took her left hand gently and slipped his ring on her finger.

"Adele, will you do me the honor of becoming my wife? Be mine forever?"

He watched with his heart in his throat as her eyes misted over and a tear leaked from the corner of her right eye. He got a little worried—for about two seconds—before her face broke out into a huge smile and she finally responded.

"Yes, Dominic. I will be yours and you mine. Forever."

He moved his hands to her face, holding her, as he

devoured her mouth. He trailed kisses down her jaw and neck before he sat back from her. He had something else to ask her, something that couldn't wait any longer. His leopard was pushing him hard to mark her and he was having difficulty restraining himself.

"There's something else I need to explain."

He moved so he sat next to her on the couch and she twisted so she was facing him with her eyebrow raised.

"Is this a shifter something?"

"Yeah, it's a shifter something."

He couldn't stop his chuckle. She really was handling the whole shifter thing a lot better than he'd feared she would.

"As well as getting married, I want us to be mated."

"And what exactly does getting mated entail? We don't have to have witnesses in the bedroom or anything, do we?"

The slight panic in Adele's eyes had him laughing; trust a female to draw that conclusion.

"No, love, nothing like that. No one extra will *ever* be in the bedroom with us."

He couldn't resist giving her a quick kiss before he continued. She was so sweet and completely adorable.

"Shifters mate for life. When we mate, I'll leave my mark on you and you on me. Others then know we belong to each other and they also know to keep their paws to themselves."

"What do you mean 'mark'?"

"We will make love and when we climax together,

claws will sprout from the fingers on my right hand and when they do, I'll scratch you. Don't worry, it doesn't hurt because it's magic, I'm not really cutting into you. You'll be left with my mark. It will look like four wide scratch marks that reveal leopard spots beneath. People who see it will think it's a tattoo."

"But how do I mark you? I'm not a shifter. This mating thing, it won't change me, will it?"

Adele's forehead was all creased up as she was obviously getting herself all tied up in knots. He'd better finish explaining this before he totally lost her to her mind's randomness.

"After I mark you, the magic flowing from me to you will allow you to grow claws, just this once, enabling you to mark me. It won't change you, you need the right DNA to be able to shift. It's not like the movies where a bite or scratch is going to convert you."

He sat silently watching the emotions flicker over Adele's face as she processed everything he had told her.

"One last question. Where will you mark me? And where do I mark you?"

"We can leave our marks wherever we want to, but traditionally the male leaves it just above the inside of his mate's right hipbone. The female leaves it over the male's heart on his left pectoral."

He watched her straighten her shoulders and raise her eyes so she held his gaze with her warm chocolate-colored irises.

"I love you, and I don't ever want to be without you, Dominic. Yes, I will mate with you."

As she spoke those words, he felt like his heart had just exploded from the sheer bliss he simply couldn't contain. Then she wrapped her left arm around his neck and pulled him in for a scorching kiss he felt all the way to his blissfully happy soul.

Jake sat down with a sigh as Sophie curled up next to him on the couch. They'd just settled Kelly into bed and were now enjoying a glass of port together. Jake had spent the afternoon going over the lists of Lost Ones, updating his own list of all the Lost Ones that were suspected of being in Australia. He'd also looked back over Choden's advice and decided it meant he didn't need to worry about the whole next Alpha thing at the moment. So he wasn't going to. The Lost Ones search would keep him plenty busy enough, especially while he was back on captain duties down at the station.

"I can feel your worry, Jake. Tell me what's troubling you."

Sophie could always read him so clearly.

"I've been going over the Lost Ones lists. There are so many and there are a lot they suspect are in Australia. I'm going to have to send out a search party I think. There's only so much you can do on the net and by correspondence."

"Which Leaps suspect their Lost Ones have come to Australia?"

"The Chilean Leap suspects that a pregnant widow-mate whose mate was murdered by the 'Caravan of Death' in the military coup of 1973 escaped the country on a boat bound for Sydney. But they got caught up trying to save the remaining shifters in Chile, by the time things settled down and they could start looking, they couldn't find any trace of her.

"The French Leap have a pregnant future-mate who went missing back in 1989. They have no idea where she's gone, so we're all looking for her.

"Then the African Leap are still searching for four families that were in Rwanda around the time of the genocide in 1994. They might have been killed but they might have managed to get away. Being able to turn into a leopard has its benefits in Africa, the only place where it actually makes hiding easier. There are more, all similar stories."

Sophie hugged him tightly and nuzzled her face into his neck.

"The Leap will help you find them. Send a small group of the unmated males out. They may even find their mates while they are off on their travels."

"Hmmm, you have a good point. I know the twins are starting to suffer for not having their mates. Xander even more so; poor man has been dreaming for years now."

"Well, there you go. Wait until the end of fire season, and sit them down to organize where you want them to go."

Jake moved to kiss his mate. He should have spoken to her about this earlier. How had he forgotten what great advice she gave?

"Alex called me earlier today."

"The detective? He wasn't too upset over Dominic killing that man, was he?"

"Honestly, I think Dominic saved him about a year's worth of paperwork. Alex had been trying to find Cole for years. He was a serial rapist and murderer. If not for the fire at the docks, he would have caught him. The fire prevented their next random drug testing of their employees. Alex had arranged to have the tests run for DNA too. They only test monthly so he was going to have to wait for the next one."

"I wonder if Cole lit that fire to get out of it."

"I don't think so. He was just a whack job and lost his temper at the captain of that ship. He'd admitted to arguing with Cole a few times before the fire."

"To think that one incident led to so many others."

"Everything that happens in this world is like throwing pebbles across water. The ripples reach out far and wide."

"Did Alex know how many women Cole had murdered?"

Jake took a deep breath as his heart ached.

"Not a final count yet. Doubt they'll ever be one. Who knows how many bodies washed out to sea and were eaten by animals. It was at least nine, including Kelly's mother."

They both sat in silence as they finished their ports. He was glad they'd found Kelly and managed to save her, but the cost had been high.

Chapter Sixteen

Adele was beyond excited as Dominic scooped her up off the couch and headed to her bedroom. She traced her fingers lightly over his dark eyebrow, down his straight nose, over his soft lips. The man was so handsome, she couldn't quite believe he was going to be hers alone for the rest of their lives. By the time they made it to the bed, her cheeks were aching from the massive grin that was plastered over her face. As he sat down on the bed with her, she caught sight of the print above her bed.

"That print. It's a photo of you, isn't it?"

Now she knew he was her *chaton* so many things were making sense, little things that had been niggling at her—all the things he'd done that had seemed familiar or feline-ish.

"Yeah, beautiful. It's me in our field. Conner came with me and took the photo."

He was looking a little sheepish, as he should. He'd been trying to pull the wool over her eyes for a while.

"This is going to sound silly, but can you please shift for me? I want to feel you nuzzle my neck in the real world."

She felt like a ditz for asking, but she needed to know his leopard in the real world, not just in her dreams.

"Love, there is nothing silly about it. And sure, I can shift for you."

He stood up with her in his arms before he gently placed her back on the bed with a kiss.

"I need to strip before I shift, or I'll shred my clothes. Hmm, I think it's only fair you strip too."

He followed up the request with that cheeky lopsided grin he knew she couldn't resist. She really needed to build up a resistance to that grin.

"You'll need to help. I can't do much with this cast on."

She didn't need to ask twice, and within moments he had her naked and back on the bed. Feeling a little self-conscious, she shuffled over so she sat in the middle. When she looked up it was to see a very naked, very sexy Dominic staring at her.

"You ready, beautiful?"

She couldn't find words, her mouth suddenly dry at the sight of all that muscular flesh before her so she just nodded. His body was engulfed in that same bubble of blue electric energy that she'd seen in the basement before his body shifted to that of her *chaton*. She smiled as she took in the beautiful creature standing before her bed.

"You are more beautiful in reality, *chaton*."

In one lazy leap, he pounced on the bed before her.

He landed lightly on his feet, the bed barely making a groan at the added weight. He padded around her, rubbing his soft fur all over her skin. It felt so good, and tickled like nothing else. She started giggling. He nuzzled against her cheek and into her neck before the cheeky boy licked her from shoulder to ear with his rough tongue.

"Oh, now, you know how much that tickles!"

She sunk her hands into his fur on either side of his massive head. Oh wow, it was so soft. She rested her forehead against his while she closed her eyes and rubbed behind his ears, just how he liked it in her dreams.

"This can't be real, it's just so...it's too much."

As if he sensed she needed something else to focus on, he shifted his head down, touching his cold nose on her nipple, then he really sent her head reeling by licking up the underside of her breast and over her nipple with his rough feline tongue.

"Ohh, okay, if you're going to start getting me all hot and bothered you better shift back to Dominic. I don't think I'm ready to be fooling around with a snow leopard—that's a little too much for me to cope with just at the moment."

Moments later Dominic—the man—sat before her. His eyes were hooded and dark with desire.

"You know, I can shift just my tongue. Did you like the feel of my rough tongue, beautiful?"

"Uh-huh."

That was about all she could manage to say. He already had her wet and hot. Her mind had gone fuzzy from the hormone overload. He chuckled as he prowled over to her and gently laid her back against the bed. Using his rough feline tongue he licked, nipped, and kissed his way from her mouth down to between her thighs where he settled in and proceeded to show her the best use for such a wonderfully rough tongue.

When he had her boneless and totally spent, he worked his way back up her body to kiss her.

He pulled back slightly and whispered a plea, "Will you let me in your body, my love, with no condom? For the mating, will you let me feel all of you?"

She didn't have to think about that one. She wanted to feel him inside her and wanted to feel claimed by him...and if she got pregnant? Wouldn't that be something, to have this wonderful man's baby growing inside her?

"Yes, Dominic. Claim me completely."

He gave her the most reverent, most powerful kiss he'd ever given her. He pulled back and rolled her over on her tummy; she looked over her shoulder with an eyebrow raised.

"This is how shifters mate, from behind. Normally I'd get you up on all fours but with your wrists, that won't be happening for a while." He pulled a couple of pillows down and tucked them under her tummy so her bottom was raised in the air. She felt so vulnerable and open to him, which she guessed was the point. She was showing him that she trusted him.

He leaned over her back, placing a fist into the bed on either side of her shoulders, he bent his head and nuzzled her neck. As he slid himself into her wet heat, he gently bit between her neck and shoulder, using the sensitive flesh to pin her under him, dominating her. She loved it. She felt surrounded and filled with Dominic's power and love. Oh, what she would give to be able to freeze time right now and feel like this forever.

Dominic had never felt such bliss. His mate was beneath him, not only accepting his dominance but moaning in pleasure from it. He began pumping in and out of her glorious wet heat. After a few strokes, he felt her walls ripple. She was getting close, which was a damn good thing because he wasn't going to be able to last long; the feel of his naked erection sliding in and out of her core was more than he could stand. After a few minutes, he felt her tighten up around him as she began to climax. He released her neck and sat back, gripping her hips in his hands and roared as he joined her.

His right hand was perfectly placed just above her hipbone when he felt the magic roll through him and his claws ripped through his fingertips and into her flesh. He dragged his hand around to her side, marking her before he placed his palm over the mark. He pulled himself from her body and rolled her over onto her back. He lifted her encased right hand to his chest. Her sharp claws looked so right coming from her fingertips. He used his fingers to help her curl the tips over and scratch down his pectoral over his heart. He then took the palm of her left hand and placed it over the mark. Satisfaction filled him and he leaned down to kiss her but didn't make it. He jerked up when she cried out and started to vibrate.

Dominic wasn't sure what was happening but he was in an instant panic—his mate was in pain. Mating wasn't meant to hurt. He reached for his phone to ring his dad to ask him for help when a blue glow started forming around Adele's body. What the hell? She was shifting? How on earth...

"Baby, don't fight it. Go with it. It won't hurt if you go with it. I don't know how or why, but you're shifting."

He saw the panic in her eyes before the blue glow engulfed her and she reappeared as a stunningly beautiful snow leopard. He reached over to stroke her fur. He was totally dumbstruck and got lost to his mind stumbling over itself. Until he heard her whimper, oh hell, bugger the whys and hows. His mate was hurting, confused.

"Adele, you're okay. You just shifted. It's okay, we'll work it all out. Dad will know why. Just relax your mind, think about what you look like as a human, and wish for it."

It took her a few minutes but eventually the blue glow began to shine and she returned to human form. Before either of them could speak, she grabbed her left wrist and screamed out in agony. Shit, the cast had shattered when she'd shifted and now her broken wrist was out of line. His heart stopped beating when she fell limp on the mattress, until he saw her chest rise and fall with breath. Dominic sunk down next to her, stroking her face and taking some deep breaths to collect himself. That was so not how he planned on finishing the mating.

Finding his pants, he pulled out his phone, rang Clint, and explained what happened. Clint told him that Adele needed to get back to the hospital ASAP to get her wrist reset and checked over. He got himself dressed. Then he put Adele in clean underwear and wrapped her up in her robe before gently carrying her out to his car and laying her on the rear seat. He locked up the house, jumped in the car, and drove to the hospital.

While Clint was x-raying and resetting Adele's wrist, Dominic rung his dad.

"Hey, son, kind of late for a phone call. Everything okay?"

"No, Dad, nothing is okay. Adele, she shifted."

"Come again? She what?"

"We completed the mating. I marked her and she marked me. Then she cried out, started shaking, and shifted to a snow leopard. I don't get it, Dad. She's human."

"I think I might know what's going on. I'll come over to explain. Where are you? At Adele's?"

"We're at the hospital. The shift shattered her cast. She shifted back and was in agony from her wrist. She passed out. So I rung Clint and brought her in. She's getting it reset now."

"Okay, I'll come down to the hospital. Go be with your mate, son, I'll be there soon."

Jake quickly got up and dressed, ready to head to the hospital. Suddenly what Choden had said to him made sense. There was no point wasting time looking for another future Alpha because Dominic was in fact mated to a shifter. He scrubbed his hands over his face as he sat on the edge of his bed. As he put his shoes on he figured he better ring Tristian and let him know they found a Lost One with a French background. He glanced at the clock, eleven forty p.m. That made it midafternoon in France. He picked up the phone and dialed. Tristian picked up on the second ring.

"Bonjour, Jake. What has you ringing me at this hour? It must be near midnight your end."

"Bonjour, Tristian. Yes, it is getting late, but this matter is urgent. I think we just found one of your Lost Ones."

"Oh, that does sound promising, tell me about them."

"It's Dominic's mate. She presented as fully human, but after mating, she shifted. I know her mother was

French, moved to Melbourne when she was pregnant."

"Do you know her mother's name? Or the year she would have moved?"

"Ahh, I don't know her mother's name but Adele's last name is Petit. She was born in 1989. November, I think."

"*Incroyable*! You found her! Oh, Remi is going to be so happy. *Merci,* my friend, *merci beaucoup.*"

"You know her father? Personally?"

"Sit back my friend and let me tell you a story."

Twenty minutes later Jake hung up the phone. Damn, he hoped Dominic and Adele handled this news well, because, depending on how fast Remi could get on a plane, Adele's dad was going to be here in a few days. He'd made the call to Tristian on speaker so Sophie would know what was going on. She gave him a tight hug and wished him luck and strength as he headed out the door to go to the hospital.

It was close to one a.m. when he walked into Adele's hospital room. She lay unconscious on the bed, and Dominic was pacing back and forth across the room at the foot of her bed. His son looked like he'd aged about ten years since he had seen him early yesterday. The anguish, confusion, and pain rolling off him cut Jake to the bone.

"Hey, son. How is she?"

Dominic raised his head to look at him.

"I didn't know it would hurt her, Dad. I don't get it. I don't understand why she shifted. I'd just told her the mating wouldn't change her and then she goes and shifts!"

Jake strode across the space and wrapped his son in a bone-crushing hug. Dominic sagged into his embrace, resting his head on his shoulder.

"She is one of the Lost Ones, Dominic. I don't know how the mating triggered the shift, but her mother was a future-mate. Her father is one of us. I spoke with Tristian before I came. I have a lot to tell you both, but I would like to be able to tell you together. Has she woken up since we spoke?"

Dominic pulled from his embrace and scrubbed his face.

"No, she hasn't. Clint said she should at any moment. He's put her wrist back in a cast. It's already healing faster now that her shifter DNA has been triggered."

"How about I go get you a coffee while we wait for your mate to return to us?"

"Sounds like a plan, Dad, because I really want to hear some answers and I'm certain she will too."

Adele awoke to find herself back in the hospital. Damn it, how the hell had she ended up back here? In a flash, the previous night came back to her. She sat forward in a rush and tried to breathe through the remembered pain. Dominic was right there rubbing her back, saying soft gentle things to her, calming her with his smooth deep voice. But it was his fault; he'd promised her the mating wouldn't change her.

"You said I wouldn't change! But I did! What the hell is going on, Dominic?"

She was pissed off. How could he lie to her about something this important? She didn't even see Jake until she heard him speak.

"Dominic knows as little as you do about what happened last night, Adele. Please, don't be angry. None of us saw this coming."

She rested her head against Dominic and took a deep breath, taking his scent deep within her.

"Please, Jake, if you have answers, can you explain them to me, to us."

She didn't have it in her to guess and play cryptic games. She heard Jake take a deep breath and Dominic's hold on her tighten; he had slipped onto the bed and had moved her into his embrace.

"Where to start...I guess I should really check a couple of things to make sure we have it right. Adele, what was your mother's name? And when did she migrate to Australia from France?"

"Her name was Fleur Petit and she migrated out in June 1989. Why? What has that got to do with anything?"

"Your father. He is one of us, and he's been searching for you and your mother since before you were born."

That sentence hit her like a bomb. Adele looked at Jake in shock. Her father? Remi Baudin, the man that had irrevocably broken her mother's heart had been looking for her?

"I don't believe you. Remi left my mother, broke her heart. When he found out about me, he literally ran from her."

"Yes, he did run, but not for the reasons you think."

Adele looked up to the door as a new deep voice floated over the room. What she saw stole her breath. A Tibetan Monk stood in her doorway, dressed traditionally in red-and-gold robing. He would only be five foot two at the most, but he had a strong aura of power and wisdom. This was a man whose presence alone commanded respect. His skin was a dark tan color, his dark hair trimmed close to his skull, and his face was serious but friendly. He looked like he couldn't be much older than twenty, but his eyes held the wisdom of an old man. Who the hell was he and why did he seem to know what they were talking about?

Jake spoke words she couldn't even begin to understand to the newcomer and then he bowed slightly. So apparently, Jake knew who this guy was. She looked over to Dominic whose mouth hung loosely open and his face looked awestruck. She gently nudged Dominic with her elbow to get his attention and cocked an eyebrow in question. He looked down at her and smiled.

"It's okay, Adele. This is Choden Sangye. He is the original shifter, and he's like our guru."

The original shifter? Guru? Adele's head began pounding and she buried her head into Dominic's chest as she became totally overwhelmed.

"Jake, my brother, have you not begun educating your newest cub? I fear we have overwhelmed the child."

"Choden, I had just started to explain. Perhaps you would like to take over. You tell our history so much clearer than I."

"Yes, I believe starting with our history would be a good place to begin. We will get to her father's story later, I think. Jake, would you be so kind as to find me a seat? We are going to be here for some time."

Adele lifted her head from Dominic's chest as she heard Jake bring a chair close to the bed. Before Choden sat down, he picked up her left hand, resting his forehead against the back of it for a moment before speaking in quiet words she didn't understand. She felt a wave of energy roll through her body and mind, leaving peace and comfort in its wake.

"Now, my child, let me tell you a story or two." He cleared his throat before he continued. "This story starts long ago with the monks who lived high in the mountains of Tibet. The monks were bonded with the snow leopards. The monks would provide shelter and medical aid, and in return, the snow leopards offered the monks protection from those who would harm them. It was a relationship that worked well and benefited both man and beast.

"In the 1750s, an elderly monk started to become concerned for the snow leopards. Their numbers were declining rapidly from hunters who sought out their beautiful and thick pelts. Together with his prodigy, a young boy who he had taken under his wing, they researched ways in which they could help protect the snow leopards that had protected them so diligently for so long.

"In 1759, they finally had everything they needed to conduct the magic that would hopefully save their friends and protectors. They had found a way to join together a man and a beast. Thus allowing the beast to shift to a man and the man to shift to a beast, enabling both to better protect themselves and others they held dear.

"Now the young monk had an extremely close bond with a young male snow leopard and they both gladly volunteered to be joined. Late at night under the darkness of a new moon, the elder monk cast the magic upon the younger man and beast. A ball of blue electric energy formed around both the man and the beast before they were raised in the air and merged into one. Upon the energy fading, the beast was revealed and the man had disappeared. The beast raised his head and roared to the sky. As he did, the blue ball of energy returned over him and he flashed into a man.

"Now, that isn't the end of the story. You see, the monks didn't realize that Halley's Comet had passed over them just as they were casting the magic. The comet strengthened the magic considerably, and along with the newly created shifter, a pair of mated shifters were conceived on each of the world's seven continents that night. The magic continues to stay with Halley's Comet and each time it passes back over the earth a new mated pair is conceived on each continent."

Adele could hardly believe what she was hearing, but then she could. It explained so much, but also bought on more questions.

"Can I ask you a question?"

She wanted to ask, but she didn't want to offend the wise—apparently very old—man before her.

"Yes, my child, ask as many as you like. It is important that you understand."

"Are shifters immortal?"

She wasn't sure how she felt about maybe living forever.

"I am the only one who is immortal. All other shifters have a human life cycle. Shifters do live longer than most humans as they don't get sick as humans do. Most shifters live well past one hundred years."

"How did you find out about what the comet did?"

"Now, that was a little embarrassing. We had no idea about the comet until later. I was fifteen when I was transformed, so shifters stay solely in their human form until their fifteenth birthdays. When they shift for the first time, it is under the rising moon on the night of their birthday. So, fifteen years after we cast the magic, we started hearing reports from all over the world, of sightings of snow leopards where they shouldn't have been. The two in Tibet came to us to seek advice and we helped them learn their skills and establish a Leap. I then took a small group of monks on a worldwide search. As we found each one, we helped them find their mate and then set up a Leap on each continent. It took many years. With the other three passings of the comet, the Alpha of each Continental Leap has conducted the Search to find the Lost Ones."

Okay, wow. Adele was no longer fifteen and she couldn't remember anything remarkable about her fifteenth birthday either.

"So why didn't I shift until last night? I'm pretty sure my mother never shifted."

"Your mother was wholly human. It is quite common for shifters to have human mates, especially the males. There has always been more male shifters born than female. Shifter DNA is strong and usually children of a shifter-human mating are full shifters, but sometimes the human DNA is the stronger and the child remains human. I can only guess that with all the trauma you have suffered in the last weeks, your shifter DNA began to surface and then combined with the magic from the mating it pushed through to the forefront causing you to shift."

"Dominic explained how the whole mating thing works, how it's predestined. How could my father leave my mother if they were mates? I don't understand how he could walk away. I mean, when I first met Dominic, I tried to push him away but couldn't do it."

"Ah, good questions, my child, very good questions. I believe you and your father have much to discuss when he arrives. As you know, a male does not dream of his mate until after she turns twenty-one. Your father met and fell in love with your mother when she was seventeen. Remi foolishly didn't seek advice. He instead crept around to see your mother, keeping it a secret. It was only when she told him about the pregnancy that he came to his Alpha to seek advice and help. So, he did indeed leave your mother, running away. He was scared and frightened of what he had done as he didn't know if she was his mate. He went straight to his Alpha for advice. His Alpha told him he should have come earlier, as he could have put his mind to ease sooner. Your mother, Fleur, was indeed his mate.

"He hurried back to return to her side, full of hope, prepared to tell her everything about him being a shifter and start their mated life together. But when he returned, your mother was gone. Your grandparents had sent her away and refused to tell Remi anything of where she had gone. The Leap monitored the family, waiting for them to contact Fleur but they never did, not even after your birth. Remi was beside himself with grief. Once your mother turned twenty-one, he started dreaming of her, and as soon as you were born, he dreamt of you. He has been a shell of a man since, haunted by the one foolish choice that has robbed him of so much."

"Does he know my mother is gone?"

Adele had tears streaming down her face. Her grandparents had a lot to answer for. Her mother hadn't wanted to leave, and now to find out Remi didn't want her to go either. How different her mother's life could have been!

"Yes, child, he knows of her passing. The day of her death was the final dream he had of her. He now solely dreams of you."

"You said we had a lot to discuss when he arrives. Are you saying he's coming here?"

"You understand correctly. As we speak, he is in a plane flying toward you. He should be here tomorrow morning, assuming there are no delays in his flight plan."

Adele didn't know what to think, her mind was overwhelmed with all the information she had received. She clung to Dominic as she tried to sort through it all. She had a father who loved her, who was coming to meet her.

"You will need some time to think about all that has happened, my child. Jake will take me to his home where I will stay. Do not hesitate to contact me if you require any more answers. I understand you have taken on the protection of a child, Kelly, who is also staying with Jake and Sophie?"

"Uh, yes, I have. Kelly is like a daughter to me. I would do anything for her."

"As you have already quite clearly demonstrated, child, you are a worthy future Alpha-mate. Strong, compassionate, and protective. You will do well. Now, Jake, please take me to meet this special young lady that has helped bring about all these wonderful occurrences."

As Jake walked out with Choden, Adele curled into Dominic's embrace and cried into his chest. She was so overwhelmed with everything and she needed to take the edge off before she could sit back and begin to process it all.

Epilogue

Six months later...

After waiting in the car for what felt like hours, Conner headed into the hairdressers to see what was taking so long. He understood it was Adele's wedding day and the girls wanted to look nice, but seriously? How long did it take to have your hair put up? He pushed open the front door and nearly plowed into a wheelchair. The young woman in the chair was quietly moving across the way, with her head down and shoulders slumped forward. Her long straight white-blond hair covered her face and had prevented her from seeing he'd come in. She quickly apologized for getting in his way, which shocked him as it was him who had come barreling into her path, not the other way around. He had just begun to tell her not to worry about it and he was sorry when a sharp high-pitched voice assaulted his ears. The girl before him visibly cringed before she raised her head to look at the tall thin middle-aged woman who'd just screeched at her. The second Conner saw her face, his instincts went into overdrive. The girl wasn't much younger than him, but her emerald green eyes shone with sorrow.

"Tina, leave young Mr White alone! You know better than to talk to customers. Now, return out the back this instant and get on with those books like you should be doing. They won't do themselves, you know."

She grabbed Tina's chair and quickly wheeled her out of sight. Once they were behind the back curtain, he heard some muffled noises but couldn't make out what was going on. He started to march toward the doorway when he heard his mother call out to him. In the time he took to look over at his mother, the older woman came back out from behind the curtain. He turned toward her with hard eyes, staring her down.

"Who was that girl? Why is she in a wheelchair?"

The woman looked down her nose at him.

"Tina is no one you need to concern yourself with, Mr White. Now, I believe your mother, future sister-in-law, and niece are ready to go."

She marched off toward his mother, Adele, and Kelly. As he turned to follow, he heard a small sob come from behind the certain. He was so going to come back here and help Tina, but not until after the wedding. If he did anything to muck up this day, he wouldn't be around long enough to help anyone. His father had given him strict instructions last night, if he valued his life and having all his body parts attached and in working order, he was to chauffeur the women wherever they needed to go, with no questions and no issues. His father had told him that no male had ever survived messing with a bride on her wedding day.

He went to his mother first, giving her a light kiss on the cheek and telling her she looked beautiful. He then moved toward Adele. His brother was one lucky man. She looked stunning, glowing with happiness, and he gave her a quick hug and a kiss on the cheek.

"You look stunning, Adele, truly beautiful."

He then turned his attention to Kelly, the sweet child had really blossomed in the last six months. She was growing more confident every day, and today, she looked stunning with her black curls all arranged on the top of her head.

"And you, little lady, are going to be the belle of the ball and you're not even in your dress yet. You better save a dance for your Uncle Conner tonight."

She blushed and giggled. He loved making the kid smile.

"Sure, Uncle Conner, I'll save you a dance."

"Well, if we're all done here, how about we head off? I do believe you ladies only have an hour before the photographer arrives."

Ha, that got them moving. Within ten minutes, they was driving out to his parents' house so they could finish getting ready.

Adele stood inside the marquee where the reception would be held later. She was waiting for everyone to get seated so she could walk down the aisle to Dominic. She was so nervous. She tugged at her dress, pulling the strapless top up a little. She loved her dress; it was made from vintage white lace. It was strapless and fitted around the bust, then flared out slightly from its empire waist, and the full skirt finished just above the ground so the toes of her shoes showed when she walked. She glanced around the marquee at the others. She couldn't hold back her chuckle when she saw Kit fussing at her dress again. Getting that woman in a dress was a miracle no one had managed before—or so she'd been told. Kit had tried to talk Adele into letting her wear the tux and being their best man, but Conner had refused to wear the dress so that switch wasn't happening. Although, the argument between Kit and Conner had been highly entertaining for everyone who got to watch.

Kit looked up and caught Adele laughing at her. She instantly stopped fussing, smiled a big plastic smile, and did a big showy curtsy just to be a smartass. Shaking her head, Adele turned toward Kelly. She looked stunning. She had put on some weight since the rescue and now had a healthy happy glow to her. Her black curls had been partially tamed into an up-do that looked amazing and elegant, especially with her dress. Both Kit and Kelly wore the same style dress, the shop had described it as a "Chic Scoop Neckline Grape Chiffon Satin Tea-Length Dress." They were retro-looking dresses that complemented their vintage lace beautifully. The deep grape color suited both girls well and the two-inch heels they each wore looked awesome as well—getting Kit into those puppies was another entertaining day she would never forget.

Hearing someone approach from behind her, drew her attention. It was her father coming to get them. Adele smiled as joy spread through her. Remi had moved to Tassie four months ago to be near her, and she was loving being able to get to know him, even though her heart ached for all the lost years they could have had, especially the years that her mother had still been alive. Both her parents had suffered greatly over the years. Remi asked her lots of questions about her mother, and they'd even gone back to the mainland to visit her grave last month. That had been very emotional for both of them.

She couldn't believe how much her life had changed in the last twelve months. She had started out so heartbreaking alone, no family or friends. Now, just twelve months later, she had a father, a daughter, a mate and soon-to-be husband, and a whole heap of friends and extended family. She had to be the luckiest woman alive.

"Daughter, you look amazing. Dominic is one very lucky man. They are ready for you. Shall we?"

He held his arm out to her and she slid her arm through his. Together they started walking toward the doorway with Kit and Kelly in front of them.

"You know, Dad, you look very dashing yourself in that tux."

She was trying to keep things light because if they started getting sentimental she would be in tears and ruin her makeup before her wedding even started.

She peeked around the edge of the marquee as Kelly and Kit expertly walked up the aisle holding their small bouquets of deep purple and white roses. She gripped her own slightly larger bouquet a little tighter as the music started indicating it was time for her to walk down the aisle to her mate. Remi leaned over and gave her a quick kiss on the cheek before they headed out the doorway.

Dominic was a jumble of emotions as he waited for Adele. He was happy, excited, nervous...and a little scared. Both Kelly and Kit had looked stunning and elegant as they had come down the aisle. The boys had been giving Kit hell about the fact she had to wear a dress, but they were all silently watching her in shock now. Who knew she'd scrub up so nicely when put in a dress? His heart had melted when he'd watched Kelly walk toward him down the aisle. Gone was the lost hurting little girl, and a confident glowingly happy young teenager was in her place. He already loved her as if she were his biological daughter. She and Adele both completed his world. He stood up a little straighter as everyone stood from their seats. His beautiful mate was on her way to be by his side; his palms began to sweat from the nervous energy floating through him.

He could hear everyone's ohhs and ahhs as Adele passed them, then finally she was in his line of sight. She took his breath away. She was stunning. Her hair was in loose waves except for a small section on each side that had been pulled back and there were tiny little flowers woven all through it. Her strapless dress fitted her perfectly, the lace looking as elegant as she did wearing it. Her father proudly walked beside her. Dominic was so glad they had found Remi; Adele had been hurting at the rejection from her unknown father. To know he hadn't rejected her, that he'd in fact spent years looking for her had helped heal her wounded heart and lessened the ache she'd suffered since losing her mother.

Remi took Adele's hand and placed it into his, officially giving his blessing to their mating. Dominic couldn't resist lifting her hand and placing a gentle kiss on the back. She smiled shyly at him, she was as nervous as he was. They stood before the minister and all their friends and family and spoke their vows, promising again to love each other forever and be by each other's sides for the rest of their lives. Leaning in to kiss his wife for the first time, Dominic figured this had to be happiest moment of his life so far. He couldn't wait to spend the rest of his life with her.

The next installment of Fire and Snow is Noble Guardian, which tells Conner and Tina's journey and will be available soon.

www.ingramcontent.com/pod-product-compliance
Lightning Source LLC
Chambersburg PA
CBHW061012120726
47910CB00006B/1892